A SAM POPE NOVEL

ROBERT ENRIGHT

For my girls,

CHAPTER ONE

'Tributes have continued to pour in for those who lost their lives during the London Marathon Bombing.'

As the news reader's calm and well-spoken words, lifted by the playful Northern Irish accent, filtered through the radio app on his phone, Sam Pope put down the block wrapped in sandpaper and reached for his phone with dusty fingers. The sun struck the screen, the spring morning offering a warmth that was usually snatched away by a chilling wind. Sam pressed the volume button on the side of the device, turning up the news report.

'Today marks the three-year anniversary of the event, one which shook this city, this country and the world, to its core. With investigations still ongoing as to who was behind the bombing, the Mayor of London has proposed a two-minute silence at ten forty-five, in respect of the civilians and police officer who lost their lives three years ago. As rows of flowers line the streets that have now been fully restored since the explosion, it is clear that those who lost their lives will never lose their place in the heart of this city. Lynsey Beckett, BBC News.'

Three years.

That was a long time.

With a resigned sigh, Sam turned the phone off, cutting

off a jovial Greg James as he offered some unfortunate member of the public a chance to be humiliated on national radio. With the phone silent, Sam shut his eyes and took a deep breath. Beyond the metal fences of the Bethnal Green Youth Centre, he could hear the London traffic, the eternal melting pot of roaring engines, frustrated yells and angry car horns. Beyond that, a few birds sang a song in one of the surrounding trees.

Three years.

So much had happened.

Sam looked down at the wooden bench which he had taken on as a project.

The bombing that had decimated so many lives had been a moment in time that would define him. Battling the eternal grief of losing his son, Sam had been hunting down criminals who had beaten the system and doling out his own brand of justice. It had been crude and offered nothing but a slight release from his pain.

The bombing was a catalyst for something so much more.

It had led to him going head to head with one of the most dangerous criminals in London, Frank Jackson, who had used his collusion with high-ranking members of the Metropolitan Police to build an empire that was untouchable by the long arm of the law. The 'High Rise', once seen as an impenetrable fortress of crime and debauchery, was brought down by Sam himself.

Floor by floor, Sam had eliminated Jackson's army, sending Jackson himself to the afterlife and exposing a despicable alliance with a high-ranking police official.

Inspector Howell.

After his arrest, Howell had killed himself in custody.

That should have been it.

But Sam's fight had come at a cost.

His best friend, Theo Walker, had given his life to

protect an innocent woman caught up in the entire conspiracy, putting himself between her and a grenade blast. Theo had been one of Sam's pillars through the destruction of his own life.

When Jamie, Sam's son, was killed by a drunk driver, it was Theo who had been there to keep him afloat.

When Lucy, who had spent many years happily by his side, walked away when it was clear the depression would consume him, Sam had turned to Theo for support and guidance. Having served together in the armed forces, Sam and Theo had built a bond that had seen Theo stand beside Sam as Lucy walked down the aisle towards him.

If Sam had been a religious man, Theo would have been the only option as Jamie's godfather.

But life had a cruel way of confirming a lack of God in the world, and watching his wife hunched over and howling in pain at the crumpled body of their dead son had told Sam clearly that there was none.

At least, not one he could ever believe in.

Theo's death was a sign.

A sign that the world was a corrupt place. That good people were killed for doing the right thing and those who were entrusted to do the right thing simply didn't.

So, Sam continued to fight.

After taking down Jackson's empire, Sam continued his war against organised crime, eliminating those looking to step into the large shoes Sam had forcibly emptied. That turned Sam onto the Kovalenko crime family, who specialised in trafficking young girls out of the country and into a life of horror. Sam brought them down, building a lasting friendship with Detective Inspectors Amara Singh and Adrian Pearce in the process.

It felt like a lifetime ago.

Especially as since then, the paths they'd walked had been forged by Sam's war and had seen Pearce retire under a cloud and Singh join a covert government operation. Pearce was now happily running the Youth Centre where Sam was working, continuing the legacy Theo had built once his deceased friend had stepped away from the armed forces. Their friendship, which had been built on trust and the unrelenting need to do the right thing, had only strengthened in the eighteen months since Sam had returned from America.

But whenever Sam thought about Singh, his heart ached.

In another life, they could have been happy. They could have made a go of it, but the world had placed them on either side of the line of right and wrong. And while their attraction and their commitment to justice had led to one tremendous romantic tryst, Sam and Singh both knew that there was no future to be shared.

Singh wanted to fight back just as much as Sam did.

Yet she was convinced that doing it behind a badge was the right way about it.

Sam's fight had taken over not just his, but their lives too, and had damaged it beyond repair. Every time he saw Pearce smile, he could see the slight pain behind his eyes. It was a feeling he shared, one that he wished didn't exist.

But they both understood why Sam had done it.

Why Pearce had helped him.

It was the right thing to do.

Sometimes, someone has to fight back against a system designed to keep the corrupt in power and the rest under their oppressive boots. That path inevitably had directed Sam towards General Ervin Wallace, his former commander during the hazy days of Project Hailstorm. Disguised as a secret, off-the-books operation, Sam and other elite soldiers eliminated targets under the pretence of liberty.

Of keeping the world safe.

Sam would soon learn the truth.

During a mission gone wrong, Sam was left for dead on the cold floor of a safe house with two bullet holes in his chest, with his life draining from him. Somehow, he was pulled out and Theo ensured he made it through. It brought a black curtain down on his sterling military career, one that would have made his long-since deceased father proud.

But things have a way of coming full circle.

As Sam had finished pulling the trigger on the final remnants of the Kovalenko family, he was accosted by a sinister American outfit known as Blackridge, tasked with bringing his former mentor, Carl Marsden to justice. The accusations of terrorism didn't fit and Sam, along with the help of a woman named Alex Stone, soon found Marsden and managed to retrieve a USB stick that Blackridge was hunting him for.

A USB stick they killed him for.

It was only when he cradled Marsden's dead body in his arms did Sam realise that Wallace was behind the entire operation, his determination to keep Pandora's box closed long enough to kill an old friend.

Alex saved Sam's life, when he was moments away from having his skull obliterated at point-blank range by a mysterious man with a grudge. Whatever Sam had been fighting for before, his motive changed.

Now he was fighting for everyone.

Fighting for Marsden and Theo's memory.

Fighting for Alex's life.

Fighting to expose the truth.

That fight led him to staging a daring abduction of Wallace on London Bridge in broad daylight, with Pearce offering his services under the strict instruction that Sam keep Singh safe. A brutal and bloody fight with Wallace's hired gun nearly brought everything to an end, but Sam, as he had found out on numerous occasions, had a body built for survival and a mind equipped to fight till the very end.

The burning memory of his son's innocent face was enough to haul him over the line.

It was enough to dig deep, finding the final remnants of soldier within him and Sam survived.

Farukh, the man Wallace had hired to eliminate Sam, was dead.

As was Wallace.

The truth of Project Hailstorm was exposed and although Sam would have to live with the demons of his past, at least he now knew they existed.

With Singh trying her best to remove him from the crime scene, Sam's injuries had made it impossible. With the police closing in and a rabid assistant commissioner baying for his blood, Sam knew there was one last thing he had to do to keep Singh safe.

He allowed her to arrest him.

The UK's most wanted man was behind bars and Singh was given a gold star and a promotion.

Sam knew she hated every second of it. Their undeniable feelings for each other only added to the guilt she carried on her capable shoulders.

But there was always a plan.

Sam's inevitable sentencing was scuppered by a forged document, sending him to 'The Grid', a maximum-security facility that didn't exist in any government book. Housing the most dangerous of criminals and the toughest of prison guards, Sam's future was to see out the rest of his life in lockdown, several feet below the ground.

But it also led him to Harry Chapman, one of the most notorious criminals the UK had ever known, and the man who had pieced together the empires that Jackson and the Kovalenkos had ruthlessly run.

He was the head of the snake.

And after doing what he had to survive within 'The Grid', Sam soon put him in the ground, along with the dissolution of his entire enterprise.

The fight should have been over then and there, and as Sam reminisced about that moment, when Singh helped him into the car and they drove to freedom, he lifted the sandpaper from the wood and blew away the dust. The sun beat down from above, bathing the garden of the youth centre in a wonderful, bright glow. Ever since he took up the role as the handyman for the centre, he had enjoyed the quaintness of the job, his interactions with the wayward kids who had turned to Pearce for guidance as opposed to the constant offers of gang life.

There was a sense of pride and self-worth in dedicating his time to a different fight, one which didn't involve death or bloodshed.

But not a day went by that he didn't think about Mac.

With freedom at his fingertips, Sam had spent the evening with Singh and his friend Etheridge, the former soldier who financed his fight against crime. With plans being made for Sam to disappear, Mac played his hand.

Having come so close to killing Sam in Rome, Mac had bided his time and hit where it hurt. He had taken Lucy and an entire wing of a hospital hostage, threatening to blow it halfway to hell if Sam wasn't handed over to him.

Sam had to go.

He had to face his past.

Over a decade before, Mac had been by Sam's side on a number of missions. As talented a sniper as Sam had ever seen, Mac was just as capable a spotter. Working alongside a soldier of Sam's ilk would only mould Mac into a valuable asset, one who would rival Sam for his effectiveness. As their reliance on each other for survival grew, so did their friendship, with Sam taking the young soldier under his wing.

Had shown him the life he could build for himself.

A life that they would value together.

Then, on a routine mission, they were spotted and, in a panic, Mac ran as an enemy chopper zeroed in on their location.

It opened fire.

The missile blew Sam from the edge of the cliff face, sending him spiralling to the town below. It should have been the end of the line but fortunately, Sam was nursed back to health by a local doctor. Mac wasn't so lucky.

Sam believed he had died.

It had been much worse.

Mac had been taken prisoner by the Taliban and spent years in captivity, where he was brutally assaulted and tortured until Wallace had found him. Sensing the opportunity, Wallace turned Mac into a ghost, using his impressive skills and ice-cold vengeance to do his bidding.

All with the promise that one day, Mac would be able to have his revenge on Sam for leaving him.

Sam willingly gave himself up, demanding the hospital be evacuated before he confronted Mac for the first time in years. With his ex-wife looking on helplessly, Sam refused to fight the man he had considered a friend, taking a beating from him before Mac was shot dead by the Armed Response Unit.

Another person who Sam cared deeply for had been killed.

As Sam thought about Mac's demise, he felt his chest tighten and suddenly, the toll of his fight rushed through his body with every injury he had sustained aching. Taking a deep breath, Sam lowered himself onto the bench, taking a few moments to collect his thoughts and allow his mind to clear.

Ever since he had returned from America, after helping Alex Stone reconnect with her family and dragging her out of an escalating drug war in South Carolina, Sam had been able to find a little peace.

Although the path he had forged was littered with the bodies of those he held dear, he at least found some solace in the fact that Alex was home with her family. It had been over eighteen months and Sam had decided not to reach out to her.

His fight was over and to move on from that part of his life, he had decided to cut ties. There had been the odd check on social media, where he could see that she had begun what seemed like a flourishing relationship with Joe Alan, the DEA agent who had helped Sam save her life.

But that was it.

Sam's fight was over and everything pertaining to that part of his life was in the past.

Alan, with the help of a shady biker gang, had faked Sam's death, allowing him to assume his identity as Jonathan Cooper and effectively hide in plain sight in London. The longer hair, dyed blonde and the thick greying beard that framed his strong jaw had done well to keep his identity safe.

It had been nearly two years since the UK had seen him marched out of the hospital in cuffs.

He was old news.

Now, he could help Pearce, try to give back to the kids that Theo had dedicated his life to and hopefully, find himself a little peace in the process.

With the sun beaming down, Sam closed his eyes and tilted his head back, allowing the warmth of the day to caress his face with its glow.

It was over.

All the pain he had put his body through, all the anguish that had racked his mind.

It was over.

'Sleeping on the job, eh?'

Sam's eyes shot open, and his gaze fell upon Adrian Pearce, who had a large, white grin across his face. Despite approaching his mid-fifties, Pearce still looked as fit and healthy as a man half his age. The only indication of Father Time's input was the white beard that ran across his jaw line, made all the more prominent in contrast to his black skin.

'I was just taking a break,' Sam replied, shutting his eyes again.

'I think you've probably earnt a few of these.' Pearce chuckled. In his hands, he held two cups of coffee from the local coffee shop, and he handed one to Sam. Pearce was always immaculately presented, and his sky-blue shirt was tucked into his navy chinos. In contrast, Sam wore an old T-shirt that clung to his muscular frame and a pair of shorts that were scuffing slightly at the hem. Pearce lowered himself onto the bench next to Sam and took a sip of his coffee.

'Thanks,' Sam said, taking a sip of his own. They sat in silence for a few moments and Pearce looked across the patio area at the other pieces of furniture Sam had sanded down and varnished, breathing a new lease of life into them.

'Looking good,' Pearce said, pointing towards them with his coffee cup before breaking into another chuckle. 'Do you remember way back when, what you said to me inside that Starbucks by Scotland Yard?'

'Just a couple of good-looking guys grabbing some coffee.'

Both of them laughed.

'If only they could see us now, eh?' Pearce said, finishing his coffee. 'At least one of us has kept up appearances.'

'Don't be so hard on yourself.' Sam joked.

'Anyways, I better get on. We have some guy coming by

in the next day or so to discuss giving a talk to the kids about mental health at some point. He seems a little too salesy to me, so I'm going to give him a grilling.'

'That poor guy.' Sam shook his head. 'He has no idea what he's in for.'

Both of them smirked and Pearce patted Sam on the knee before pushing himself from the bench. The first time the two of them had met, Pearce was working for the Department of Professional Standards, and he'd interrogated Sam regarding an assault on a criminal who'd beaten the system.

This poor guy stood no chance.

As Pearce headed into the Youth Centre, Sam took a final sip of his coffee and then looked at the coarse area of the bench, sizing it up before another intense session of sanding begun.

It was a world away from his war on crime.

And for the first time since Sam had lost his son, he at least felt a modicum of happiness.

CHAPTER TWO

'Nice one, Linz.'
'Great stuff.'
'You nailed it.'

Lynsey Beckett smiled politely at her crew as they packed away their gear, running an awkward hand through her light brown hair. As always when she was on camera, she felt awkward by the amount of make-up that was slapped on her face and she felt like someone else.

It was a great gig she had.

One that any journalist, especially at her tender age of thirty-one, would die for. To be a news correspondent for the BBC was an incredible achievement, and it was merited. Born and raised in Belfast, Lynsey had sparkled at university, blossoming not only into a wonderful reporter but a quite striking woman. Her brown eyes matched her hair, and they contrasted with her pale skin and sharp features.

The university life also allowed her to discover who she was as a person, finally able to break free from the shackles of a strict, religious family who had nothing but good intentions.

Although her faith had lapsed numerous times, she still wore a crucifix pendant around her neck, a reminder of where she came from and to her, a connection to her parents who she hardly saw. They were born in Belfast and would die there, not wanting to explore the world or even contemplate the thought of a world outside of Northern Ireland.

They disapproved of her moving to London when the offer came from the BBC, her father remonstrating passionately that the news needed to be reported there in Belfast.

He had a point.

But Lynsey wanted more.

She wanted to see the world, investigate crazy stories and shine a light on the things people wanted kept in the dark. Uprooting and moving to London at the age of twenty-five had seemed daunting at first. She had hoped that living in Belfast would prepare her for London, but the capital city was a different beast entirely. It took her a few weeks of battling homesickness and loneliness until she struck gold and moved into a house share with two other young professionals, both of whom were as dedicated to their work as she was.

Luckily, they also liked to play just as hard and soon, a friendship blossomed among the three of them. Rosie was a year older and working as part of the crew for a famous photographer and Sue, who was a proud and feisty Brazilian woman, was another year older and already held a rather senior position within an accountancy firm.

Six years later, Rosie and Lynsey had been joint maids of honour at Sue's wedding and while she had moved on to wedded bliss, Lynsey loved her frequent visits to the flat to keep the old traditions going.

She had found her family.

A few semi-serious relationships had almost blossomed

into something more but Lynsey's promotion to an in-the-field correspondent put love on the back burner. She wasn't against the idea of settling down, and as she had turned thirty-one a few months prior, she had felt the very first tick on her biological clock.

But it wasn't the priority.

Nor was reporting on the three-year anniversary of the London Marathon bombing, despite the undoubted air play it would receive and the impact it would have on her ever-rising stock.

Lynsey was working on something else.

Something big.

Ever since her thirst for journalism became apparent, she had always had dreams of writing an exposé on a ground-breaking discovery. Something that would shake the nation to its very core. Despite the horrendous nature of the bombing, she didn't discover it. Sadly, those who suffered from the blast were the ones who went through the ordeal.

The rumours that it sparked Sam Pope's war on crime were exhilarating, as was everything to do with the man, but that had been unearthed by the late Helal Miah, a man she had respected from the first time she'd laid eyes on his work.

His death, in uncovering the vile truth of General Ervin Wallace, had hit her hard.

She had respected the man for his no holds barred approach to journalism, even though he pushed the boundaries so hard that he fell through.

That was the life she really craved.

The danger of knowing you were rattling the right cages and knowing that the words she committed to the page could be just as life changing and as dangerous as the bullets in a gun.

The BBC offered a great wage, a sturdy pension and

wonderful security. She knew that with her charming accent and pretty smile, she would most likely be groomed for one of the top spots in the next five years or so.

But she aspired to more.

She had given up her life in Belfast for more.

Scuppered her relationships for more.

And what she was working on could possibly be that ticket to the life she craved. On a few occasions, she had reached out to Nigel Aitkin, the editor of *The Pulse*, and while he was interested in having her on board, his scepticism of the BBC meant he didn't take her entirely seriously. Major news networks always have an agenda. Their allegiances to political parties often undermined the truth. It hurt Lynsey to hear she had been tarnished with that brush, but while there was a BBC lanyard around her neck and her face on their news broadcasts, she respected his decision.

But what she was working on would change not only his opinion, but her entire life.

As the BBC van side door slid shut, one of the apprentices returned from the local Costa with a tray of coffees, the crew welcoming her back with a big cheer. Lynsey smiled, remembering her own nervousness when she broke into the business in Belfast. Those days were filled with long hours and shite pay, but the sense of being where she belonged got her through. Lynsey made an effort to thank the apprentice personally, recalling the thrill she had received when the lead reporter acknowledged her as part of the team. Sipping her coffee, she glanced nervously at her watch. While the report she had recorded earlier had already gone out on the breakfast radio, there was now the painstaking session of working with the editing team to ensure their recording was stripped down into a three-minute segment on the evening news.

Lynsey had plans that night.

A place she needed to be and a large step towards completing her project.

Anxiously, she glanced down at her watch again, drawing the attention of Drew, her camera man.

'Everything all right, Linz?' He spoke in his usual gruff voice. The man was a teddy bear and Lynsey enjoyed his company.

'Yeah, just need to get this piece edited quickly today, is all.'

'Big plans tonight, eh?' Drew raised his eyebrows jokingly. The man had been happily married for years and had a couple of kids he adored. He was also constantly ribbing her for her failed romances. 'What does this hipster do? Perhaps he runs an organic fart smelling chamber or something ridiculous.'

The crew laughed and Lynsey mockingly held up a middle finger to him. Drew rallied the rest of the crew and they all embarked upon the vehicles, ready to head back to the studio in White City. Lynsey finished her coffee, popped the corrugated cup in the recycling bin nearby and followed suit, her mind racing with the thought of her project, and how tonight could be the night she painted a target on her back.

It was a sobering moment for Sean Wiseman the first time he had reconnected with his mother. It had been over five years since he'd last spoken to her, and although the journey he had walked since then had been one of pain and discovery, it was still heart breaking upon his return.

The first thing he'd noticed as he clambered the graffitied stairwell that ran through the centre of the block of flats like a crooked artery, was how impoverished the entire area was. The Heaton Estate in Neasden was a known criminal hotspot, and it was where Sean had begun his regrettable descent into the underworld, but what broke his heart was that it was the best his mother could do. Throughout his entire childhood, he wondered where his father had been. Without one single recollection or memory of the man, Sean had never badgered his mother for answers. There was a silent acceptance that the man didn't exist and now, as he approached his thirtieth birthday, Sean realised how hard that would have been for her.

Deep down, he had blamed her. For years.

And she knew it.

When he'd finally decided to reach out and show her that he'd turned a corner, he did so with trepidation. Despite living below the poverty line, Sean knew that his mother had worked effortlessly for him to not follow the gang life that had infiltrated the area like a disease. She worked two jobs, with a combined salary of barely minimum wage and instead of thanking her, he had thought her a failure.

Now, as he sat in the front room, watching her through the serving hatch as she made a cup of tea in the kitchen she kept so tidy, he scolded himself for how naïve he was.

The woman was strong.

She had been dealt a horrid hand by life, their situation exacerbated by his low life of a father and a government that looked out for the *haves*.

To them, the *have-nots* didn't exist.

'Sean, honey…' His mother's voice echoed through to the living room. 'Do you take sugar?'

'Just pop your finger in it.'

Sean smiled as he heard his mother giggle. Born in Nigeria, she had moved to the UK when she was four years old and been in North London for nearly fifty years. With money in short supply, she had never gone far, but she had refused his help. He could still hear her words when he cried as a child at Christmas, when all he had was a small toy to play with.

'*We are not poor, Sean. Not when we have each other. We are rich because we have love.*'

Those words haunted him his entire teenage life, especially when he and his best friend, Elmore Riggs, began working for the local drug dealers. At just thirteen years old, Sean was the top bread earner in the house, but his mother refused it. She would clutch her *Bible* and tell him that he may as well shake hands with the devil if he wants to make money that way.

But Sean ignored her. With Elmore pushing him further down the rabbit hole, the two of them soon became dealers themselves. Eventually, that escalated to Elmore being a hired muscle and when he assaulted a rival and removed his eye, he spent seven years in prison. By then, the gangster life had run its course for Sean, and he took up his studies again, his analytical brain seeing him gain a few qualifications which his drug money had paid for.

He was ready to leave the life behind.

Until Elmore was released.

With his reputation enhanced, and his thirst for life rejuvenated by his incarceration, Elmore made serious plays that soon found him within the inner circle of Frank Jackson aka 'The Gent', one of the UK's most notorious criminals and the man who ran an off-limits building where criminals were offered sanctuary and the police were offered their every desire.

Elmore took Sean with him, harnessing Sean's intelligence to increase his footing and soon, Elmore was one of the most feared men in London. When Sam Pope put several bullets in Frank Jackson's chest, Sean wanted to give the game up for good.

Elmore wanted to seize the throne.

As Sean watched his mother walk into the front room with two cups of tea, he offered her a thankful smile. She placed it on the coaster, the steam rising from the mug and running over an old, black and white photo of his mother as a child.

'Thank you.'

'So, tell me…' His mother dropped into her chair with an audible groan, and it dawned on him that she was getting old. She was in her early to mid-fifties, but a life of hardship had caused bones to creak before their time. 'Is there a lady I should know about?'

Despite his dark skin hiding the blush, Sean could feel his cheeks warming with embarrassment.

'Nothing concrete.'

'Concrete?' His mother jokingly snapped her fingers. 'I want to be a grandmother!'

Sean smiled and sipped his tea. The flat, where he had spent so much of his life, felt tiny. It caused another ripple of regret to echo through his body.

Despite the size.

Despite the location.

She had always made it feel like home.

Sean could feel his mother's gaze resting on him and he greeted her with a grin.

'I've been too busy studying,' he said proudly. 'I'm a fully qualified social worker now. And I volunteer a lot at the Bethnal Green Youth Centre.'

'I always knew you were clever,' his mother said with a beaming smile. 'Always with your head in the books. It always hurt me to see you throw that away.'

Sean looked down at his hands which rested in his lap, allowing the guilt of his estrangement from his mother to wash over him. His life could have been so different.

Alongside Elmore, he had everything.

A nice flat. Money. An endless line of cheap women

who enjoyed the lifestyle and would lie with him to stay within it.

But the scar on the back of his hand was a permanent reminder of how close that life had taken him to death's door.

The skin where the bullet had ripped through his hand had healed over in time, giving a smooth finish and a lighter shade. But the damaged nerves had only partially recovered as the bullet Sam had blasted through his hand had done its job.

Not only did it convince Sean to give up Elmore's location.

But it gave him all the motivation he needed to quit the life. To do something better.

To *be* something better.

Since that moment, and a subsequent run-in with a vicious Ukrainian gangster, Sean had followed Sam's advice and visited Pearce at the youth centre, and his life changed forever. Suddenly, the only thing he wanted to do was to help guide kids following the same steps he had, and move them to a better path.

He had worked tirelessly to get the right qualifications, volunteered at the local council and made the right in roads to becoming a social worker. Now, fully qualified and with a burgeoning reputation, Sean finally felt that not only had he done something with his life, but he was finally doing something to make up for his past.

His mother's words still hung heavy in the air, and he leant forward and cupped her hand with his. She noticed the scar but said nothing.

'That's why I need to help these kids,' he said passionately. 'So they don't make the same mistakes I did. Right, I need to make a move. I've got a few more appointments this afternoon and then I'm attending a seminar later.'

Sean stood, followed by his mother, and he leant down,

his wiry frame causing him to tower over her. He planted a kiss on her forehead, the first time he had shown his mother that level of affection for years. He felt her shake and so threw his arms around her, the two of them holding each other tight.

Whatever pain or animosity that had driven a wedge between them had evaporated. Time had passed, lives had changed.

At their core, they were mother and son.

But from the life they had, they were all they needed.

'You're a good boy, Sean,' she finally said, wiping away a tear. 'Just don't spend your life working. Find a nice girl and give her everything. You don't want to be alone.'

Sean stepped back and wiped away his mother's tears before walking towards the door, lifting his satchel from the floor as he did.

'Don't worry, Mum. I'll be fine. Besides, you were alone, and you turned out pretty great.'

Sean opened the door and flashed a grin at his mother, who approached him. She ran the back of her hand across his cleanly shaven face and looked at him with love.

'I was never alone. I had you.'

They hugged once more, made a promise to see each other that Friday and Sean set off, walking through the dilapidated building that for so many years he had called home.

And for the first time in what felt like years, he had a reason to return.

CHAPTER THREE

'The thing people try to skirt around these days is the fact that mental illness is a pandemic. The number of lives destroyed by mental illness is comparable to some of the worst diseases the world has ever known. And while they encourage people to get vaccinations or teach about the impact of such outbreaks in schools, there is still a stigma around mental health that just won't go away.'

All eyes were glued to the stage, just as Adam Bridges wanted. As a leading spokesman for Head Space, one of the leading organisations tackling mental illness, Bridges had carved out a sterling reputation for getting the message across. At just thirty-four years of age, he could command entire conferences of teenagers, or stuffy boardrooms full of directors. It didn't matter what walk of life the audience was from; Bridges would have them eating out of the palm of his hand.

He craved the attention.

He always had.

Everything about him, from his walk to his hair cut, was pre-meditated. Paid handsomely by Head Space to spread their message, he ensured the clothes he wore were tailored to his gym-built physique. His neat, perfectly styled hair sat atop a handsome face with a strong jaw. Behind two rows of straight, white teeth was his biggest asset.

His silver tongue.

Bridges had the 'gift of the gab', speaking with such confidence and conviction that he could turn most situations to his favour. Coupled with his good looks and infectious charm, the man was catnip for CEOs and directors, all hoping to show the world that they wanted to help. In reality, it was good PR for their companies and a sizable amount of cash to Head Space, but Bridges didn't care.

His bonus cheques were always loud enough to drown out any lingering doubts he had about how genuine the company truly was.

Money made the world go round.

That was fact.

And if his organisation made a truck load while trying to at least help people, he could sleep well at night.

Besides, turning down the advances of powerful women was a perk of the job, especially as his tastes were for men just like himself.

As he peered out across the conference room, he revelled in the glow of the spotlights pointed on stage, the Head Space logo illuminated behind him. Several cameras were trained on him, with his talk about the work being done to raise awareness of mental health, particularly in teenagers, being beamed LIVE on Head Space's website, along with multiple networking channels.

Bridges was the face of change.

His immaculate grin luxuriated in it.

'As part of the next phase of fighting this war, and believe me, this is a war, is for someone to go first. We need someone to be bold. Someone to be brave. Someone to say, we want to listen. And Head Space waited for that voice and it never came, so we have decided, as of now, to take the lead to a brighter future for all of us. While there will be some generations who deem mental illness as weakness, we want the future generations to confront it. To accept it and most of all, understand it.'

Bridges took his rehearsed pause, knowing the following round of applause was incoming. It sent a tingle down his spine, knowing that every media outlet, school representative and social worker in attendance was hanging from his every word.

'So we have created the 'Out Loud Initiative'. The single goal is to make talking about mental illness, and seeking help, as natural as asking a friend for a lift home. To make discussing depression or, God forbid, suicidal thoughts, as easy as chatting about the weekend's football scores.' Bridges was in full flow, parading across the stage with the mic affixed to his expensive blazer. 'It won't be easy. Of course, it won't. The generations who tell young boys to 'man up' are the ones who are still raising our target audience. But this is a new world. Kids today, teenagers today, they have their finger on the pulse. They have seen the world that's been left for them, and they want it to change. They want to mould it into a more accepting and more caring future. The media, they will peddle a 'Be Kind' slogan when a tragedy befalls someone who they incessantly hounded, purely to cover their tracks. We don't want that. We want this world to be better. We want our children to be safe and most importantly, if they are struggling, we want them to know they are not alone.'

Bridges clenched his fists. He wondered how many people were wiping away tears at his words. Would this speech reach national news?

It was very exciting.

All he had to do now was finish strong.

'Head Space is committed to working towards that world. To making it a place where talking out loud is welcomed, not stigmatised. And if you believe in this initiative, let me know and say it proudly and say it… out loud.'

A thunderous round of applause echoed through the conference room, alongside the scraping of chairs as a few people stood abruptly, providing Bridges with the standing ovation he knew he deserved. Camera flashes flickered like a disco light, and he ensured he breathed in and set his shoulders straight. After a few moments, the applause began to die down, and he meandered to the side of the stage, twisting the cap off a bottle of water and taking a large gulp. His assistant quickly reminded the audience about the London 'super tour' that Head Space was embarking on, visiting schools and youth centres and that all interested parties should sign up via the website. Bridges walked back to the centre of the stage and waved goodbye to everyone, laying on his appreciation thick.

As he scanned the first few rows, he noticed the attractive woman trying her best to get his attention, her piercing eyes wide with intent. He rolled his, knowing that he would most likely have to turn down her advances.

She was holding onto a press card which was attached to a lanyard and as he squinted, he made out the initials.

BBC.

National news.

Instantly, Bridges motioned to his assistant to hand her a microphone. As the young man scurried to oblige, Bridges cleared his throat, ready to rubber stamp his slot on the news and the undoubted boost to his bonus cheque.

The woman was handed a mic, and Bridges afforded her his best smile as she began to speak in a thick, Northern Irish accent.

'Mr Bridges, my name is Lynsey Beckett for *BBC News*. Thank you for that wonderful presentation and I think we can all agree that the 'Out Loud Initiative' is a fantastic idea and a worthy cause.'

A few woops of agreement echoed from the room, along with a small clap. Bridges nodded his appreciation.

'Thank you, Miss Beckett. It's good to see so many people eager to share our vision.'

'Well, that's what I wanted to discuss with you, if I may. It is my understanding that the CEO of Head Space, Nicola Weaver, is also a shareholder at Prime Pharmaceuticals who happen to be the market leader for the mass production of antidepressant, Lonoxidil.' Lynsey could see the sudden flash of anger in Bridges' eyes. She had to ignore it and push on. 'With the rise of deaths from the overuse of this drug, and Head Space's recommendation for them, is there a genuine cause for concern that perhaps the vision of your CEO and Head Space as a company is more focused on the potential value of mental health as opposed to tackling it.'

'Ladies and gentlemen, that's all for tonight. I'd appreciate it if everyone could treat this so-called reporter's clear slander as exactly that. Good night.'

Bridges pulled off the microphone with disdain and tossed it to the floor, before marching off the stage, berating his assistant for not fielding the question before it was asked. Having grown up as an openly gay man, Bridges had suffered horrendous verbal abuse, but it had never bothered him.

What bothered him was being made to look foolish.

Especially in front of so many people.

Part of him wanted to confront that Beckett woman and let her know how dangerous allegations could be.

But that wasn't his job.

Mrs Weaver had ways of handling bad press and he was certain that once she saw the allegation, she would move swiftly to quash it. She was a powerful woman, as rich as she was terrifying and unfortunately for Lynsey

Beckett, it would probably only take a phone call for the story and her career to evaporate.

At least that was the best-case scenario.

The worst-case scenario caused Bridges to shudder, and he appreciated that his role never meant he had to get his hands dirty.

But as he marched through the back exit of the conference centre to the luxury car that would take him to his hotel, he did wonder about whether or not Beckett had truly understood what she had done.

There were some cages that were not meant to be rattled.

From a young age, Sam had been a man of routine. It had been instilled in him by his father, Major William Pope, who had been a proud military man. As respected as he was feared, Sam's father had navigated his way through a phenomenal career by using diplomacy instead of aggression, and for that, he was remembered fondly by all those who had met him.

But a man of William's ilk never missed a meeting and was regimented to the minute.

It was one of the many qualities he had passed down to Sam, and even though Sam's military days were long since over, old habits died hard.

With everything he had been through, from his attempted murder that ended his career, to the death of his son, to his war against crime, Sam had always had a reason to continue.

Something to fight for.

But it had been over eighteen months since he had gone to war to return Alex Stone to her family and, with the help of a hardened biker gang and a trustworthy DEA agent, faked his own death.

The government had registered his death on their records, and he was no longer a person of interest.

Sam was a ghost.

The long, highlighted hair, along with the thick beard skewed his identity enough, with the tabloids only ever showing a clean-shaven military photo.

He was yesterday's news.

Now, he was just Jonathan Cooper, a quiet man who worked as a handyman for a youth centre.

But his mind was still that of a soldier, and he found himself in the gym, sticking religiously to an extensive workout routine that kept him in prime condition. As he thrust the barbell upwards, he appreciated the effect a healthy routine had on his mental health. He had ample opportunity to give up and drink himself to death, allow the pain and loss of his own family to finally clamber up and snatch him away from the world. With no clear mission ahead, the demons were lurking ever closer to the surface.

It was why Sam had happily worked for nothing with Pearce, donating the minimal salary back to the youth centre.

It was also why he had quit drinking, knowing it would only take one lonesome, drunken stumble down memory lane to take him back to a dark place from which many people never return.

And it was why he dedicated an hour and half every evening after he finished work to the local gym, pushing his body and his muscles to breaking point to keep them working. After years of fighting for his country, from both sides of the law, Sam had put his body through the wringer.

He had been beaten, shot, stabbed.

Over a decade earlier, he had been blasted down a cliff face by a rocket.

His body should have been nothing but a bag of bone shards, yet here he was, in a physical condition that the young pretenders posing in front of the mirror could only dream of.

Sam was built to survive.

And if he stopped, then the sand in his hourglass would start falling again.

Sam grunted through the last few lifts and then slammed the barbell back onto the rack with a heavy clunk before pushing himself to a seated position. His pectoral muscles were burning, the tissue ripped by the heavy workout, and as he drank his protein shake, they would soon get to work rebuilding themselves.

It was a routine in which he found comfort and familiarity.

But the truth was, he was tricking his body into thinking it was fine, when really, it was as broken and as damaged as the life he had once led.

As Sam stood, he wiped down the machine and nodded to the young man who appreciated the vacancy. Finishing off his drink, Sam approached his rucksack, which he had stashed in the corner, threw his bottle inside, and then looped it over his broad shoulders. The gym was part of a chain, offering a twenty-four-hour facility and a cheap membership.

It also offered showers that Sam would have avoided even on his worst missions.

It was only a mile and a half from the gym to the Blackstone Estate, where he'd rented a small flat ever since moving back to the capital. Besides, he could use the warm down.

Jogging through the streets of London, he thought back to over two years before, when he pounded the pavement of Naples, building his strength back after nearly being killed by his former friend Mac.

He had come a long way since then.

A lot had happened.

But it was now in the past. It was time to move on and lock that part of his life away for good. It was why he had moved to the estate. Despite the good people he'd met locally, the estate, which was on the outskirts of the London Fields in Hackney, had a reputation for crime and poverty, with the desire to live there replaced by a necessity for most. Sam's friend and former ally, Paul Etheridge, had left him a small fortune when he went dark, a way of funding Sam's fight against injustice.

But now the fight was over, Sam refused to use the money, only taking what he knew he had in savings and from his military pension. Etheridge was a computer genius and would find some way of accessing the money despite Sam's demise.

Sam planned to pay him back every penny.

It only took him twelve minutes to turn the corner onto the estate, the large concrete structures jutting from the estate like jagged teeth, all of them composed of numerous flats too small for the occupants. The landlords didn't care about the conditions, just as long as the rent was paid on time.

Sam had been shocked at how easy it was to find a private landlord who asked no questions, especially when he offered a year's worth of rent up front. It also meant they didn't do any digging into Sam's background, especially when he wasn't sure exactly what history Etheridge had fabricated for Jonathon Cooper.

The estate was covered in graffiti, and as Sam slowed to a brisk walk, he could feel the eyes of a group of young men loitering on the flyover. As a white man, he was a minority in the area, however he hadn't come across any problems with the local gang. Just like his routine, Sam's automatic absorption of detail hadn't left him either, and he clocked eight of the young men watching him. Two of them sat on bicycles, while one of them was on his phone.

The gang were known for selling drugs and were involved in a 'war' with another local estate, according to Sam's neighbour, Jess. Sam had scoffed at the description of war, having fought alongside soldiers in the heat of battle. But to Jess, who was a single mother just trying to keep her daughter safe and make ends meet, life on the estate was tantamount to a war zone. Sam's flat wasn't in one of the large high rises, but one of the small houses on the side street. The owner, in an attempt to maximise profits, had split the house in two, with Sam occupying the small, four-room abode up the stairs, while Jess lived on the ground floor. Over time, they'd become friendly, although Sam had made it clear he had no interest in a romantic endeavour when she had made a drunken pass at him one night. Despite her initial embarrassment, the two of them had moved past it quickly and forged a solid friendship. Jess had only just turned thirty-one, but having been a teenage mother, had a daughter on the cusp of turning sixteen.

Jess was a proud woman, working a job as a cleaner along with a few evenings in one of the local pubs, refusing to live on benefits. Sam had offered a couple of times to help her out financially, but she had refused, although had leant on him a few times when their landlord had refused to fix issues in the house.

As he approached the door to the house, which then split off into two front doors, it flew open, and Lily, Jess's daughter, stormed out, screaming obscenities back at her mother who watched on with quiet resignation at the door. Sam popped his earphones from his ear, but Lily ignored him, stomping past him and back towards the estate.

Despite Jess's best efforts, Lily was becoming enamoured with one of the gang members and understandably, Jess was terrified of what might happen. As Sam approached the gate to the small courtyard out front, Jess clicked her lighter and shook her head.

'Sorry about that, John.' She offered a defeated smile.

'Don't be silly.' Sam waved it off. 'You okay?'

'Not really. But I have to go to work, so I have to just hope she doesn't do anything stupid.'

'She's a bright kid. Besides, I'll keep an ear out for her.' Sam placed his hand on Jess's shoulder. She smiled and gripped it with her own.

'Thanks, John. You're a good man. Tell me again, how are you single?'

Sam felt himself blush slightly and it was the only time he had been thankful for his beard.

'I prefer it that way.'

Sam stepped past Jess, the thick, heavy stench of smoke filling the air, and he did his best not to show his disapproval. As he stepped into their cramped landing, he slotted the key into the lock and pushed open his door. Behind him, Jess flicked her cigarette and reached in for her bag and coat.

'Oh, and John, word of advice.' Jess smiled cheekily. 'Don't have kids. Trust me, they cause you nothing but pain.'

Sam smiled politely, and then stepped into the stairwell up to his flat. He closed the door behind him, leant against it and instantly, visions of Jamie flooded his mind.

He slowly slid his back down the door, allowing the pain of his loss to flow down his cheeks.

CHAPTER FOUR

Six Years Earlier...

The constant hum of noise that emanated from any hospital was one of the things that had always made Sam nervous. Whenever he had entered the white, repetitive walls of a medical centre, he had always been a little on edge by the constant buzz of activity. As a trained soldier, one of the greatest marksmen to have ever held a rifle for his country, he would have assumed it wouldn't have even registered with him.

But it always did.

The relentless noise of people working their hardest to keep people alive.

His job meant that a life could be ended in a split-second decision, usually by the retraction of his finger and a squeeze of a trigger.

But in a hospital, people were working round the clock to keep people alive, responding to literal life or death situations with the skill and calmness beyond anything he had ever experienced.

A soldier on the front line was a brave man.

A nurse or a doctor on an emergency ward was something else entirely.

While his unease within a hospital was offset by his undying respect for those who dedicated themselves to medicine, on that fateful night, none of it registered.

The world had gone silent.

Black.

A light shut off.

Somewhere down the hall, in a private room, he could hear the pained cries of his wife, Lucy, as a grief counsellor sat diligently by her side, trying their best to help the woman through the loss of her son.

Their son.

Sam hadn't said a word since he'd let out an anguished howl of pain upon the sight of Jamie's body, his broken frame crumpled on the side of the road, his lifeless eyes staring out towards him. It was a memory that had carved itself into Sam's brain and heart for eternity, a pain unlike anything he had ever felt before.

That evening had been one of celebration.

Having recovered from the bullet wounds that had cut short his military career, Sam had enrolled as a Metropolitan Police Officer, excelling through the long, arduous training plan at the Hendon Police College. As an elite soldier, interest in Sam was high, with a clear path marked towards the Armed Response Unit being mapped out for him, either as a response officer or as a firearms trainer.

Either way, with his skill and capability, Sam was destined for a well-respected career.

After years of fighting overseas and surviving some of the most dangerous off-the-books missions, a training job within the Met sounded like a dream.

It meant more time at home with Lucy.

More time with Jamie.

But that evening, as he drank merrily with his best friend, Theo, Sam had watched a young man drunkenly stumble to his car, drop into the driver's seat and turn the key. Sam went to intervene, but Theo turned his attention away and the man drove drunkenly into the night.

That man was Miles Hillock, and on that journey home, he veered off the road and killed Sam's son.

Alongside the heartbreak of his five-year-old boy being snatched from the world, Sam's guilt hung heavy like a cinder block around his neck.

All he'd had to do was the right thing.

Stop Miles from getting in that car.

But he didn't.

And now Jamie was dead.

If he'd been asked, Sam wouldn't have recounted his journey to the hospital, his mind frozen in disbelief since the harrowing vision had greeted him as he stumbled home. A catatonic pain had encompassed him and as he finally looked down the corridor, he saw Theo standing, arms folded, talking to a couple of police officers.

Everyone's face was one of sadness. All of them were suffering from the death of a child, but Sam didn't register it. There was nothing anyone could say, nothing they could offer that would ever fix what had broken that night.

Theo nodded his appreciation to the officers, even gently patting one on the shoulder before he shuffled further down the corridor to the Costa Coffee machine, which loomed over the hallway. The clunky machine spat out a couple of sloppy coffees and charged Theo a small fortune before he marched back towards his best friend.

'Sam, take it,' Theo said, his words laced with heartache. 'It will help.'

Somehow, the message got through and Sam reached up and took the cup, not even thinking of thanking him. Theo sat on the uncomfortable plastic chair beside Sam and took a sip of his drink. They had built a friendship that verged on brotherhood while they'd served together, and Theo knew he didn't need to offer Sam words of encouragement or pity.

He just sat with him.

It might have been minutes.

It may have been hours.

Sam would never know, and Theo would never tell. The grief counsellor emerged at some point, explaining to them both that Lucy had cried herself to sleep, and that rest would do her the world of good. Theo thanked her politely, but Sam just stared ahead, wondering how any part of the world made sense.

How could he fight for so long and survive so much, only to have the one thing he fought for be ripped away from him? Throughout all his missions, Sam had come across some of the most heinous and vile people imaginable. While many of them had faced their own demise at the end of his rifle, so many of them roamed the earth, stepping down on those who were just trying to get by. And while a world could allow people like that to not only exist, but thrive, someone as innocent as his son could be cruelly taken away by a young man who didn't give a damn about the law. Every fibre of Sam's being wanted to roam the hallways of the hospital, looking for the man responsible for his son's death and put that man in the ground.

Miles Hillock.

He had committed the name to memory, knowing that he was the cause of a pain that would follow Sam like a shadow until the day he died.

With his heart shattered into a million pieces, Sam wished for that day to be sooner rather than later.

After an undetermined amount of time, Sam spoke, stirring Theo awake from the light slumber he'd fallen into.

'I should have stopped him.'

'What?' Theo mumbled, embarrassed that he'd been asleep.

'I should have stopped him.' Sam spoke slowly, staring at the wall before them. Tears ran from his red eyes down his stubbled cheek and dropped to the tiles below. 'I saw him get in his car, and I didn't stop him.'

'Sam, don't do this,' Theo said, resting his hand on Sam's shoulder. Sam jerked it away.

'But I didn't. Did I? I saw a drunk man get in his car and drive away and I did nothing.' Sam shook his head, the tears now rolling out in uncontrollable waves. 'Think of everything we did, Theo. All

the missions. All the people we saved. Somehow, somewhere, I thought that what we were doing would make this world a better place. Every time I went out there, I made a promise to come home to Jamie. But after all that, it took something as stupid as letting a drunk get in his car to fuck it all up.'

'Sam, it's not your fault.' Theo could feel his own voice cracking. 'Look, buddy, I know it hurts. It's always going to hurt. But your wife is in that room over there, going through the same thing as you. You have to fight again, Sam. For her.'

Sam wiped his eyes with the back of his wrist and took a deep, cleansing breath. He nodded, patted Theo on the knee, and then lifted himself from the chair. From the ache in his body and the numbness in his back, he'd been sitting for hours.

'There is nothing I can do for her that will ever make this right.'

Theo looked up at his friend, completely heartbroken.

'Sam, you can't make everything right. It's not how the world works.'

Sam drew his lips together, nodding a final thanks to Theo.

'Someone has to try.'

With that, Sam turned and slowly wandered down the corridor before opening the door to the private room. Taking a deep breath, Sam stepped into the darkness, ready to join his wife in their life destroying grief.

―――

It had been a trying afternoon and Pearce sat back in his chair, rubbed the bridge of his nose and let out a well earnt sigh. Ever since he'd taken on the role as Bethnal Green Community Centre Manager, Pearce had felt a new lease of life. He had loved his job as a detective inspector for the Met. His uncompromising morals and quest for justice soon saw him as the scourge of the bent copper.

The Department of Professional Standards investigated the actions taken by the police officers, and Pearce was at the forefront. With his smooth talking and severe backbone, he terrified many officers.

He was also despised by a number of them, seen as a traitor by a bunch of people who were swimming against a tidal wave of bureaucracy and public distrust.

But he was good at his job.

He had kept the police on the straight and narrow and most importantly, it had brought him to Sam Pope, a man who had changed his life irreversibly. Although he could never fully condone the path Sam had taken, the more involved he became with Sam, the more he realised he was a necessity. While Sam had his own reasons to fight, Pearce wasn't blind to the fact that there were places the police couldn't go, and several processes and procedures that tied their hands behind their back.

In most instances, a police officer would need written permission just to knock on someone's door.

Sam blew them open with a twelve-gauge shotgun.

For one whole year, Pearce had looked the other way, settling up with his conscience when Sam got results. It was only when Pearce had to break the law himself, by assisting a daytime raid of a high-ranking general in public that he knew he'd gone too far across the line to ever make it back in one piece. The decision to retire was an easy one to make.

With a great pension, Pearce stepped away and ever since Theo had given his life in the fight, he'd been volunteering to try to fill the hole the man had left behind.

The council wanted someone not just to run the youth club but the entire community centre, and with Pearce's stellar reputation and commandment of respect, he got the job.

The pay was low.

The hours were long.

But Pearce loved it.

Now and then, there were aspects he didn't enjoy so much. As with every job, he had to grit his teeth and get through it, and when Adam Bridges had left his office, Pearce was relieved. The man meant well as far as Pearce could tell and he was clearly passionate about the 'Out Loud' initiative he had discussed with Pearce, which was certainly intriguing.

But there was something off about it, too.

Years as an untrusting detective made those red flags a deeper shade of claret and as much as Pearce wanted to get invested in the idea, he didn't find one word out of the man's mouth to be genuine. Bridges was certainly a smooth operator, combining good looks, a charming smile along with bucket loads of charisma.

Many people would be lured in by him, Pearce was sure of it.

And while pushing the younger generation to discuss mental health as openly as they do their physical health was admirable, slapping a banner across it made it feel more like a PR campaign rather than a movement.

Pearce leant forward and picked up one of the leaflets from the information pack Bridges had left on his desk and looked over it.

He had made real progress with the majority of the kids who had found their way to the youth centre, many of whom didn't have anywhere else to go. With the poverty in the area on the rise, many of the teenagers came from broken homes, or worse. At the youth centre, a place of trust that Theo had established before his untimely murder, they had a voice.

They had people who would listen.

More importantly, they had hope.

Hope that there were people out there who gave a damn about them, and Pearce found, quite quickly, that he did. The idea of unleashing Adam Bridges on them felt like a violation of the relationship he had built with them, and the last thing he wanted was to pressure any of them to talk beyond their comfort level.

Pearce glanced up at the clock.

It was quarter past six.

With no club on that evening and the weather offering a rare, enjoyable spring evening, Pearce smiled and stood, stuffing the leaflet into his pocket and reaching for his sports jacket. He slid his arms through and then headed to the door, knowing he would catch Sam on his way through.

Sure enough, as he approached the back courtyard, he could hear the relentless scratching of the sandpaper as Sam ferociously hammered the wood. Pearce had offered him the budget to buy an electric sander, but Sam had relented. As Pearce watched him, he could see why.

Whatever Sam used to keep bottled up was getting harder to contain, and he channelled that into the project of upcycling the patio furniture. He was doing a good job, but Pearce knew that it meant more than that.

With his fight over, Sam was looking for meaning in a world that he had turned his back on.

However Pearce could help, he would.

'Don't you ever get tired?' Pearce interrupted as he stepped into the forecourt. 'I'm knackered just watching you.'

Sam stood up from the bench, which was on the verge of completion. He would need to paint the entire piece with a nice varnish, but he couldn't help but be proud of the job he'd done. A bead of sweat dribbled down his forehead, and he swept it away with a dusty hand, smearing it across his head.

'It'll be worth it.' Sam smiled.

'Well, I think you've done enough for the day. Come on, I'll buy you some dinner.'

'Thanks, but I've got the gym.'

'You can miss one day.' Pearce insisted. Sam rested his hands on his hips. The gym had been part of a routine that had kept him sane and pain free for over a year.

But Pearce had done more than that.

An evening of good company was worth skipping a session for, especially as Jess was working that evening thus denying Sam any chance of a conversation later.

'Let me clean up, and I'll be with you.'

Pearce smiled warmly as Sam tidied away the courtyard and then nipped inside to his locker. A man of basic tastes, he swapped his plain black T-shirt for another and sprayed some deodorant. Pearce sometimes felt ashamed of his designer clothes when he was with Sam, knowing the man held little stock in fashion.

But Sam never said anything.

It was a foolish stick to beat himself with, especially when he did so much for so many. Sam reappeared in the courtyard, a clean T-shirt stretched across his muscular torso, and water splashed into his long, blonde hair.

'Let's go.' Sam nodded, before lifting his hand. 'Oh, by the way, I found this in the bathroom.'

Pearce held out his hand and Sam put the empty prescription box in his palm. The name of the patient had been removed, but the name of the drug was clear as day.

Lonoxidil.

Pearce opened it and removed the foil packet, but it was empty. A look of worry spread across his face, and Sam looked at him.

'Everything okay, Adrian?'

Pearce took a moment to collect his thoughts and then nodded, before heading to the door.

'Hey, Sam, do you mind if I invite another person to join us?'

Sam shrugged and the two men headed out of the side gate of the youth centre, as Pearce pulled out his mobile phone to make the call.

CHAPTER FIVE

The spring evening brought with it a gentle breeze, and Sam was glad he had brought his jacket. The beer garden was surprisingly vast for a pub in London and the majority of the wooden tables were occupied with groups of co-workers, all enjoying the Friday evening and the promise of a hang-over fuelled weekend to come.

Sam tried his best to block out memories of his drunken evening with Theo the night of his son's death and looked at the Diet Coke on the bench before him. It had been eighteen months since he had tasted alcohol, sitting in the same beer garden opposite the same man.

Pearce raised his IPA to his lips and took a sip, before resting it down and enjoying the comfortable silence between them. Sam appreciated Pearce's company, and the fact the man knew about the personal demons he was constantly battling. Throughout his entire fight against the criminal underworld and corrupt elite, Pearce had been more than an ally. He had been a friend, and now that the fight was over, that friendship had truly blossomed. There was no need to force a conversation for the sake of filling the silence, and Sam was eternally thankful for Pearce's understanding.

A young waitress approached the table, clearing away the empty plates, and Sam offered her a smile, which she returned.

'How's Jess?' Pearce asked, lifting his drink again.

'She's okay. Her daughter stormed out of the house yesterday. Was a bit of a scene.'

'She's always welcome at the centre, you know that, right?'

'Oh, I've mentioned it a few times to both her and Jess.' Sam shrugged. 'But Jess thinks she's hanging around with the gang on the estate and she doesn't want to listen.'

'It must be terrifying for her.' Pearce shook his head. 'The Blackstone Estate isn't the safest place for anyone, let alone a fifteen-year-old girl. Hopefully, she isn't stupid enough to go too far down that rabbit hole.'

Sam took a sip of his Coke and felt helpless. Jess was a wonderful woman, who had done her best with what she had to provide a stable life for Lily, but all that good work was being eroded by the lure of the streets. Every night, Sam had to fight against every fibre of his being not to step in and eradicate the gang that haunted the estate like a violent spectre.

But he had turned over a new leaf.

He was at peace with himself. Although he had broken his promise to his son to not kill again, he had at least fought back against those who treated the system as a joke, and who profited from the pain and misery of others. His legacy was vilified by most quarters of the press and his actions were as violent as those who he had put in the ground.

But it had been the right thing to do.

Sam wanted to help Jess to steer Lily back onto the path she had worked so hard to forge.

But he couldn't go back there.

With a resigned sigh, Sam looked at Pearce helplessly.

'What am I supposed to do?'

'I don't know.' Pearce smiled and lifted himself from his chair. 'But I know just the person to help.'

Sam followed Pearce's gaze and arched his neck to see Sean Wiseman stepping into the beer garden, a wide grin on his face as he waved to them. Sam could feel the smile crawl across his face as he watched the young man stride across the grass to their table, his satchel swinging from his shoulder. Sam shot a glance back to Pearce, who beamed with pride, and their embrace was that of a father hugging a son.

Pearce was certainly a father figure for Sean, and ever since Sam had directed Sean to the youth centre, the man had turned his life around.

It had been two and half years since Sam had accosted Sean's car on a dual carriageway on a rainy night in Holborn, taking out the vehicle with a well-placed shot. After removing the driver from the equation, Sam had come face to face with Sean for the first time, berating the wannabe gangster into giving up his boss, Elmore Riggs. To put an exclamation point to the end of Sean's criminal career, Sam had blasted a bullet through the back of the young man's hand.

Sam regretted it now, knowing his mission had taken control of his mind and he had been needlessly aggressive.

But Sean saw it as a reminder of who he had been and how far he had come. While he had lost some of the nerve function, the scar that spiralled out from his hand was a map of his success.

He had since dedicated his life to helping the helpless, and Sam had nothing but respect for the man.

Pearce slapped Sean on the back and they both took their seats, as another round of drinks came to the table.

Sean gave Sam a bit of lip about his sobriety, to which Sam threatened another bullet through the hand.

The three of them chuckled.

A friendship had been born out of Sam's mission, with Pearce and Sean joining the fight to help people in their own distinctive ways. It had bound them together, and the conversation was light and breezy as a few more drinks followed, with Sean's skipping of a good dinner coming back to haunt him. As Pearce dug around in his pocket to find his wallet, he tossed his keys onto the table, along with the empty packet of Lonoxidil.

Instantly, Sean's eyes lit up.

'What the hell is that?'

'Oh, it's just a keyring.'

'No…' Sean rolled his eyes and lifted the empty packet. 'This.'

'Oh, yeah. It's one of the reasons I invited you. Sam found it in the bathroom at the centre.'

Sean looked to Sam who nodded to confirm.

'Jesus. This is bad, Adrian. I thought the talk we did last year had finally got through to them. This stuff is like cocaine to these teenagers.' Sean cleared his throat, embarrassed. 'Not that I know what that's like.'

'Relax.' Pearce chuckled. 'You're not that guy anymore, and we aren't the people we once were, either. But yeah, you're right. We need to do something about it.'

'Do you want me to give another talk?' Sean shrugged, sipping his drink.

'Actually, I had some overbearing guy turn up in my office earlier today. He was a bit much, but he was running a program designed for teenage mental health.'

'It wasn't Head Space, was it?'

Pearce clicked his fingers and pointed at Sean to confirm. Sam watched silently, noticing the worry in Sean's eyes.

'That's the one. Seemed a bit pushy, but I guess it couldn't hurt for him to—'

'It could hurt. A lot.' Sean interrupted and Pearce turned to him with a raised eyebrow. With a sigh, Sean flashed a glance to both men and then explained the session he'd attended the night before, where Adam Bridges had schmoozed the entire room into buying into the 'Out Loud' initiative and drew a rapturous round of applause for aligning so many companies into fighting the battle on mental health. It wasn't until Lynsey Beckett, the BBC reporter intervened and embarrassed the man on stage by revealing damaging links between Head Space and the manufacturer and distributor of Lonoxidil, coupled with accusations of collusion and an intent to supply.

'Seriously, she was incredible,' Sean continued, his face twisted in a smile. 'No fear at all. Just went straight for the throat.'

'And you believe her?' Sam finally joined the conversation, his hand gently resting around his glass of Diet Coke.

'Absolutely. She's a great reporter and she had proof.'

'You saw it?' Pearce asked, running his fingers across his beard and loathing the ex-smoker within.

'A little.' Sean looked at them both sheepishly. 'I kind of asked her out after the event. To talk more about the story and stuff.'

'Yeah, right.' Sam ribbed, and Pearce laughed as Sean squirmed in his seat.

'When are you seeing her?' Pearce asked, a serious tone to his voice. 'It would be good to get a little more information before we let this guy loose on the kids.'

'Agreed.' Sam nodded sternly. Somewhere in the back of his mind, he could feel that instinct to get involved twitch. A voice, calling from the darkness, telling him that he could get the truth his own way.

Sam ignored it.

That part of his life was over.

'I'll message her now. See if she's free tomorrow.' Sean said, his hand shooting for his phone and he shuffled with excitement at the thought of contacting her. As Sam watched his friend click away at the screen of his phone like a horny teenager, he hoped he was wrong.

Sam wanted to believe that people were intrinsically good.

Wanted to.

But couldn't.

As Sean tapped away on his phone, a jovial Pearce ordered one final round of drinks and Sam cleared his mind and focused on enjoying the company.

It was another late-night dash to the express supermarket before it closed, but luckily, Lynsey made it before they'd closed the doors. Another late night in the office had seen her write up a scathing article on the 'Out Loud' Initiative, tying in numerous reports of Head Space's involvement with the Lonoxidil addictions that were plaguing the teenage population.

Her editor had been uneasy with the subject matter, noting that their CEO, Nicola Weaver, was a friend of the chief editor and a generous benefactor for numerous charities.

But Lynsey wanted the truth.

Not the reputation or the glory.

There was a story to tell and a genuine problem to fight and she wasn't going to let the notion of someone's good standing in the media be used as a shield to protect them from the truth. It had been a long time since she had attended Church, but growing up, she had been badgered with the notion that people needed to own up to their sins.

That God was the only one who would judge them and that he offered forgiveness for those brave enough to come forward.

Over time, her faith had waned, but her commitment to the truth had never faltered.

Staring at the remnants of the microwave meal section, Lynsey selected a passable-looking pasta dish and headed towards the self-checkout, picking up a bottle of wine on the way through. As she reached for the bottle, a large, gruff looking man offered her a warm smile, before stuffing his hands into his leather jacket.

Another creep.

Lynsey rolled her eyes and headed to the checkout. She scanned the items and then waited for someone to confirm her age. She sighed quietly as the shop assistant hit the '*visibly over twenty-five*' button on the screen, reminding her that she had hit thirty.

She wasn't longing for a husband or a baby just yet, but it was always horrible to be reminded that her carefree days of her twenties were in the rear-view.

As the machine asked her for her payment method, her phone buzzed, and a smile spread across her pretty face.

It was from Sean.

After the talk the night before, and her confrontation of the repugnant Adam Bridges, Sean had approached her with a gentle smile. At first, she thought he was another leech who recognised her from the television, which then apparently gave him the right to demand a photo.

But he was different.

Kind. Softly spoken.

But most importantly, invested. He was a social worker, working with local youth centres to tackle the very problem Head Space was creating.

He was also handsome, and with her train deadline fast approaching, she had cut the conversation short but had given him her number.

Fancy a drink tomorrow? It's Sean btw. X

Lynsey pressed her card against the contactless machine, slipped her meal for one into her handbag and then headed to the door, her face blushing from the excitement of a drink the following evening.

She wasn't craving for a husband or a relationship.

But she had needs.

Plus, the idea of a night of good company and intelligent conversation was appealing and she stepped onto the street, looking at her screen.

With her attention focused on the flirty message that was forming beneath her fingertips, she didn't notice the man from the supermarket approaching her from behind. As his footsteps echoed behind her, she spun in fear, only to be greeted by his grin.

One of his teeth was horribly stained.

His thinning, black hair clung to his skull like a weed, and his chubby face was covered in patchy stubble. He stood at over six feet two and was stocky. A lifetime of gym memberships had given way a little to Father Time and his stomach was slightly paunched against his jacket.

The smile quickly faded.

His words came out in a thick, Cockney accent.

'Lynsey Beckett.'

She stayed quiet. He pointed to her lanyard, which still hung from her neck, revealing her identity and place of work.

'Can I help you?' she snapped, taking a step back, her right hand fumbling for her keys in a vain attempt to intimidate. The man chuckled at the idea and lifted his meaty hands in faux fear.

'I just wanted to introduce myself. My name is Daniel

Bowker. It would be in your best interests to not publish your article tomorrow.'

'What article?' Lynsey questioned, playing dumb. Bowker sighed, as if he'd played this game a hundred times before.

'The one about Head Space. It would cause problems.'

'So?' Lynsey tried to hide the quiver in her voice. She had failed. 'What's it to you?'

'I'm the person powerful people send for when they have problems.' Bowker grinned his crooked smile. 'And you are very close to being a problem. Understood?'

'Are you threatening me?'

Bowker chuckled, fixing the collar of his jacket before popping his hands into his pockets.

'Put it this way, love. If you publish that article, you are going to find out exactly why people like me exist.' Bowker's cold, dark eyes bore a hole through Lynsey, who could feel her knees buckling with fear. 'Good night.'

Bowker stomped off into the London night, leaving Lynsey rooted to the spot, the fear holding her in its cruel clutch. After a few moments, she realised she was crying, and she wiped away the tears with the back of her hand, her fingers still clutching the phone.

It rumbled.

It was Sean.

Before she even thought about reading his message, Lynsey took a few moments to compose herself. A very clear threat had just been made against her, from the company and CEO she was investigating.

It was meant to scare her away.

All it had done was confirm to her that she was right. As a terrifying thought of the repercussions raced through her mind, she hailed a passing taxi to take her home, with her resolve to expose the truth stronger than ever.

CHAPTER SIX

'Looking lovely, Janice. Loving that hairdo.'

Bridges flashed his million-pound smile in the direction of the office manager, who waved him away with a roll of the eyes. Janice had worked for Head Space since its inception and while she was extremely diligent in her role, Bridges had tired of hearing about her failed love life and cynical take on the world. As a gay man, he had no romantic intent at all, but he found himself perpetually wound up whenever she dismissed his compliments.

It wasn't that he truly meant them.

It was the fact that every other woman in the office was like putty in his hands.

Bridges had never made it clear that he was homosexual. He wasn't ashamed of it. In fact, he was as proud of his sexuality as he was of his central role to the organisation. The power of his charm was a valuable weapon in his arsenal, and he wasn't prepared to sacrifice it for some brave notion of equality.

He did what he had to do.

That's how people got ahead in life.

It's what had helped to pave the way to his immaculate

office, and as he walked past the banks of desks in the open-plan part of the office, he couldn't help but feel a smug sense of superiority. Hunched over their desks were plenty of lower paid people, all clicking away at their keyboards, running in the hamster wheels he'd helped create.

One or two of them may make a step up one day.

But none of them possessed even an iota of his charisma or drive and for that, he held no sympathy nor respect for them. As he approached the door to his private office, he took a final swig of his coffee and dropped the cup in the one of the many recycling bins dotted around the floor.

Head Space cared about the environment, too, and published a very generous report on their green policy and drastic reduction in emissions.

Bridges chuckled to himself.

Mrs Weaver was one hell of a CEO.

That much he did know.

She did what she had to do.

That's what she'd told him multiple times as he ascended the ladder. His turn of phrase and broken moral compass caused her to radiate towards him like a moth to a flame. With the right tailor and clear direction, Mrs Weaver had turned Bridges into a one-man PR Machine, and the bonus cheques he received for the business he pulled in were eye watering at first.

Now, they were par for the course.

Whatever she wanted the message to be, Bridges wove the narrative. He had reporters eating out of the palm of his hand, whether that be at social events or charity fundraisers. There had even been a time where he had blown a senior figure within one of the major media outlets, then threatened to out him to the press.

Bridges did what he had to do.

Mrs Weaver would have approved.

However, as he stepped into his office, the scowl on her face told him she wasn't there to offer her highly coveted praise.

'Mrs Weaver. What a lovely surprise.'

'I thought you said this wasn't going to be a problem.' Weaver snapped, waggling a newspaper at him. As with any bubbling tension, Bridges used his chiselled grin to cut through it like a knife through warm butter.

'I don't know what *it* is, but you know me. Nothing is a problem we can't solve.'

As Bridges approached her for their usual embrace, she stopped him by slamming the newspaper into his solid chest. There had been the odd occasion where she had been a little too forward with him. As a powerful woman approaching her sixtieth birthday, Weaver ensured that her appearance was immaculate, but sometimes, she needed something a little more to validate her beauty.

Bridges did what he had to do, but as she paced his office with her hands on her hips, he didn't think she would appreciate an advance.

'You said it was handled.' Weaver pointed a perfectly manicured finger in his direction. 'You promised.'

Confused, Bridges unfolded the paper, which Weaver had opened at page four. The headline was damning:

'Mental Health Organisation with ties to drug epidemic: New initiative seeks to prey on those who need help the most.'

The edges of the newspaper rustled as Bridge's fingers curled in anger. He scanned the paragraphs, noting his and Weaver's name several times, the slanderous words calling them nothing more than 'high-end drug dealers'.

It was preposterous.

Bridges wasn't an idiot. He knew Weaver had irons in many fires, and the fact she had someone like Daniel

Bowker on retainer told him some of them weren't legitimate.

Bridges' eyes locked onto the name of the writer.

Lynsey Beckett.

His eyes squinted with anger and suddenly, Weaver's presence became clear. After he'd reported back Beckett's probing question at the conference the other evening, she had instructed him to contact Bowker. It was a side of the job Bridges hated.

Bowker was a heinous excuse for a human being, but he certainly had his uses. He operated a seven-man crew, masquerading as a private protection business. Essentially, they were muscle for hire and, with a man with as little regard for humans as Bowker sat in the top chair, they took on whatever job they were offered.

As long as the money was good.

Bridges had given Bowker the name and instructed him that Beckett worked at the BBC. That was all he needed, and Bowker had given his word that it wouldn't be a physical solution. A clear threat to her personal safety should have been enough.

It had been on multiple other people.

There had been something in Beckett's eyes, a steely determination that had alarmed him. She had got hold of a thread, and it was becoming abundantly clear that she was willing to pull on it as hard as she could.

What she would unravel would destroy an awful lot of work and make a lot of wealthy people very unhappy.

As he glanced up from the paper, he could see the venom emanating from Weaver's stare.

'Fix this,' she demanded. Her words were cold.

'Leave it with me,' Bridges assured her, putting the paper down on his desk. 'I'll get this discredited by lunch.'

'We both know that a woman like that won't stop just

because we trash her case.' Weaver sighed, straightening her silk blouse. As always, she was dressed impeccably. 'You will need to take steps.'

Bridges felt his stomach flip with disgust.

He was a lot of things.

Narcissistic. Selfish. A snake.

But he wasn't a criminal.

Not in the true sense of the word.

But as Weaver headed to the door, she shot him one final glance over her shoulder, and gently nodded. His hand shook and he slid it under his leg to keep it from showing.

The nod was a silent order.

As the door closed behind Weaver, Bridges rocked back in his chair and took a moment to collect his thoughts. Then, with a heavy sigh, he lifted his phone to call a dangerous man to tell him he hadn't done his job properly.

Bridges had to do what he had to do.

But as he heard the gravelly tone of Bowker on the other end of the phone, he wished he had any other job in the world.

As Sam turned the corner onto the Blackstone Estate, he slowed to a brisk walk, allowing the gentle breeze to cool him. It had been another successful day.

A quiet one, with Pearce called to various meetings and only a few kids showing up to use the youth centre as a place of study. Sam had watched on from the courtyard, applying a final varnish to the bench he had proudly refurbished with his own two hands. Considering he had spent his entire life using them to kill people, he was impressed with how the bench had turned out.

It kept his mind off the past.

Kept his head clear.

Gave him a purpose.

Pearce had dedicated a lot of time to the local kids regarding the importance of their education and had therefore given them access to use the centre for a quiet area to dedicate their time to their work. Many of them came from rough places or from broken homes that offered little value to their future education.

Sam lived in one such area, and as he admired the graffiti that lined the first building of the estate, he sighed. Countless times, he had thought about cleaning it himself, but he knew it would be a thankless task. The hope that it would tap into a dormant community spirit was a fool's errand, and the reality was that the graffiti would return and most likely spread to his front door.

Sam didn't want to invite that attention to Jess's doorstep, and with his new life of simplicity and calm, he too didn't want the hassle.

As he walked, Sam stretched out his back. The slow ache of a vigorous weight session after work had started to take effect and he could feel his muscles wrestling for space. Now and then, he would feel a wince of pain in his spine, with his mind flashing back to his brutal fight with the Hangman of Baghdad, where Sam had his back sliced open.

Farukh didn't survive.

Sam had.

He always survived.

That pain, along with the rest of the injuries he had suffered through his war, was becoming less frequent with every week. Sam was under no illusion that most of it was in his mind. His brain was reaching back to his former life, sending messages to Sam that there was still a war to be fought. But by dedicating himself to the youth centre and keeping his body and mind in the best shape possible, Sam was doing well to ignore the call.

As he walked past the first block of flats that comprised the estate, he could hear the murmurs of an argument, a woman's voice bickering with peril. Sam quickened his pace, rounding the building until he arrived at the courtyard that separated the large decrepit block from the next.

Lily.

Jess's daughter gesticulated at the gang before her, their smug grins causing Sam's fists to clench. It was clear that she was trying to leave, but the young man she had become increasingly more enamoured with was refusing to let go of her arm. To hammer home his control, three of his friends had stood around her, their hoods up and their chuckles ringing loudly.

'I want to go home.'

Lily pulled back again, trying her best to wriggle free from the boy's grasp. With a nonchalant shrug, the boy let go of her sleeve, and she stumbled back before losing her footing and crashing backwards onto the hard pavement.

She yelped in pain.

The group laughed loudly.

Sam tried his best to keep to his new path.

But it was no use.

'Hey!' Sam called out, his deep voice echoing off the surrounding concrete and sending the whole scene silent. The four boys turned in a mixture of surprise and annoyance, with the ringleader snarling angrily as Sam stormed towards them. The others adjusted their positions, standing behind him, all of them doing their best to convey the amount of danger that Sam was walking toward. As he approached, Sam noticed a few twitches of apprehension among the gang. Still wearing his gym clothes, Sam knew that his muscular frame was daunting, and he stomped towards Lily, who was trying to scramble to her feet. Sam leant down and offered his hand.

He could see the humiliation in her pretty face, but her eyes conveyed an anger at his intervention. With a disgruntled mutter, she took his hand, and he hauled her to her feet.

'Let's go,' Sam said sternly. Lily huffed and turned, stomping away from the gang who hurled a few derogatory slurs in her direction. The leader of the group, the one who had sent her tumbling, held out his arm with a smirk, her handbag hanging from his ringed fingers.

'Oi, bitch. Forget somethin'?'

The others laughed as she turned back, her eyes red with tears and Sam took a deep breath.

His fight was over.

He kept telling himself that over and over again.

As he watched Lily continue to walk away, her arms wrapped around her body, he turned back to the gang who were laughing among themselves. Sam took a few steps towards them, his eyes glued to the leader of the group. One of them noticed his approach and all of them turned, chests out and jaws straight.

An attempt at intimidation.

Sam stopped a few feet from the ringleader, catching them off guard by his lack of fear.

'Give me the bag and that will be the end of it.'

'Man, fuck you, white boy.' The leader spat, kissing his teeth. 'Do you know who the fuck we are?'

'Man, fuck this pussy up.'

'Yeah, Jamal. Shank this bitch.'

'Jamal,' Sam said firmly, ensuring the boy understood he knew his name. 'Just give me the bag and I'll go.'

With his crew egging him on, Jamal took a few deep breaths, psyching himself up to prove his toughness. Sam had already clocked the nerves and watched carefully as the young boy's hand slid into the pocket of his hoodie, most likely for a weapon. Knife crime was a horrific plague upon the city of London, especially among the teenage gangs that felt they had no other options.

If the government wouldn't help, they had to fend for themselves. As much as Sam deplored the idea of young kids carrying weapons, he understood that desperate people did desperate things.

Nervously biting his lip, Jamal stepped forward, stopping a few inches from Sam.

'You're in a dangerous place, bruv.'

Sam leant in. His voice cold.

'So are you.'

Sam's threat rattled Jamal, who quickly tried to re-establish control. As he withdrew his arm, Sam's arm shot forward, his hand wrapping around Jamal's forearm and locking it in place like a mechanical vice. The gang member yelped in shock and Sam shot his other arm out as if to strike him.

Jamal threw his other hand up to block the blow.

His surrounding friends jumped back.

But the blow didn't arrive.

In his panic, Jamal had dropped the bag to the floor and Sam leant down and retrieved it from the floor. He waggled it gently at the gang, looking each of them dead in the eye as a warning. He released Jamal's arm and then marched away, heading after Lily who had disappeared around the corner and was heading for their flat. As the gang watched Sam leave, Jamal hurled some abuse at him, calling him a dead man.

But Sam had heard a lot worse.

From a lot tougher.

Eventually, he caught up to Lily, who had regained her composure, and he slowed to a walk, accompanying her as they approached the street that their respective flats were on. Sam held out the bag and Lily took it, not even offering Sam a courteous glance by way of a thank you. Sam walked silently beside her before opening the gate to their building and letting her step through. She stormed to the door that led to the small entrance and headed straight for the door of her flat.

Sam headed to his.

It was a Wednesday and he knew that Jess worked an evening shift at a local supermarket nearby.

'I'm upstairs if you need anything.' Sam shrugged, before slotting the key into the lock of his door and it clicked open. As he stepped through into his stairwell, Lily leant against the frame of her own front door.

'Thanks.' She practically had to force the words out. 'Back there. Thank you for helping me.'

'You're welcome.' Sam offered her a smile.

'I thought he liked me, you know…'

'Take it from me, Lily. If you spend your time with bad people, bad things happen. I know things are tricky, but your mum is out there, working two jobs to give you as much as she can. Just try not to make things harder for her, hey?'

Lily wiped her eye with her sleeve and took a deep breath. Judging from the look of contemplation on her face, Sam knew he had got through to her.

'There are a lot of bad people around here,' she finally said. 'So why did you help me?'

'Because it was the right thing to do.'

'You're all right, John. You know that?' Lily finally smiled. 'But be careful. Jamal can be dangerous.'

'I'll take my chances.' Sam chuckled, knowing that Lily was unaware of who he truly was. With one final sigh, Lily turned back to the door and pushed it open.

'Goodnight, John.'

'Goodnight, Lily.' Sam nodded and Lily disappeared

into her flat and the door closed. Sam stood for a few moments, juggling with an unusual feeling. He closed the door and climbed the stairs to his own flat and as he entered, he realised that the strange feeling was one that had been absent for a long time.

He felt good about himself.

CHAPTER SEVEN

Daniel Bowker was a man of simple pleasures.

From a young age, he had never been one to toe the line, and his attitude had led to a failed education. With an absent father and a selfish mother, Bowker had grown up marching to the beat of his own drum. For fifteen years he had run roughshod over the estate in Lewisham. Mixing with the other tearaways, the only place Bowker had found structure was in the unrelenting code of the streets.

Several scrapes had moulded him into a tough kid and when he stumbled across a boxing club on his fifteenth birthday, he found a place to make him dangerous.

Every day, he hit the bags.

Bowker had always been a big kid, but by his seventeenth birthday, he stood at over six feet tall without a shred of fat on him. Soon after that, with his coach spurring him on, Bowker began to enter the local boxing circuits, amassing a terrifying knockout streak due to his relentless assault on his opponents. His 'go for the throat' tactics were unruly and drew the ire of many boxing aficionados, but the wins racked up and soon Bowker was being touted as a potential pro.

But boxing federations had rules and policies, all of which he had felt caged him from being the fighter he was destined to be. By the age of twenty-one, he had failed one drug test too many and was banned from competing professionally.

Instead of hauling himself back on track, he followed the cocaine further off the rails into the world of bare-knuckle boxing, where once again, he built a reputation as a man without a limit.

They nicknamed him 'The Reaper'.

And for numerous opponents, he more than lived up to the billing. By the time the fifth person had died by his hands, he found invitations drying up, with the underworld wanting to protect their investments.

It was a backhanded compliment, but one that had left him without a steady income and more importantly, a sense of purpose.

There was no glitz or glamour to the life he had led. But soon, a crime boss named Harry Chapman reached out, needing a problem solved before an impending court date.

Bowker took the job, sent a clear message to a key witness by breaking her husband's spine, and was paid handsomely.

No fuss.

Whatever the request, Bowker obliged.

Men.

Women.

Even children.

Had he had even the slight remnants of a conscience, maybe he would have spoken out, but Bowker didn't care. He understood that rich and powerful people were willing to exercise both attributes in order to remain in their thrones. While beating a teenage boy was done by his hand, the order came from a moral-less bastard who sat behind an oak desk in a fancy office, fawning for the public.

Bowker wasn't the real villain.

He was just an instrument in ensuring the real ones were never caught.

While the money rolled in from his rich clients, Bowker had never been lavish. The flat he was sitting in was modest. Its furnishing bought from a chain store that offered quality relative to its prices. The wide-screen TV was a budget brand and was only ever used for boxing or mixed martial arts events.

There were only three items within the confines of Bowker's flat that were reflective of the vast fortune he had amassed from the crimes he'd committed.

The punchbag in the spare room, the mattress on his bed, and the record player that sat proudly by the window in the living room. Beyond that, the money went either on his private security business, or his penchant for prostitutes.

Either way, Bowker had more money than he ever needed.

A man of simple pleasure.

What he truly desired was what he had when he had stepped between those ropes all those years ago.

Fear.

The fear of the man opposite, looking him in the eye and realising that his luck had run out. That no amount of training could ever prepare him for what Bowker offered.

That their time had run out.

Once he'd forged his reputation, he had set up his own personal security firm. Throughout his life on the streets and the trail he had blazed through the underground boxing circuit, Bowker had met many like-minded individuals, all as gifted with their hands as they were vacant with their emotions.

He reached out.

Built a seven-man crew that were at his beck and call.

Clients stacked up.

Problems were solved.

Now, in his mid-fifties, Bowker didn't even need to lift his own fists to handle a problem and cash a large cheque.

He only needed to lift his phone.

Simple pleasures.

As he sat back on his sofa and sipped his beer, he groaned slightly as the prostitute's head bobbed up and down on his lap, pleasuring him for a hefty fee. The vinyl spun on the record player, the smooth jazz filling the apartment in its cool, off-the-cuff melody.

Simple pleasures.

All of it was interrupted by the shrill, piercing ring of his phone. With a sigh, he lifted it.

Bridges.

'What?' he grunted.

'Mr Bowker?' Bridges' voice stammered. Bowker rolled his eyes. For all the slick talking and polish, Bridges was a weak man.

'What do you want?' Bowker looked down at the woman, indicating for her to continue. She obliged.

'Umm… that problem we spoke about the other day?'

'The reporter. Yeah. What about her?'

'Did you read the paper today?'

'I don't read the papers,' Bowker snapped. 'Nothing about this world interests me.'

'Well, it seems like the message wasn't clear enough.' Bridges paused, clearly scared of offering criticism. 'Mrs Wea…'

'Let me guess… you want me to send another message?'

There was a knowing silence.

Bowker smirked, waiting for Bridges to locate his balls before he could answer.

'Yes. Perhaps a little stronger this time?'

'That will cost more,' Bowker said, taking a deep breath as his companion quickened her pace. 'The bigger the mess, the bigger the clear up.'

'Money isn't a problem.'

'When?'

'Tonight?' Bridges was panicking. Clearly, he had given his word that things wouldn't get this far. 'We believe she is preparing another article for tomorrow…'

'I don't give a shit,' Bowker interrupted. 'Consider it done. I'll be in touch.'

Bowker cut off the call and tossed the phone onto the sofa beside him. A ripple of anger coursed through his body. The thought of his intimidation not working was insulting. Beyond the damage to his pride, it was an easily solvable situation. He would call his right-hand man, Benny Hicks and get him to dig up what they needed.

But that call could wait.

He tilted his head back, took a sip of his beer and let the jazz seep through him, as the woman brought him to the finish line.

Simple pleasures.

―――

Sam stood at the back of the main hall; his muscular arms folded across his broad chest as he watched on with interest. He'd caught a glimpse of himself in the reflection of a window and barely recognised the man staring back. His hair was thick, pushed back over on itself and tucked beyond his ears. The usual dark colouring had been lightened with highlights that clashed with the thick, dark beard that was tinged with grey.

He was unrecognisable to the clean-cut soldier he had been, and while it was a necessity to live his new life, it always caught him off guard. Combined with the impressive physique his newfound gym addiction had moulded; it was like looking at a completely different person.

The hall was packed, with over fifty teenagers all shifting uncomfortably in the plastic seats he'd laid out in neat rows, their eyes transfixed to the front where Sean stood, talking passionately about the dangers of reliance on medication to deal with mental health problems. Dressed smartly in a shirt and chinos, Sam was impressed with the man Sean Wiseman had become. More impressive still was how, despite coming from a troubled background, Sean had pushed himself into a position where these kids trusted every word he spoke. Many of them came from similar backgrounds, whether that be through hard financial circumstances or broken homes. However it had happened, many of them had been let down with little option for a change.

In Sean, they had a role model. Despite everything Sam had done, the punishing fight against organised crime, he could never be the symbol of a better life that Sean was.

Watching Sean answer the concerns of the crowd, Sam felt a sense of pride. Judging from the look on Pearce's face, who stood behind Sean with his hands casually in his pockets, Pearce felt it too. After Sam had destroyed the Kovalenko empire over two and half years ago, he'd sent Sean to Pearce as a way out.

Sean's life had been hard, dragged along a bad path by the wrong people and Sam knew if there was one person who could bring him back from the brink, it was Pearce. As expected, Pearce did exactly that, but he didn't just save Sean from a life of crime. He pushed him into a completely new one. And as Sean qualified as a social worker and took an active role in ensuring the children who relied on the youth centre never ventured down the same roads he did, Sam could see Pearce's parental pride blossoming.

Although Pearce had been married in his younger years, he had never had a child. His commitment to his job of investigating corrupt cops had superseded his commitment to his wife, and they parted ways just shy of his fortieth birthday.

In Sean, Pearce had found a son.

In Pearce, Sean had found a dad.

Sam couldn't think of a better role model for the young man, and for the kids in attendance, he couldn't picture two better people for them to look up to. It made him shuffle uncomfortably on the spot, knowing the things he had done were so far beyond the line that he had to fake his own demise to lead any sort of normal life.

He had done bad things for the right reasons, but there should have been no way back.

Sam knew he was lucky to have his freedom and watched on with interest as Pearce stepped forward, his brow furrowed with authority as he addressed the room.

'If any of you have any concerns around your mental health or the use of Lonoxidil, then I want you to come and see me.' He offered them a smile. 'Day or night. Over the phone or in person. We are always here for you, you know that, right?'

The kids all nodded, and Pearce then let them go about their business, as the majority of the older teens congregated around the pool table while some of the younger ones rushed to the back courtyard. Sam had already packed away his tools for the afternoon, so there was little worry for them to be unsupervised. As a few of them rushed past him, they smiled and greeted him, a few of the teenage girls giggling shyly. Sam laughed and then approached Sean, who Pearce had already patted proudly on the back.

'Good stuff.' Sam nodded.

'Thanks,' Sean said dryly, knowing Sam's praise wasn't always forthcoming. 'Let's hope it sinks in.'

'I'm sure it will,' Pearce said, before taking a quick sip from his water bottle. 'These kids are smart. Plus, they know you know what you're talking about. Imagine Sam trying to deliver that message?'

'Hey, I can be nice,' Sam said, faux offended.

Sean lifted his scarred hand.

'Yeah, real nice.'

All three men chuckled and then looked around at the harmonious room. Sam felt a little jolt of pain in his chest, his heart aching at how proud he knew Theo would have been at the good work that had been done in his name.

The same name that hung above the door in his memory.

Unlike Sam, Theo didn't get a second chance after doing the right thing, and it was another driver for Sam wanting to leave everything behind. To forge onward with a new life, where he made a difference in a different way.

'Oh, by the way, I'm seeing Lynsey tonight,' Sean said, trying hard not to boast.

'Nice,' Pearce said approvingly, like a proud dad who had just heard his son had popped his cherry.

'I'll ask her for more information about Head Space and—'

Pearce cut him off with a wave of the hand.

'Just go and have a nice time. If it comes up, ask a question or two, but don't press the issue.'

'But I thought...' Sean began and again, Pearce cut him off.

'Just don't do anything to fuck it up.'

Again, all three men chuckled before Sean said his goodbyes to get ready for his date. As he bounced towards the exit, Sam stepped next to Pearce, his arms folded.

'I thought you wanted him to get more information?' Sam asked.

'I do.' Pearce shrugged. 'But I kind of feel like the kid could do with a nice evening out.'

Sam agreed and the two of them walked casually towards the back door, ensuring that those who were in the courtyard weren't getting up to any mischief. As they walked, a few of the teenagers tried to goad Sam into a game of pool, which Sam temporarily put on hold. Pearce spoke with a few of the elder kids about the centre being open later that evening for movie night, which they ribbed him for his usually poor taste in films.

Everyone laughed.

A happy vibe buzzed throughout the entire youth centre.

Somewhere within himself, Sam wondered if he had finally found a modicum of contentedness.

CHAPTER EIGHT

Twenty Months Ago...

'You sure about this?'

Paul Etheridge looked up at Sam with his eyebrows raised. The sun gleamed off his shaven head, his hair having long since given up the fight. The man had been transformed since Sam had walked back into his life, demanding his help in tracking down Jasmine Hill, a young girl who had been snatched from her world for a fate worse than death. Back then, Etheridge had focused on the wrong things. He had an unlimited flow of cash from his private internet security firm, a trophy wife, and a massive house.

But it had rendered him hollow.

It wasn't until he'd been brutally tortured by Mac that he found his purpose. Shedding the materialistic life, he had sold his company, accepted the divorce from his wife and then tricked the government into thinking he had moved abroad for an early retirement. But he hadn't.

He had gone to work.

Despite the crippling knee injury that Mac had inflicted, meaning a lifetime limp, Etheridge returned to the exercise regime of his early military days, a time where he toured with Sam and Theo and was indebted to both of them for saving his life.

Now, as he looked up at Sam, he looked at him as an equal, not as the man Etheridge wished he was.

The respect was mutual, and Sam nodded to respond to his question.

'I'm sure.'

'Once we do this, there isn't any going back. It's done.'

'I'm ready for it to be done.'

'Okay. You're the boss.' Etheridge gave a mocking salute, drawing a wry smile from his friend. It had been three days since Etheridge had hijacked a prison convoy taking Sam to a lifetime of incarceration. They had got away swiftly and now Etheridge, just like Sam, was a wanted man. The original plan had been a success, with Sam being sent to 'The Grid' due to Etheridge's intervention, where he was able to bring down Harry Chapman.

Sam had taken off the head of the snake.

Chapman had ties to Frank Jackson, the Kovalenkos and most of the drugs and guns coming into the country.

They had stopped him.

It was only the emergence of a ghost from Sam's past that threw the entire plan into chaos, with Sam willingly stepping forward to protect his ex-wife.

Etheridge respected the decision. So had Amara Singh.

But it meant Sam had stepped back into the arms of the law and there wasn't any chance of a reprieve once he was behind bars. So Etheridge had ensured he never arrived and since then, they'd laid low in a safe house, where Etheridge had used his expertise and contacts to create entirely new identities for them.

They were bullet proof.

They could have walked away for good, but Sam had one final promise to keep. Etheridge had placed a small fortune in a bank account for him, telling him to use it to make the world a better place. Sam said he would use it to help Alex Stone, but then that was it.

And with this final decision, Etheridge knew Sam meant it.

The fight was over.

With a sigh, Etheridge lifted the large wooden crate lid and slid it across the top of the crate, concealing the last remnants of Sam's arsenal.

Sam had referred to it as his rainy-day fund, a stash of weapons in case he needed to fight back.

But with the fight over, Sam wanted to draw a line under it and move on.

Try to rebuild.

Try to forgive himself.

Once the lid was aligned with the edges of the crate, Sam picked up the nail gun and blasted the lid down, the nails ripping through the wood and locking it in place. Etheridge had already organised the courier to collect the crate and ship it off to the nearest military base, ensuring that the weapons Sam had used to disperse his own brand of justice would be placed in the right hands.

As the final nail shot through, Sam lowered the gun and took a sigh.

A weight seemed to lift from his shoulders, and he looked at Etheridge with a smile.

'*That feels good. That was everything, right?*'

'*Sure,*' *Etheridge replied unconvincingly, a wry smile across his lips.* '*You know that once you're back from the States, I won't be able to help you get any more?*'

'*Yeah, yeah. I know. You're going off the grid.*' *Sam made his hand move like a mouth.*

'*I'm serious. I'm in the wind.*'

'*I told you. I'm done.*' *Sam put his hands on his hips and looked out over the Thames. They had transported the guns to an abandoned fishery near the river, ensuring the crate was collected from there to cover their tracks. Sam thought back to when he had launched himself from New Scotland Yard into the river before him.*

It had been a long journey since then.

A lot of criminals had died by his hand.

A lot of lives had been saved.

But now, with the likes of General Wallace and Harry Chapman dead, he had reached the end of his journey. Discovering that Project Hailstorm was nothing more than an elite kill squad doing Wallace's bidding had ripped Sam's remaining heart fragments in twain, but he had at least put some of that right.

He had one last promise to keep, to return Alex to her family and then he could get to work on the one he had made to his son.

That he wouldn't kill anymore.

And as they made their way back to Etheridge's car, leaving the crate on the concrete for the delivery van, he knew that he would no longer have the weapons needed to break that promise again.

He didn't foresee a happy life ahead.

Jamie's death would hang heavily around his neck until the day he died.

But he could at least try to live a better life.

Walk a better path.

They both entered the car and sat in silence for a few moments, watching as the courier arrived and the driver suspiciously looked around. The package was as described and eventually he shrugged, lowered the ramp at the back of his van, loaded the crate onto the trolley and then began his work.

Moments later, the courier and the crate were gone.

Sam started the engine.

Etheridge chuckled.

'You know. I'm going to miss this,' Etheridge said, looking out of the window at the capital city, the sun shimmering across the windows of the numerous skyscrapers.

Sam slid the car into gear and pulled away.

'I'm not.' Sam said firmly. 'I'm ready for it to be over.'

———

Sean had never been to an upmarket restaurant in his life, let alone one of the top Japanese restaurants in London. Having grown up in poverty and then the inevitable descent into gang culture, the nearest he had come to fine dining was a takeaway from a fast-food chain. Before he left his flat to meet his date, he had stressed for ages on the appropriate outfit. He would never want to admit it, but he had been inspired by Pearce's commitment to grooming and ensuring that he always dressed smartly.

Since forging that relationship with his mentor, Sean had quietly gone about copying his wardrobe and now had a plethora of smart shirts and chino trousers to choose from.

But was it too smart?

Should he play it more casual?

Eventually, he had gone with a white shirt and navy trouser, along with a smart pair of trainers. It certainly worked, as when he met Lynsey Beckett out the front of the restaurant, she smiled and complimented him immediately.

It settled his nerves, and the peck on the cheek she gave him put a massive grin across his face.

She'd come straight from work. Another hard day on the journalism grindstone and Sean found himself fascinated by how intricate her job was. He had always assumed the reporters he saw on TV were just the pretty faces bringing the news to life, handed their lines to memorise like a stage actor. It turns out every news story Lynsey presented was the result of her hard work. She was given a lead, and she investigated and the more she spoke, the more Sean was engrossed.

When the waiter came for their order, he startled Sean, who had been lost not only in her Northern Irish accent, but in her dark eyes.

The following exchange with the waiter had Lynsey in stitches. Not only did Sean struggle to understand the man's broken English, but it soon became very clear that he had never had sushi in his life. Eventually, he took

Lynsey's recommendation of some salmon maki to start, followed by some duck gyoza and a chicken katsu dish.

Despite a gentle ribbing from Lynsey, Sean saw the funny side of it and explained how he had never had sushi before. The conversation turned to his life, and Lynsey sat intently, listening to every word as Sean discussed his childhood. It was a world away from her strict upbringing in Belfast. Every hurdle she felt she had overcome paled in significance to hardships Sean had battled. She encouraged him to continue as their starters arrived, stopping only to show him how to use the chopsticks provided.

Sean had never felt closer to someone.

There was something about Lynsey, the way she maintained eye contact as he spoke, how she gently reached for his hand as he spoke about the wrong turns he had been forced to take.

Everything came out.

The time with Elmore Riggs, the drugs, and the criminal path he had walked.

But there was no judgement from Lynsey.

She held his hand, stroking it gently as he explained how he had turned his life around, and was now on the same trajectory as her, championing the expulsion of companies like Head Space who were seeking to profit off the fragile mental health of today's youth.

Whatever connection was building between them, it was magnetic, and had never felt so comfortable talking about his past.

Lynsey's thumb stroked the back of his hand, her pale skin a stark contrast to his darker tone and her thumb rested on the scar tissue that dominated it.

'What's this?' she asked tenderly. Sean's hand seized slightly with discomfort.

'A reminder,' Sean eventually said.

'A reminder of what?'

'Not to go back to where I came from.' Sean chuckled. 'Would it be insane to say that a friend did this to me?'

Lynsey leant forward and to Sean's shock, planted a gentle kiss on his scar, before placing her other hand on top of his.

'A little.' She smiled. 'But I think having a reminder of where you have been is essential to know where you're going.'

The waiter came along with their bill and Sean, trying to be wildly chivalrous, demanded to pay. Lynsey put him square in his place by assuming a BBC reporter got paid more than a civil servant, and they laughed as they agreed to split it. Once outside, Lynsey told Sean that he better call her soon as he opened the door for her Uber. He agreed and then, to his surprise, she kissed him.

Throughout his life, Sean had been with a few women, mainly on drunken or drug-infused binges during his time in Elmore Riggs' gang.

But never had he experienced a kiss like this. With the light breeze swirling around them, he felt their passion and attraction grow as they held each other for a few moments. He gently pulled away, planted another kiss on her forehead, and told her he'd think about it. She jokingly slapped him on the arm and got into the cab. As it drove away, Sean resisted the urge to fist pump, checked his watch, and figured he'd get back to the Youth Centre before the end of film night.

They hadn't discussed Head Space in too much detail, but what Lynsey had shared with him was proof enough that Bridges and the whole operation was dangerous. With Sam retired, he hoped maybe Pearce would have some contacts still in the police who could get involved.

With the thrill of his blossoming relationship pumping through him, Sean decided to walk the three miles across London to Bethnal Green, allowing the warm evening to guide him through the streets and his mind to wander about the possibilities of a future with Lynsey.

Before he knew it, he was at the gates of the youth centre and he marched through, a spring in his step.

As the door shut behind him, a black Mercedes slowed to a stop outside, the driver killing the engine. Benny Hicks was a rough-looking man, his head shaved to the scalp and a thick beard protruding from his strong jaw. His gloved hands reached inside his leather jacket, where he retrieved his phone and dialled a number.

'Bethnal Green Youth Centre.' He spoke, his words cold. He nodded. 'See you in ten.'

Hicks tossed the phone onto the passenger seat and stared at the building. The lights to the main hall were on and he could hear the hushed noise of people inside.

He lit a cigarette and waited, counting as the youngsters began to filter from the building and out into the night.

Bowker and his boys would be there shortly.

CHAPTER NINE

As the credits began to roll, Sam looked around the youth centre, watching as the approving smiles of the teenagers lit up the room brighter than the lights ever could.

For once, Pearce has got his movie choice correct, and those in attendance were thrilled as the latest Marvel movie played out before them. While certainly no film goer, Sam was aware of their existence, with the posters of the latest films dominating every billboard or bus in London. To him, they were a bit far-fetched, and it felt like a month didn't pass without a new logo and famous face plastered next to the famous logo.

But he knew he wasn't the target audience, and as the action sequences ramped up, so did the excitement in the room. Sam couldn't help but enjoy the action, chuckling to himself at the implausibility of it all. Considering the situations the last three years of his life had brought his way, he was of the belief that most things were possible.

But maybe not superpowers.

A few teenagers waved to him as they made their way to the door, and he offered them a polite nod.

While they were friendly towards him, they knew he

wasn't as easy going as Pearce or Sean. Ever since he had returned and begun working for Pearce, Sam had kept his head down, working diligently to maintain the youth centre and improve it. He wasn't there for the interaction or for the events that Pearce enthusiastically ran. But he was always willing to chat with the kids, especially those who were there to escape what was happening outside the walls. He would offer them advice or sometimes just an ear.

Sometimes, some people just needed to talk.

One of the older kids, a sixteen-year-old named Curtis, had approached Sam once when he was re-plastering a wall and began to quiz Sam about the process. Happy to share, Sam invited Curtis to help and by the end of the day, the two of them had done a pretty good job. Since then, Curtis had always stopped to discuss DIY with Sam. Considering the enthusiasm with which the young lad spoke, Sam didn't have the heart to tell him he was learning as he went.

The kid was genuinely interested and by some of the work Pearce had agreed to, showed true understanding of some of it.

In the six months that he'd helped Sam with odd jobs, Curtis had decided he wanted to be an electrician and Pearce had already scoped out some apprenticeships for him. Sam watched as Curtis sat in the front row, his arm around his girlfriend, discussing the upcoming movies and how they would tie into the one they had just watched.

'Enjoy that?'

Pearce's voice cut through Sam's focus, and he turned to his friend with a shrug.

'Bit much at times.' Sam mused. 'But it was pretty fun.'

'I know. If only it was more realistic, like taking on an entire motorcycle gang with a broken wrist.' Sam chuckled as Pearce pushed the main doors open and put them on the latch before turning back to the room. 'Right, it's late. Is everyone okay to get home?'

The remaining teenagers mumbled their response and began to rise from their seats, all of them thanking both Pearce and Sam for the film. As they filtered out, Curtis told his girlfriend to hold on a second and walked over to Sam.

'Hey, JC,' he said, unaware of Sam's true identity. 'You about this Saturday?'

'I can be.' Sam smiled. 'What's going on?'

'I noticed there was a few flickering lights in the guy's bathroom, and I ain't back here till then. Was hoping you could hold off and wait till then and I could help you?'

The electrical issues in the bathroom were on Sam's to-do list, and he shot a quick glance to Pearce, who nodded instantly.

Ever encouraging.

'Sure.' Sam nodded. 'Nice and early though.'

'You bet.' Curtis waved to Pearce and then held his fist out to Sam. 'Catch you then.'

'You have my mobile number. Make sure you let me know if you can't make it.'

'For sure.'

Sam bumped Curtis's fist, much to Pearce's amusement, and watched as the young man caught up with his girlfriend by the door. Just as they were exiting, Sean stepped through the door, greeting them both, before bounding into the now empty auditorium. Pearce had lifted the first chair to begin to stack them, when his eyes lit up.

'Evening,' Pearce said with a smirk. 'Stood you up did she?'

'Ha.' Sean mocked. 'Actually, quite the opposite.'

'She sat you down?' Sam asked with a shrug, looking at Pearce.

'That doesn't sound good.' Pearce agreed. Both of them chuckled as Sean looked flustered by their gentle ribbing.

'Fuck you both.' He laughed, heading to the refreshment table and the slim pickings the teenagers had left behind. Sam lifted a chair and began stacking his own pile. The good mood that had followed Sean into the building had swarmed around him. The last six years of his life had been one long, brutal fight against his grief.

It was nice to experience true friendship again, and the camaraderie he shared with both Pearce and Sean was welcome.

It was genuinely nice to see the young man so happy.

And to see the smile on Pearce's face.

As Sean tucked into the rogue packet of crisps that had been left behind, Pearce sighed.

'Go on then, Romeo. How did it go?'

'She is incredible.' Sean was almost bursting out at the seams. 'She's so smart and just talked about everything. I mean, we spoke about my life before and what we are both trying to achieve now. The evidence she's collecting is just amazing.'

Sean took a moment and then looked at both Sam and Pearce.

'I think someone's in love.' Sam chuckled.

'No, I just—'

'It's okay, son,' Pearce said calmly, resting a hand on Sean's shoulder. 'It's great to see.'

'But she told me so much stuff. About Head Space and the links to Lonoxidil—'

'It can wait,' Pearce said, ushering Sean to the pile of chairs that he'd finished stacking. 'I'm more interested in how you got on than that. So, help Sam take these to the storage room, then why don't we go for a drink? Sound good?'

Sean nodded eagerly, and Sam rolled his eyes. Pearce turned towards the snack table, clearing up the empty packets and paper cups that had been left, as Sam lifted his stack of chairs with ease. He headed towards to the door on the far side of the hall. The storage cupboard was down the end of the corridor. As he strode towards it, Sean hobbled behind, his arms struggling under the weight of the smaller stack he had been awarded.

They disappeared out of the hall and Pearce smiled to himself, excited to hear about Sean's date. He seemed so happy, and Pearce was heavy in the thinking that a girlfriend would be the making of the man. As he collected the empty packets and put them into a bin bag, his attention was quickly averted by the sound of footsteps entering the youth centre, and as he turned, the door to the youth centre slammed shut.

'Can I help you gentleman?' Pearce asked, trying desperately to mask the concern in his voice.

With a blistering right hook, Bowker almost took the punch bag clean off the hook. Instead, it rocked back on the chain, its fixture straining against the ceiling of his warehouse. Bowker had been using the place as an office of operations ever since he had started up Stonewall Security Ltd. Despite the ridiculous sums of money the rich were willing to spend on their problems, Bowker had never invested much of it back into the premises.

It was a long-term lease on a large, open plan floor and that was it. The electrics worked. The single toilet was plumbed in.

That was enough.

In the years since, Bowker had installed a private gym, giving his employees and himself access to all the machinery and weights they needed to keep themselves fit for the job. Like Bowker, a number of them had a past in boxing and Bowker was more than happy to provide the necessary equipment to keep their skills sharp.

He even invested in an old boxing ring that sat in the middle of the warehouse. Although none of his employees were willing to step between the ropes with him.

His reputation as 'The Reaper' preceded him.

The one time one of them did, he walked out with a broken jaw.

Benny Hicks had forgiven him for it, chalking it up to a fair beating. Since then, when Bowker wanted to put on the gloves, the only opposition he faced was the relentless swing of the punch bag.

That evening, he needed to let off a little steam.

The call from Bridges had pissed him off and an hour of hitting the bag was the perfect remedy to calm down. The rest of his boys had been assembled, Bowker sending out a group message to say that they had a job that evening. Hicks, as his trusted right hand, was sent to follow the young woman who hadn't got the message.

Lynsey Beckett.

As thunderous fist followed thunderous fist, Bowker knew what was really the crux of his anger. Not that another enjoyable evening had been ruined, but that he hadn't scared Beckett enough. He had made it very clear that she was a marked woman, yet she still went ahead and published her article.

It emasculated Bowker in a way he wasn't used to.

Most of the time, when one of the rich pricks who acquired his service needed someone to change direction, a simple visit from Bowker was all that was required. He was a strapping man of considerable size, and most cowered when he alluded to the consequences.

But not Beckett.

Was he losing his touch?

Had he gone soft as the hands of Father Time ticked by?

As he battered the tattered leather that hung from the ceiling, he doubted it. Despite losing some of his muscle mass, he was still a physical unit with a deadly pair of hands. In the ring, there was nobody who could match him and if Lynsey Beckett needed a stronger message, then he was happy to oblige.

Step one was a visit from Bowker.

Step two was slightly more rudimentary.

In the far corner of the warehouse, the other six men who represented Stonewall were biding their time. A card game was playing out between four of them, with an ever-growing pile of cash building in the middle. Smoke billowed around them as they gambled. The other two were sitting on the beaten sofa Bowker had placed in the corner, opposite a semi-decent TV.

There were no channels, but they seemed engrossed in whatever DVD they had put on.

Despite the prudent furnishings of the base, all of them were paid handsomely by Bowker, and considering the steep rise in price that Bridges would be paying for step two, all of them were more than content with biding their time.

Connor and Jimmy Stokes were brothers, sitting on either side of the poker table. Both in their forties, with a lifetime on the streets of Liverpool and were as nasty as they were close. They did everything together, and when Bowker needed more than one person to change their mind, setting the Stokes boys on them was tantamount to tossing a live grenade into the room.

Also playing poker was Pavel Bezdek, who Bowker had heard speak maybe no more than twenty times in the decade or so he'd known him. Bezdek was from the

Czechia, where his parents suffered horrendously during the conflicts. Orphaned at fifteen, Bezdek came to England for work and soon found a fruitful living on the underground boxing scene. When Bowker offered him a steadier job, he graciously took it and, since then, had been loyal as a dog.

The remaining player was Mickey Turner, as cockney as Bowker, but half the size. But what he lacked in size he made up for with sadism, and while Bowker didn't condone the actions, he was sure that Turner had done more than just intimidate some of their targets.

On the sofa, Paul Creek and Lemar Taylor were quietly watching the film. Creek was a fellow boxer, a man who had taken Bowker to his limits a few times when they were younger. When Bowker had to forcibly retire due to his drug use, Creek stepped into his shadow and forged a semi-decent career. Never challenging for titles, but he did find himself on numerous undercards for well-paid shows. As age caught up with him, he turned to Bowker, who was happy to oblige him. Lemar was from Hackney, coming up through the ranks in one of the estate gangs before his own boss fell foul of Bowker himself. Lemar watched as Bowker bludgeoned the man to death with a crowbar and was told he needed to work off the debt or face a similar fate. That was eight years ago, with the debt repaid within two. But Lemar was a cold, calculating bastard and Bowker saw him as an asset.

Hicks, however, saw him as an intruder, and was always one racial slur away from a fist fight. Hicks, despite his incredible loyalty to Bowker, was a known racist with ties to the National Front and made it clear his disdain for having to work with Lemar.

Although Bowker was of the opinion that most disputes could be handled in the ring, giving Hicks licence to attack Lemar wasn't good for business.

Taking a deep breath, Bowker lifted his gloves, pulling the Velcro strap back with his jagged teeth and then sliding his hand out. As he removed the other glove, his phone pinged.

It was Hicks.

At dinner with her boyfriend. Follow?

Bowker's meaty thumbs slapped the screen of his phone.

Follow him.

A thumbs up emoji returned, and Bowker went to the sink in the dilapidated rest room and cleaned up. He pulled off the sweat stained T-shirt to reveal his broad torso. The muscle definition had waned slightly, leaving him with a slight sag on his pecs and a gut that just poked over his trousers. The tattoos that once proudly adorned his physique were faded, a sad memorial to the specimen he once was. Tufts of grey hair sprouted across his chest and stomach, and he tutted at his own reflection.

Perhaps his life had become too simple.

He marched back to his sports bag and removed his jeans and shirt, changing quickly before running a comb over his thinning hair, refusing to face reality and admit defeat in his battle with baldness.

Half an hour passed when he received a call from Hicks. He had followed Beckett's boyfriend back to a youth centre in Bethnal Green.

Bowker smirked. The youth centre was only a ten-minute drive from Mile End where their base was.

He'd have this sorted in no time.

As he headed for the door, Jimmy Stokes looked up from his card game. The others followed his gaze.

'We moving, boss?'

'I can handle this one,' Bowker said assuredly. 'You guys sit tight.'

A few murmurs of boredom echoed behind him as he

marched outside to his black Range Rover, and he pulled out into the cool evening. With little traffic, Bowker pulled up outside of the youth centre less than twelve minutes later. Smoke filtered out from the window of Hicks's car, and he stepped out.

'A few kids stayed late for some reason.' Hicks shrugged, tossing his cigarette. 'Probably some nonce running the place.'

Bowker ignored Hicks's vile accusation and carefully looked up and down the street.

'How many people inside?'

'No idea. Beckett's fella turned up, and then some teenagers filtered out. Maybe they were trespassing?'

'Maybe. What does her fella look like?'

'I don't know. Some black bastard,' Hicks said with a sneer.

Bowker ignored the needless racism. For a man who did unspeakable things for money, he didn't exactly have the moral high ground. After watching the last few teenagers disappear down the street, he nodded to Hicks.

'Let's go in and meet him, shall we?'

Bowker smiled evilly and Hicks's eyes lit up with excitement as they set upon the front door of the Bethnal Green Youth Centre, looking to send a message that would get the job done.

CHAPTER TEN

Pearce watched tentatively as the two men filtered into the hall, the rehearsed routine playing out in front of him. The smaller, balding man was well built, but he patrolled the room like a security guard, checking the windows were closed before heading towards the door that Sam and Sean had passed through a few minutes before. The man peered out into the corridor, a swastika tattoo visible behind his ear and partially covered by the thick beard. After a few seconds of looking down the hallway, he turned back to his boss and nodded, before he stood in the doorway to prevent any hope of an exit.

Pearce sighed with relief.

Sam and Sean were out of sight.

He turned his attention back to the large man who was clearly in charge. His broad frame was tight against his leather jacket and his stubble-covered chin was pulled tight. The man looked around the room, eyeing the remaining rows of chairs, and then looked up at the projector screen.

'Movie night?' he asked politely, his Cockney accent thick and laced with menace.

'I mean it's not quite the IMAX, but it works,' Pearce responded. 'Sorry, can I ask who you are?'

Bowker ignored Pearce's question again and then looked to Hicks, who stood, arms folded, covering the exit. Without looking, Bowker raised his meaty hand and pointed at Pearce.

'Is this the guy? Little old, isn't he?'

'They all look the same to me.' Hicks shrugged. Pearce frowned at the racist remark and turned back to Bowker.

'Look, you guys need to leave otherwise I'll…'

'What?' Bowker turned sharply. 'Call the police? How quickly do you think I could snap your fingers, son?'

'I don't want any trouble.'

'I know.' Bowker grinned, showing his stained teeth. 'Now, the thing is, me and my friend here are looking for a black kid who was out with a woman this evening. A woman who didn't listen when I spoke to her. Now, I don't think a young white woman would be interested in an old bastard such as yourself, so if you know where he is, it would be in your best interests to tell me.'

Pearce swallowed. The men were looking for Sean and by the looks and sounds of things, they weren't there to present him with an award. The two men had strategically cut off either of his viable exits and Pearce knew, despite his background of police training and pretty decent boxing record, there wasn't any way of fighting his way out.

Over the last few years, he had bonded with Sean, watched him grow from a misguided kid into an upstanding man, who clung tightly to his convictions.

A man who was making a difference.

A man who had a bright future.

Pearce knew that calling for Sam was an option, but considering the turmoil the man had walked through, he was now trying to leave that world behind. Pearce didn't want to bring him back into it.

But he could still act as Sam would.

By doing the right thing.

'Oh Lynsey?' Pearce said casually. 'Yeah, we ate not too long ago. Lovely young girl. A little misguided, but we have fun.'

'Lynsey Beckett?' Bowker raised an eyebrow.

'Yeah. She's a reporter for the BBC.' Pearce held the terror in his voice. 'Do you know her?'

Immediately, the air was driven from Pearce's body as Bowker swung a fist so quickly his arm had been a blur. The full weight of the man was expertly driven into his concrete fist, and it slammed into Pearce's stomach with tremendous velocity.

The man hit like a pro.

Pearce hunched over, gasping for air, and then dropped to one knee. Bowker eyed him up, looking a little suspicious. He turned back to Hicks.

'Are you sure this is the guy?'

As the man muttered with his colleague, Pearce looked across the youth centre to the door. The bearded man stood in the way, but just behind him, peering through the crack of the door, was Sam. Even from across the room, Pearce could see the anger in his eyes, and he begged Sam to look at him.

Eventually he did, and he raised his eyebrows as if asking Pearce for permission.

Despite the pain pulsing in his stomach, and the very likely threat of more to come, Pearce took a breath and shook his head slightly.

Sam looked shocked, but Pearce ignored him, pressed one hand on the floor and pushed himself back to a standing position. Bowker looked at him, almost impressed.

'Look, mate, let's not do this,' Bowker offered. 'Either you tell me where I can find Beckett's boyfriend, or I will take this entire building apart until I find him. Then, if I don't, I will take you apart until you tell me where I can. Do you understand?'

Pearce gingerly pressed a hand to his aching stomach and nodded his head.

'I get it. You're envious that a guy my age can attract younger women.'

Bowker drove another fist into Pearce's stomach, but at the last minute, Pearce swerved his body to the side, dodging the blow. The man's sizeable frame stumbled toward him, and Pearce threw his leg forward, tripping the man who crashed onto the wooden floor, the room shaking as he thundered against the ground. A grunt of shock echoed from the man's accomplice.

Not for what Pearce had done.

But for what would be the coming retaliation.

Embarrassed, Bowker tried to laugh it off, pushing himself to his knees and turning to Pearce.

'Nice footwork. You box?'

'I did,' Pearce responded as calmly as possible. 'A few years back when I was still an officer.'

'You were a pig?' Bowker stood, dusting down his knees. 'That's a shame. See, I boxed pretty much my whole life and one thing I always wanted was to step in the ring with a filthy fed and knock seven shades of shit out of him. Unfortunately, we don't have a ring here.'

Bowker lunged forward with deadly intent, and he drove another into Pearce's stomach, this time connecting with devastating effect. Pearce hunched over in agony, only to be met with a raised knee that drilled him in the side of the jaw, sending him sprawling across the wooden boards. Bowker, whose eyes sparkled like a shark who had just caught the faintest whiff of blood, readjusted his jacket and then reached into his pocket. Before he could reveal what was waiting for Pearce, everyone's attention turned to the entrance of the building. Without realising the situation at hand, Curtis bounded into the room.

'Hey, JC, about this...'

Curtis didn't even finish his sentence, the fear of the situation before him causing the colour to drain from his young face. Pearce was on the floor, blood trickling from his split lip while a hulking man stood above him, his fists clenched and fury in his eyes. Beyond him, on the other side of the room, another man watched on with pleasure, but his eyes landed on Curtis and lit up with delight. Being from an estate and escaping the gang culture, Curtis always thought he had the inbuilt toughness needed to survive on the streets if he ever needed to.

But he froze.

Whatever he had walked into, he shouldn't have.

Quickly, he tried to leave, but the bald, bearded man with a crazed stare stepped forward, his grin revealing his crooked teeth.

'Who do we have here?'

Hicks spat sadistically, reaching into his pocket and to the horror of Pearce and the sheer terror of Curtis, pulled out a Glock 17.

'Jesus Christ, what the hell are you doing?' Pearce yelled, fighting back to his feet only for a boot to crash into his ribs, sending him sprawling

Things were escalating.

As Pearce laid helplessly on the floor, he watched in despair as Hicks raised the weapon, aiming it squarely at Curtis, who went a deathly pale as fear enveloped him.

———

Sam placed his stack of chairs in the storage cupboard, bending his knees to lower the weight and taking the pressure off his spine. He waited patiently as Sean stumbled in behind him, straining under the weight of those that he carried.

'Need a hand?'

Sam chuckled and Wiseman shot him a glare before dropping them into the space Sam motioned towards. As he did, Sean reached for his back, over emphasising the struggle. Sam rolled his eyes.

'Oh, I'm sorry,' Sean snapped sarcastically. 'We can't all be hench as fuck.'

The two of them laughed, but Sam's head snapped to the doorway, the sound of footsteps and voices carrying through the corridor. Sean heard them too and stepped towards the door, only for Sam to pull him back.

'Stay here.'

Sam's words were as stern as that moment over two years ago, when he put a gun to Sean's hand and told him his days on the wrong side of the law were over. Sean nodded and stepped back into the room. Sam carefully inched out of the room, enough to hear the gruff Cockney accent demand to know where the person out with Lynsey Beckett was.

They were here for Sean.

Sam peered through the crack where the door hung from its hinge, his days as a sniper helping hone his vision and quickly assess the situation. The view was obscured by the clear outline of a bald man. Judging from the echo of the voice, whoever was blocking the view wasn't the one talking to Pearce.

Which meant Pearce was outnumbered.

Which also meant, whoever these men were, they weren't here to pat Sean on the back for scoring a date with a BBC reporter.

Sam heard Pearce respond, followed by the unmistakable thud of a fist being driven into his friend's stomach. As Pearce gasped for air and collapsed to the ground, Sam felt his knuckles whiten as his nails dug into the palms of his hand.

'Sam, what the hell is happening?'

'You need to leave,' Sam whispered, turning back into the room. 'As quietly as you can. Go. Now.'

Before Sean could respond, Sam stepped out of the room and shuffled silently down the corridor, keeping his back against the wall. Sean ducked his head out, resisted every temptation to follow him, and then quickly headed to the back door that led to the courtyard, ensuring his steps were as silent as possible. Sam continued down the corridor until he reached the door, then pressed his eye to the crack between the edge of the door and its wooden frame. Taller than the bald man standing in his way, he looked over at Pearce who was on his knees, his hands clutching his stomach as he tried to gather his breath. His attacker was a large man with thinning hair, decked in a black leather jacket and walking with the swagger of a man who had done this multiple times.

A professional.

Sam felt his fists clench again.

The image of his friend being attacked was a strong call to go back to his old life.

Pearce shot a glance his way, making clear eye contact.

A shake of the head.

Sam grit his teeth in frustration. Pearce was willing to take a beating to keep Sam out of it. Throughout his crusade against crime, one of the biggest shining lights was Pearce's commitment to the greater good. In his eyes, taking a few licks to keep Sam on the right path was worth it.

Sam hated it, but he stood his ground.

Pearce got back to his feet as his attacker made it clear that unless he gave up information on Sean, it would happen again. Pearce shot back with a snarky comment and the man lunged forward, only this time Pearce sent him sprawling to the ground. As his attacker hit the ground, the man standing a foot in front of Sam took a foot forward, his hand reaching into his jacket.

Was he armed?

Sam absorbed every detail and watched as the burly attacker got to his feet, a smile spread across his world-weary face. As he and Pearce exchanged more words, the man caught Pearce with another blow to the stomach, followed by a crunching knee to the face. Pearce hit the ground, bloodied, and Sam felt every muscle in his body tighten.

He wasn't worth this.

Pearce didn't deserve to walk through hell to keep him safe.

As Sam struggled with his dilemma, the sound of the front door bursting open echoed through the hall and all eyes turned to the entrance way, as the eager footsteps approached.

Curtis.

The young boy froze at the sight before him, and Sam felt a ripple of fear shudder through his body. These men were dangerous, and most likely not in the habit of leaving witnesses in a fit state to identify them. The bald man by the door stepped forward, a hint of excitement in his voice as he reached into his jacket.

'Who do we have here?'

The man stepped away from Sam's obstructed view, his hand freeing itself from its jacket, most likely with a weapon in tow.

Pearce's horrified scream filled the room.

'Jesus Christ, what the hell are you doing?'

Everything happened in a split second. Sam knew that he walked a tightrope where he could easily fall back into the life he had led before. The promises he had broken to his deceased son would come crashing down around him once more, and the very real threat of being revived from the dead would see him locked away and the key disintegrated.

His next moves would need to be careful.

Precise.

As Curtis raised his hands in fear, only one thought penetrated Sam's brain and took complete control.

Do the right thing.

Keeping the weight off his feet, Sam stepped out from behind the door and approached the bald man, who had his Glock trained on the teenager. As the man slowly approached Curtis, his boss, who loomed over Pearce, turned to look at him. As he did, his eyes widened in shock as he saw Sam less than a metre behind his comrade.

'Hicks, behind you.'

Hicks spun, trying his hardest to turn the weapon on Sam. Expertly, Sam lifted his hand and wrapped his fingers around Hicks's wrist. With his thumb and index finger, he dug into the pressure points on the man's wrist, relinquishing his hold on the weapon. Sam slid his hand around the bottom of the gun and as soon as he solidified his grip, he drove his elbow down the length of the man's arm and steered it viciously into his bearded jaw.

The man hit the floor; his eyes wide in shock.

It had happened in a matter of seconds, and now he looked up at the muscular man who had trained the gun directly at him.

'Get up,' Sam demanded, motioning for the man to back away towards his colleague. 'Curtis, move away from the door and get behind me.'

The hall was deathly silent as both obliged, as Curtis, shaking with fear, scarpered across the hallway until he was safely behind Sam. The bald man spat blood onto the floor and stood to the side, while his boss stood, hands in his pockets and a defiant look on his face.

'Who the fuck are you?' the man asked, his words heavy with rage.

'You okay?' Sam asked Pearce, ignoring the man. Pearce got to his feet and nodded, wiping the blood from his mouth.

'I said, who the fuck are you?'

'I'm the janitor,' Sam responded, raising the gun so it stared directly at the man's forehead. 'Who are you?'

'My name is Daniel Bowker.' Bowker regarded Sam carefully, his eyes squinting. 'Do I know you?'

Sam shook his head.

'I doubt it.'

'You look familiar to me. Have we met?' Bowker looked to his colleague and then back at Sam. 'It's your face. I've definitely seen you before.'

'You must have me confused with someone else.' Sam felt a slight discomfort, his new identity under threat. Bowker's smirk dissipated, replaced by a thunderous frown.

'I'll keep racking the old brain. In the meantime, I feel obliged to tell you just how big of a mistake you have made.'

'Is that so?' Sam shrugged. 'I think you need to leave. Both of you.'

Bowker smirked and took a step forward. Sam straightened his arm, insinuating that he would pull the trigger. Bowker held his hands up in surrender.

'Let's stay calm. It's not like you're actually going to pull that trigger.'

'Try me,' Sam said coldly, his eyes fixed on Bowker, his stare unwavering. After a few seconds, something seemed to click, and Bowker's smirk turned to a vicious snarl. He took a few steps back, his eyes locked on Sam.

'You're in a very dangerous place, son.'

Sam kept the gun trained on him.

'So are you.'

Bowker bared his teeth, like an attack dog ready to pounce. From the man's reaction, Sam was sure he wasn't used to being threatened. Pearce slowly got to his feet and stumbled towards Sam, who kept his gaze and more importantly, the gun fixed on Bowker. After a few tense moments, Bowker relaxed and patted his colleague on the arm.

'Let's go.'

Hicks rubbed his jaw and looked at Sam.

'You made a big fucking mistake, buddy.'

Sam said nothing. The two men quickly stormed out of the youth centre, and it wasn't until the door of the centre slammed shut that Sam eventually lowered the gun. His fingers were locked around the weapon comfortably, as if reacquainted with an old friend.

It had taken a lot for Sam not to pull the trigger.

The two were bad news, clearly hired to do unspeakable things to Sean. Luckily for him, he had a friend as loyal as Pearce and knew a man as capable as Sam.

'I'm fine, Curtis. Really,' Pearce said reassuringly to Curtis, who handed him a tissue. Pearce dabbed at his lip, the tissue turning red instantly. 'That was dangerous, John.'

Keeping up appearances in front of Curtis, Sam nodded his agreement.

'I know. I don't know what I was thinking.'

'Are you kidding me?' Adrenaline took control of Curtis. 'That was fucking awesome. The way you took his piece and jacked his jaw. Can you teach me?'

'None of that was awesome,' Sam said coldly. 'Do you understand me? That was a bad situation and luckily, we got out of it.'

'But still… you're full of surprises, JC.'

'Come on…' Pearce interjected. 'Let's get you home.'

Pearce, still holding the tissue to his lip, jingled his car keys in the other. As Curtis said his goodbyes and headed to the door, Sam stepped in close to Pearce, lowering his voice.

'Are you okay?'

'I'll be fine.'

'They'll be back.'

Both men looked down at the gun in Sam's hand, hesitant to make any suggestions. Eventually, Pearce pulled the tissue away and offered Sam a smile.

'We'll figure something out.'

Curtis waited patiently for Pearce as he shuffled uncomfortably to the door, his body still adjusting to the clubbing blows he'd been dealt. Curtis threw up a hand to wave to Sam, and he nodded in return. As the door shut behind them, Sam stood silently, his finger still resting gently on the trigger. Muscle memory could have sent that entire situation down another path, but it was his dedication to his new life that stopped it.

But a feeling hung heavy in his gut that it would be tested again.

And he was worried that what was coming would mean there was no other option.

CHAPTER ELEVEN

Sean had barely slept a wink.

The terror of the evening before had revisited him over and over once he had returned to his flat, and it wasn't until Pearce called to tell him he was okay that he finally stopped chewing his fingernails. Despite a few bruised ribs and bust lip, Pearce said he was okay and that luckily, Sam had intervened.

Sean suggested they go to the police, but Pearce made it clear that was a no-go.

The risk of them discovering Sam was too strong.

But what Pearce said next was what had resulted in a sleepless night and now, on a fresh Friday morning, a heavy reliance on coffee.

Whatever Lynsey Beckett knew, some very bad people wanted it kept quiet.

And they were willing to go through Sean, an innocent man, to make that point as clearly as possible.

The reality of the situation hit Sean like a slap to the face and the fact that Pearce took a beating on his behalf only made him feel worse. Having never really known his dad, and only recently built a bridge with his mother,

Pearce was the closest thing Sean had to a father figure. Although their relationship was built on friendship, it was Pearce who had taken him in when he was at his lowest ebb. Having been brutally attacked by Oleg Kovalenko a few days after Sam's intervention, Sean had nowhere to go.

His life alongside Riggs had been eviscerated by Sam's gun and the seeds they had sewn had landed him in hospital.

Pearce had guided him down a better path.

Without questioning his past, Pearce had opened the door of the youth centre to Sean and put him to work, giving him a sense of purpose. As the days and weeks rolled by, he watched as Pearce made time for every single child who came through the door and gave all of them his undivided attention. As their bond grew, Pearce explained the legacy of Theo Walker, a good friend of Sam's, who had sacrificed himself to save an innocent woman and her husband.

A man who had dedicated himself to keeping soldiers alive and who had served his country as a medic with distinction. Theo had come from the same streets as Sean and, as Pearce divulged more about the man, Sean couldn't help but be inspired.

He could help them the same way.

With money tight, Pearce made a plea to the council to put a basic salary against Sean's role. Pairing that with the money he'd saved during his time running with Riggs, Sean enrolled on an Open University course and worked his way to the required qualifications to become a social worker.

Every time he doubted himself, Pearce stepped in.

Whenever he hit a wall, Pearce gave him a leg up.

Just as a father would.

And last night, when faced with two men with bad intentions, Pearce took Sean's place without hesitation.

The man had given so much to Sean, to help get him on the right track and now, through no fault of his own, Sean was in another bad spot.

He had agreed with Pearce to lie low for a few days, until Pearce and Sam could figure out the next steps and then said his goodbyes. Luckily, Sean's shift pattern meant he had the Friday off and so he tried to go back to bed, hopeful of a few hours of much needed sleep. When it didn't come, he decided to have another cup of coffee and possibly try the home workout Sam had drawn up for him a few months previous. Sean had begged Sam to whip him into shape, but the desire to look good and the dedication needed were two very different attributes.

But he couldn't concentrate.

It wasn't that he was worried for his own safety, but the fact that Lynsey was the real target.

If they'd tried to get to her through him and failed, what would they do next?

Sean messaged her, asking to take her to lunch, and she quickly agreed and after a quick shower, he bounded out of his flat and headed to the Underground station, ready to navigate the labyrinth of train tunnels to Shepherd's Bush, where the BBC headquarters proudly stood. The forecourt was awash with abstract art sculptures, and an entire parade of shops and eateries lined the large buildings. It was like its own little metropolis, with hundreds of young, enthusiastic workers scurrying around like an ant colony. A few streets away was the Kiyan Prince Foundation Stadium, the home of Queen's Park Rangers Football Club.

Previously named Loftus Road, the stadium was renamed in honour of a youth team player who had tragically lost his life in the ever-growing epidemic of knife crime.

Another stark reminder of why Sean did what he did.

The darkness of the loss of a promising life was offset by the bright smile of Lynsey Beckett as she walked out of the BBC building, her lanyard hanging from her neck and covered by her brown hair that swayed gently in the breeze. As her eyes widened with happiness as he smiled, Sean felt a twinge in his chest, fully aware that he was falling for her.

But that twinge wasn't of love.

It was of fear.

Fear of what might happen to her.

They didn't have long, as Lynsey was due to head out on scene for a report for the six o'clock news, so they grabbed a sandwich from the on-site Pret a Manger and sat on a nearby wall that enclosed a well maintained flower show.

'This is a lovely surprise,' Lynsey said with a smile, gently resting her hand on his. Electricity sparked between them.

'What, a tuna baguette?'

She chuckled and flirtatiously slapped his arm. As Sean watched her smile, the severity of the situation began to ebb away, replaced by the possibilities of their next date. What could it lead to?

'Everything okay?' Lynsey asked, a gentle concern hanging from her words.

Sean took a deep breath and then relayed everything that had happened the night before when he had left her. As he explained the attack on Pearce, he omitted the interaction with Sam. The last thing Sam needed was a BBC reporter knowing he was hiding in the same city. Sean's tale may have been a little different to the actual facts, but the point remained the same.

Lynsey had rattled the wrong cage.

But judging by the defiant shake of her head, she wasn't planning on backing down.

'If someone is willing to go to these lengths to shut me up, then I'm on the right scent,' she said angrily. 'I'm sorry about your friend, but I can't allow them to brush away the truth.'

'But you could get hurt?'

'The BBC has people to protect us. I'll tell them a threat has been made against my boyfriend and they'll make arrangements for both of us.'

Sean leant back; his eyebrows raised.

'Boyfriend?'

'Shut up.' Lynsey shoved him, her cheeks turning an embarrassed shade of pink. 'I have to get back. Call me later?'

Sean nodded, and then to his surprise, Lynsey leant forward and planted her lips against his. The sound of the entire city disappeared, and Sean found himself lost in the kiss, his hands raising up to cradle her face and the two of them locked in position for a few more seconds. Gently, he pulled away and looked at her, her eyes still closed.

'Boyfriend?'

Lynsey shoved him again.

'Aren't you going to be late to see your mum?' she asked.

'Oh shit.' Sean suddenly checked his watch. He'd made plans to see his mum that afternoon, another step across the bridge they were building together. 'I'll speak to you later... girlfriend?'

Lynsey leant in for another kiss.

'If that's the case, you better tell your mum about me.'

Sean grinned, kissed her, and then watched as she returned to the building. As she disappeared beyond the glass and the levels of security, Sean realised he couldn't wait to tell his mum.

She would be thrilled.

After he saw her, he would drop in to see Pearce and let

him know that Lynsey was making arrangements to keep them safe until everything blew over.

With a fresh, positive perspective, he dashed across the lavish forecourt of the BBC Headquarters, back towards White City Station, unaware of the two men following him.

―――

As his eyes scanned across the text message that had appeared on his phone, Bowker could feel his grip on the device tightening.

We paid the money upfront as asked. Get it done.

There was something about Adam Bridges that caused his temper to bubble under the surface. On the one occasion Bowker had met him, he'd been thoroughly unimpressed. Bridges was a well-groomed, silver-tongued poster boy. There was nothing about him that Bowker found genuine and having grown up on estates and in boxing rings, Bowker appreciated the sincerity that came with the struggle of both paths.

Bridges had nothing that Bowker respected.

The man was clearly homosexual, but Bowker didn't care about that. Whatever people wanted to do in their own time, he didn't care. His closest ally, Hicks, was an open racist, but as far as Bowker was concerned, the man was still as loyal as a dog and as vicious as one to boot.

Bridges was a fake.

A man who believed he was in control because the person who controlled the purse strings had ordered him to make the call.

What angered Bowker most about the text message wasn't that the little runt had tried to exert some non-existent authority, but the fact that he was right. Bowker had built his entire business and reputation on the fact that he delivered. Most of the London underworld knew who he was. While he didn't dabble with organised crime, they knew well enough to stay out of his way. He was a dangerous man, paid by extremely powerful people to eradicate problems.

But he had failed.

He had been paid to do a job and didn't deliver.

Now Bridges was throwing around demands for him to put it right, and as much as he wanted to pin Bridges to the wall and demonstrate his prowess with a punch bag, Bowker knew he needed to suck it up and deliver.

The old man who had stupidly taken the beating last night clearly wasn't Beckett's boyfriend, but no man willingly steps into those shoes unless he cares.

The boy's father?

An uncle?

Whoever he was, Bowker made a mental note that should shit really hit the fan, targeting that old man may lure the boyfriend out into the open. It would be like injuring one of the herd to draw the rest out.

With a sigh, Bowker's thumbs hit the screen, and he sent his response.

Will be done within the next 24 hours.

It was a bold claim, considering they had nothing to go on. The ex-police officer he'd beaten last night was never going to give the boyfriend up and as frustrating as that was, Bowker could respect it. At that moment, there was a knock on Bowker's door and he strode to answer it.

Crystal.

As a man of simple pleasures, Bowker's remedy for a stressful situation was, as always, to hire the services of Crystal. He didn't have time to court women the old-fashioned way, and the idea of entering an emotional relationship with someone else had no appeal. Soon, they would expect more from him than he was willing to part with and it would get in the way of the life he had built.

With Crystal, the rules were clear.

No talking.

No play acting.

He paid her, and she serviced his needs however he deemed fit. Silently, he poured her a glass of Scotch from his drinks table and then walked back to the sofa in his modest flat. She eyed him up, perhaps with disgust, but he didn't care.

He paid good money, and she charged a hefty price.

As she drank her drink, Bowker undid his belt before pulling his jeans and boxer shorts down to his ankles and then sat back on the sofa, the leather cold against his bare buttocks.

'That bad a day, huh?' Crystal chuckled dryly, before knocking back the last of her Scotch and removing her coat to reveal the skimpy negligee beneath. Bowker raised his eyebrows in agreement and then watched as she sauntered towards him, before lowering herself slowly to her knees before him and burying her face in his lap.

He let out a groan of pleasure as she began, trying his best to collect his thoughts now he was in a calmer state.

There was one other question he needed answering.

Who was the janitor?

Bowker could have sworn he'd seen the man before.

Perhaps in the boxing ring? The man was certainly built like a prize fighter and the way he'd disarmed Hicks and put him down so swiftly told Bowker that the man was trained.

Military?

Bowker had known a few ex-Paras who'd fallen on hard times and had used their skills on the streets to make ends meet. There was a chance that they'd crossed paths, but Bowker was certain he'd seen the man before.

Certainly, he recognised the man's eyes.

Whoever he was, Bowker had already promised Hicks his revenge and had made it clear that once Beckett's boyfriend had been taken care of and she got the message loud and clear, he would let Hicks off the leash.

Despite the mysterious janitor's size, Hicks was a different beast entirely, and Bowker had no doubt his confidant would take a sick pleasure in bathing in the janitor's blood.

However, Bowker was curious to know who he truly was. The way he held the gun, the lack of fear of what he was faced with.

It gnawed at him like a toothache and in his frustration he pressed his hand down on Crystal's head, enjoying her gasps. His phone buzzed, and he relinquished his hold, annoyed that Bridges was about to ruin the exceptional blow job he was paying good money for.

As he read the message, his eyes lit up with excitement.

It was Jimmy Stokes.

Bowker had sent him and his brother, Connor, to camp outside the BBC studio to keep an eye on Beckett.

Boyfriend in our sights. Will follow and let you know where.

Whatever reprieve the old man and the janitor had earnt for the young man was now redundant. The Stokes brothers would track him to his next location, and Bowker would move in. He could afford no more screw-ups.

This time, he would take the entire crew.

It might have been overkill, but Bowker couldn't take any risks. If the boyfriend was with the janitor, then Bowker didn't expect it to be easy.

If he was on his own, then God have mercy on him.

Bowker responded to the message and then tossed the phone onto the sofa. Crystal lifted her head, panting slightly as she drew her breath.

'Good news?' she asked, her hands firmly gripping him.

'Exceptional news,' Bowker sneered. 'Now take that off and get on the floor.'

Smirking as she stood, Crystal began to slowly remove her clothing as Bowker watched with evident excitement. His team had come good for him and by the end of the day, the problem would have been eradicated.

Job done.

Then he could deal with the janitor.

Simple pleasures.

As Crystal took her place on the floor, bracing herself for what was to come, Bowker pulled his t-shirt from his portly body and positioned himself behind her, ready to get his money's worth and to work off the last remnants of a needlessly stressful situation.

CHAPTER TWELVE

One thing Sam never did was panic.

His father, William Pope, had been a heavily respected General within the British Military, setting an example for Sam and every soldier who passed through his command based on his unflappable integrity. There were those who joined the army to get their hands on guns. Those who had no other option, who saw it as a way out of the life that fate had delivered them to.

Then there were those who just wanted to make the world a better place.

With his calm, soft voice, General William Pope had been dismissed as a pacifist, clashing with several other senior officers over their gung-ho approach to freedom.

Despite the backlash to his proposals, Sam's father commanded the respect of his men and through every battle that he co-ordinated, he never panicked.

Not once.

It was one of the admirable traits that he had passed on to Sam, their bond growing stronger when Sam's mother left when he was too young to have forged one with her. The life of a military wife was a hard one, and during the years Sam had been married to Lucy, he came to forgive his mother for walking away.

The terrifying reality that your husband wouldn't come home.

The cold sweats they would wake up in during the night, when a ghastly memory infiltrated their dreams.

The constant moving.

Through the separation, Sam's father had always put Sam first, stepping away from a field position to something more bureaucratic, leading with his mind from behind a desk than behind a gun on the battleground. When Sam found himself in trouble at school, his father had reasoned with him with diplomacy instead of anger, guiding him to make the right decisions.

To do the right thing.

It had been ingrained in Sam from that moment on. His father's ideals may as well have been injected into his veins.

Even during his final days, where he suffered a heart attack, there was no panic.

The man was made of stone, and it was another attribute Sam inherited, making him an ice-cold marksman during his years as a sniper.

Now, with his war on crime behind him, Sam had settled into his new routine. His days working at the youth centre filled him with a sense of purpose. His friendships with Pearce, Sean, and Jess nullified any loneliness he felt.

He was calm.

But after the attack on Pearce last night by Daniel Bowker and his associate, Sam felt the edges of his tranquil life beginning to fray.

Whatever they had wanted Sean for, it wasn't good. Considering they'd traced him based on his blossoming connection to Lynsey Beckett, Sam had deduced it was linked to her work. Sean was adamant she had information on the pharmaceutical company peddling dangerous drugs to uneducated teenagers, branding it under a catchy slogan and an empty campaign.

Clearly, she was right, as people like Bowker don't go hunting for your nearest and dearest unless you've pissed off the wrong people.

Sam sat in his apartment, watching as clouds began to overcast, the promise of a springtime storm looking to be fulfilled. The city of London was a majestic spectacle, especially in the sunshine, but replaced by a thunderous storm, it became a different beast.

Dark.

Grey.

A concrete jungle tinged with the smell of damp and an overwhelming sense of foreboding. During his war against crime, Sam had seen the worst of the city, turning over the dirtiest rocks to find the worst incumbents. He remembered the faces of every criminal he had put down. From the Mitchell Brothers who worked diligently for Frank Jackson to Buck in an underground bunker in Italy. There had been so many, and Sam had wandered down that path far enough to know exactly the kind of person Bowker was.

Someone relentless.

Someone who wouldn't stop.

But that wasn't what had caused a mild panic in him. It was the threat of being recognised. Of course, a man of Bowker's ilk, a career criminal operating in London, would have paid special attention to Sam's crusade. He fit the profile of one of Sam's targets and in all honesty, Sam was perplexed as to how Bowker had never flagged on his radar.

Until now.

Now he was, and Bowker had recognised him. And

while he couldn't place Sam's identity to his face, it was a dangerous place to be.

Not for Sam.

But for everyone he'd surrounded himself with.

A light rain began to patter against the window of Sam's flat and he looked down at the book on his lap. He was halfway through *The Fellowship of the Ring*, trying his utmost to keep his promise to his son and read as much as possible. Considering the rave reviews and the rabid fanbase, Sam had expected a more thrilling read, but he would persevere, even if a fantasy world wasn't really his cup of tea.

The cold, harsh reality of the world had made fantasy impossible.

Besides, he couldn't enjoy his day off knowing that Bowker was out there hunting for Sean. Pearce had told Sam he had had spoken to Sean, and he had relayed that Lynsey's company would provide protection for them both until it all blew over. It was a small victory, but it still sat uneasily in Sam's gut that it might not be enough.

His mind raced to the handgun he'd removed from the clutches of Bowker's associate, and Sam wondered if he would need it to fix the problem himself.

He hoped he didn't have to.

That life was behind him. Pearce had insisted on taking it, promising to hand it in to an old colleague at the Met.

But as Sam looked out over the morbid sky that promised to ruin the Friday night of many young Londoners, he felt the familiar sense of foreboding seeping through his body.

There were some things you couldn't come back from and somehow, Sam had managed it.

He had reclaimed a life.

Although it still echoed with the pain of his son's death

and was bathed in the blood of the criminals he had killed, Sam had made it out the other side.

But he wasn't calm.

Not when he felt that Daniel Bowker was a problem that wouldn't just disappear. With the need to clear his head, Sam changed into his running gear and headed out into the grim afternoon that welcomed him. As he began to jog through the estate, he hoped that the chill of the rain and the relentless hum of London life would drown out the doubts that had begun to sprout in his mind.

―――

Fridays were usually a little quieter at the youth centre, which, on this particular one, Pearce was relieved about. As he sat at his desk, working through the usual paperwork that the local council demanded he provide, his body pulsed with agony.

Daniel Bowker hit like a pro.

It had been over a couple of decades since Pearce last took off his boxing gloves, but even then, in the healthy competitive boxing league among the different police forces in the UK, Pearce had never been rocked with fists so deadly.

The two clubbing blows felt like they'd scattered his internal organs and he'd spent all day expecting blood to appear in his urine. Luckily, that hadn't been the case, but every movement he made was accompanied by a dull, aching sensation emanating from his core.

His split lip, he was less worried about.

To the few kids who had passed through that day, he had told them he had tripped while carrying a table and split his lip on the furniture.

One of them even said he looked bad ass.

But his relief for the day wasn't due to his physical

anguish. It was the constant worry for Sean. Whoever Bowker was or worked for, it wasn't good. They were clearly targeting Sean and the previous night after he'd dropped Curtis home, Pearce had returned to the centre to check on Sam. His good friend had dedicated himself to a life of peace and had been afforded a second chance when there never seemed like one.

Pearce didn't want that to slip.

If he had to protect Sean, he would, but he didn't want Sam to be pulled back into a world where he thrived.

Pearce's mind had been put to rest by Sean's phone call earlier in the day, explaining how Lynsey was organising protection through the BBC until Bowker and whoever else was gunning for them had been caught.

That made him feel a little better, but Pearce hadn't been pleased that Sean had risked his safety to do so.

But the kid was clearly smitten, and Pearce understood Sean's desire to play the knight in shining armour. However, judging from the callous beating Bowker had handed him, Pearce was certain that Bowker and his friend were not interested in being part of a fairy tale.

As the afternoon began to wind down, Pearce began to tidy up, gingerly shuffling around his office as he returned documents to folders and looked forward to a weekend off. As he slid a folder back onto its shelf, he grimaced.

'You really need to work out more.'

Sam stood in the door, his damp running gear clinging to his muscular frame. The heavens had opened twenty minutes prior and had been relentlessly pattering Pearce's window. Judging by the state of Sam, he had run through the brunt of it.

'I know, right?' Pearce smiled. 'It's almost as if I deserved those punches.'

'You are a madman,' Sam said, shaking his head. He looked around Pearce's pristine office. The tidiness of the man had always been something Sam respected, and it gave a great insight into how he had been such a successful and feared detective. 'How you holding up?'

'Well, I'm not pissing blood, which is always a plus. Apart from that, I feel my age.' Pearce lowered himself into his chair. 'You good?'

Sam folded his arms and shuffled uncomfortably, amazed at Pearce's sixth sense when it came to him.

'I don't know, Adrian.' Sam shook his head. 'I got a bad a feeling about this. About Sean and this girl. Look what they did to you.'

'I told you. I'm fine.' Pearce tried to hide his wince of pain. 'Besides, Lynsey has the goddamn BBC looking out for her. They'll have this sorted soon enough. You just make sure you keep your head down.'

Sam sighed and then nodded, looking at his friend with concern before turning and heading towards the door. Just as he was about to exit, Pearce spoke up.

'Thank you, by the way. For stepping in. I know it wasn't easy for you.'

'That's the thing.' Sam shook his head in frustration. 'It was easy.'

'You're not that guy anymore, Sam.'

Sam ran a hand through his long, wet hair, the slickness making it glide through his fingers with ease.

'Then who am I?'

Before Pearce could answer, Sam left the room, trudging back towards the entrance to the youth centre before stepping out into the rain. As he broke into a run and pounded the pavement, Pearce sat back in his chair and sighed. There was so much turmoil and conflict embedded in Sam, and it broke Pearce's heart to watch him try to move on.

Move forward.

Sam had killed a lot of people, all in the name of what

he perceived as justice, and now, with the fight over, it clearly hung from him like a medal of dishonour. Pearce knew Sam was a good man and the new path he was walking had a few different outcomes at the end of it.

The path he was on before had only one outcome.

It was just a matter of when, not if.

It was why Pearce had taken the gun from Sam, which was now safely locked in the desk just beneath his hands. Pearce would hand it in over the weekend, but for now, he wanted to do as little as physically possible.

After another hour or so, the sky had darkened, the absent sun setting behind a myriad of rain clouds, which continued to lash the city with reckless abandon.

Pearce was ready for a quiet night, a few beers, and maybe a takeaway.

As he packed up his satchel, his phone began to shimmy across his desk, the vibration echoing loudly in the empty centre.

It was Sean.

Pearce lifted the phone to his ear, greeting his friend with the usual rapport they had built over the years.

But as he heard the muffled sound of a familiar voice on the other end of the phone, Pearce's brow furrowed in a horrified, angry frown.

Within seconds, Pearce was pushing his body through the pain barrier, as he raced through the rain to his car, with the freezing cold downpour welcoming him to the horrifying evening ahead.

CHAPTER THIRTEEN

TWO AND HALF YEARS EARLIER…

'Hello, young man. Can I help?'

Pearce watched as the young man lifted himself from the steps to the youth centre, a look of discomfort splattered across his bruised face. Whoever he was, he had taken a beaten, with his eye swollen and bruised and a few cuts sporadically placed around his face. His right hand was heavily bandaged, and Pearce could see the man's discomfort.

Not from the pain.

But for why he was here.

Clearly, the man was from the streets. Although he was winding down his career as a detective for the Met, Pearce had spent many years working the beat and he knew the pressures of gang culture and those who fit the remit for entry.

Here, a young black man stood, his clothes and his disposition told Pearce he'd been down a hard path and now, he was looking for redemption.

'Err, I don't want to get into any trouble.' The young man insisted as he raised his hands in protest.

'There's no trouble here, son.' Pearce smiled. 'I don't allow it.'

The young man smiled, his youthful exuberance peeking through the brutal scars.

'Well, I was sent here by Sam Pope. He said this was the place to come if I needed help.'

Pearce stopped in his tracks and shook his head, smiling. It had been six months since Sam Pope had come onto his radar and since then, the man had led Pearce on a merry chase for his own sense of morality. For so long, the world had been black and white to Pearce.

There was the law, and you were either on the right side or on the wrong side.

But Sam had found a small pocket where the lines blurred and painted everything a shade of grey.

And the more he let Sam off the leash, the further he painted the world in that new shade.

'He wasn't wrong.'

Pearce extended his left hand, ensuring he aimed for the healthy hand as a sign of friendship. A look of relief fell across the young man's beaten face and Pearce motioned for him to follow as he ventured in from the cold. Winter had hit London with a vengeance, and the icy rain had chilled the young man to the bone. As they stepped into the main hall, Pearce walked across to the kitchen area and clicked on the kettle before removing two mugs from the cupboard. With authority, Pearce turned to his guest, his arms folded across his chest, and he observed him carefully.

'So, you going to tell me your name?' Pearce eventually asked.

'It's Sean. Sean Wiseman.'

'Name's Adrian,' Pearce said with a smile. 'So why are you here?'

As Sean reflected inwardly and struggled to find the right words, Pearce dropped tea bags into the mugs and then poured in the piping hot water. As he walked to the fridge for the milk, he looked at Sean, encouraging him for an answer.

'I don't know really…'

'Can I hazard a guess?' Pearce chuckled, as he carefully poured *milk into the cups.* 'From the look of your face and hand, I'd say you're in a pretty tough spot. And considering you said Sam Pope sent you here, then I imagine you aren't exactly surrounded by people who can help you. How am I doing?'

Pearce offered the tea to the young man who took it gratefully with his functioning hand.

'Pretty spot on.'

'Look, there is only one path that man is taking and unfortunately, it isn't lined with roses. So, no bullshit, are you a gang member?'

'I was,' *Sean said with a hint of shame.* 'You gotta do what you gotta do to get by.'

'And how is that working out for you?' *Pearce said jokingly, smirking as he took a sip. Sean raised his heavily bandaged hand.*

'Not great. But I'm done with it.'

'Are you?' *Pearce's tone changed, the authority of a senior police officer seeping through.* 'See, this is a safe place. The kids we have coming in here, they're from the same place you are. But they want to be better than their surroundings, so instead of running in gangs or breaking the law, they come here. Now the man who set this whole scheme up, he gave his life to save an innocent woman. His name was Theo Walker, and he was a good friend of Sam's. I didn't really know him that well, but it's not hard to respect a man who dedicates his life to helping others. So, we do our best. We support the kids who come through here, whether that's with schoolwork or just simply to make the right decision. Now the fact Sam sent you here instead of putting a bullet through your skull means he must think there's more to you than who you have been. So, are you done with it?'

For the first time in his life, Sean felt a sense of parental guidance. It was a strange feeling. His father had left before his memory had allowed him one cherished moment and his mother was either working or drunk. He had had to fend for himself, and with his best friend Elmore Riggs, they had survived.

But they had done it the only way Elmore had known.

And it had cost him his life.

'I'm done with it,' Sean said with clarity. 'I want something better. To be better.'

Pearce smiled and stepped forward, patting Sean on the shoulder.

'Good to hear. Now follow me, I'll give you the tour.'

'The tour?'

'Well, you don't get tea for free in this place. So, let's put you to work, shall we?' Pearce chuckled and started striding across the hall towards the door at the far end. Sean quickly downed the remnants of his tea and placed his mug in the sink before scurrying behind him. As they walked, they spoke freely, and the seeds of a very fruitful friendship were being sewn.

Almost immediately, Sean knew that following Sam's advice and meeting Adrian Pearce would be the catalyst to a better life.

―――――

Despite the unfortunate shower that was hammering from the evening sky above, Sean bounded out of his mother's apartment block. The Heaton Estate had been a dark, lonely place for Sean as he had grown up, but now it represented something unfamiliar.

Home.

With every visit to his mother, Sean was feeling more of a connection to his upbringing and the poor choices he made, although out of desperation, were becoming clearer with every return.

For so long, he had loathed his upbringing and blamed his mother. But now, as he matured, he saw how the system was built to work against people like his mother, and he appreciated just how hard she'd worked to keep him fed and clothed.

As for their relationship, a smile grew across his face as he recollected the look on his mother's face when he told her about Lynsey. Despite it being really early days, his mother was ecstatic at the thought of her son meeting a girl and the subject of grandkids erupted within seconds. As they both laughed it off, Sean couldn't help but feel excited about the prospect of a future with her. While he omitted the current predicament they were facing with regard to their safety, Sean was confident she would have it organised soon. She had even sent him a text to say that her boss had organised a flat for them to stay in.

Just the two of them.

An excitement rushed through his mind at the thought of what might happen and as his smile grew, he reached into the pocket of his drenched jacket for his phone. Pearce would no doubt be worrying about him and the least he could do would be to let Pearce know that it was sorted, so the man could enjoy his weekend. As Sean thumbed through his phone, grumbling as the rain smeared across the touch screen, he felt a twinge of guilt for what had happened to Pearce.

Those injuries he was sporting were meant for Sean, and he couldn't believe that Pearce took them on his behalf.

The Heaton Estate was dark and beyond the few buckets of brightness offered from the street lights, most of it was enveloped in shadows.

It's why Sean didn't realise he wasn't alone as he turned into the alleyway that cut through the estate and led back towards Neasden Underground Station.

As the phone began to ring, he turned a corner in the dark, secluded alleyway, and came face-to-face with Daniel Bowker. Sean's face dropped and as his hands lifted in immediate surrender, he was certain he could hear Pearce's voice cutting through the downpour.

'Hello, mate.' Bowker grinned, his jagged teeth ground together like broken glass. 'I think we need to talk.'

Sean spun on his heels in panic, turning to escape, and as he did, a clubbing blow collided with his stomach, driving the air out of him and causing him to stumble forward. His phone fell to the ground, clattering into a puddle, but before he could follow it, Jimmy Stokes pulled his fist back and then wrapped his arm around his neck, dragging him back towards the alleyway.

Through the sharp, panicked intakes of breath, Sean's voice cracked with fear.

'Please. Don't hurt me.'

'Oh, we both know that isn't an option.' Bowker spoke calmly, motioning for Jimmy to bring Sean forward. As Sean struggled, Connor appeared from behind Jimmy, slapped Sean with a gloved hand, and then helped his brother fulfil Bowker's command. Disorientated from the pain, Sean looked around the narrow alleyway. Beyond the pouring rain and the menacing figure of Bowker, he could make out the figures of four more men. Trying his best to concentrate, he noticed that one of them was black and another was short. The other two were stocky men, similar in stature to Bowker who leant forward, and, despite the briskness of the evening, the pungency of his breath hung heavy in the air.

'You have to understand, mate. This is just business.'

'I don't have much money…' Sean began, only for one of the men holding him to wrench his arm backwards. With the tendons in his shoulder straining to breaking point, Sean howled in agony.

'I'm not here for your money, son.' Bowker offered him an apologetic shrug. 'However, I do have a reputation to uphold and unfortunately for you, your friends damaged that reputation last night. Now, I usually like these things to be clean, you know? Concise. But sometimes…'

Bowker snapped forward, his fist clenched, and with the accuracy of a homing missile, he drove a clubbing haymaker right into Sean's cheek. The blow knocked Sean into a daze, and he lost balance, slumping lazily in the grip of the two men, who let him crash onto the cold, wet concrete. Bowker looked at his fist and stretched out his fingers, before turning back to Sean, who murmured in pain on the ground.

'...a message needs to be crystal clear.' Bowker looked at the six men, his entire crew minus Hicks who had his own business to handle. 'Try not to kill him.'

With those haunting final words echoing in the dark, wet alley, Bowker stuffed his hands into his pockets and began to casually stroll back towards the estate, knowing that not even the worst that it had to offer would never step up to him. Sean heard the man's footsteps splashing as he left, and with his vision beginning to unblur, he could see the feet beginning to circle in on him, like a pack of wolves surrounding the weakest of the herd. Desperation began to ricochet through his body and Sean tried to pull himself up to all fours, hoping he could somehow escape the inevitable.

With his scarred hand pressed flat against the concrete, he watched in horror as a thick, black boot was driven down onto it with the full weight of one of the attackers. As the sole crunched against his squashed bones, Sean let out a guttural roar of pain. The man held his foot in place, pinning his decimated hand to the ground and, as Sean yelled out for help, one of the other men saw their opening and drove his own boot forward.

The steel-capped boot caught Sean square on the side of the jaw, dislodging the bone and shattering it in one swoop. The pain was excruciating and, as Sean's head snapped to the side, a splatter of blood and a couple of teeth burst forth into the rain. With the pain beginning to take control of his body, Sean closed his eyes, trying his best to focus his mind on something or somewhere else. Another heavy blow caught him hard in the ribs, and although his body twitched on impact, the pain of the blow was just absorbed by the rest of it.

Sean's mind raced to Lynsey, her smile and the kiss they had shared, and he tried his best to return to that moment, to feel her lips on his again. The rain splashed against his bruised face, and he could feel two people dragging him to his feet, his slack jaw hanging sloppily in his mouth.

He thought of Pearce and the wonderful relationship they had shared, the countless evenings spent working through his qualifications and discussing a better tomorrow.

One of the attackers rocked him with another ferocious right hook, snapping his head back and shattering the cartilage in his nose.

Sean went limp, slumped in the grip of his assailants as the blood poured from his obliterated nose and down his useless jaw.

He thought of his mum. A few streets away and probably still beaming at the presumption expectation of grandchildren. The time they'd wasted over the years and the desire just to hug her one last time.

With the sand in his hourglass emptying, Sean felt the warm sensation of a blade being plunged into his side, the burning pain roaring through his body and threatening to bring him back to consciousness.

But it was hopeless.

The men released their grip and for Sean, the two second collision to the concrete felt like it lasted a lifetime. He felt like he was floating, looking down on the faceless attackers who had surrounded him and looking out beyond the sickening assault. Sporadically, he could see Pearce, his mother, and of course, Lynsey.

All of them were smiling in his direction, all of them telling him he would be okay.

Sean also saw Sam, the man who had saved him from himself and put him on the path to a happier life.

But then he collided with the concrete with such a velocity, his skull hitting the wet pavement with a sickening thud. As the consciousness seeped from his skull among the trickle of blood, Sean's final thoughts were with Sam.

And how he wished he'd been here to save him.

The final sound he heard was of the multiple footsteps of his attackers as they abandoned him to the dark, wet alleyway.

Then everything went black.

CHAPTER FOURTEEN

The bright blue lights of the emergency services had bathed the estate in an ethereal glow, illuminating the rain as it fell from the sky. The brightness guided Pearce, who felt his fingers clench the wheel until his knuckles whitened.

He felt sick to his stomach.

He had done ever since he'd answered his phone.

Every second since he'd turned the key in his engine had felt like an hour. Pearce had pulled out onto the street and hurtled down the road as fast as he could, the rain clattering against his windscreen as his wipers worked tirelessly to clear them.

It felt like they were falling in slow motion.

Throughout his decorated career as a detective, Pearce was renowned for keeping his cool. Being unflappable made him the perfect man to throw into a room with a corrupt copper, knowing they would aggressively proclaim their innocence. There was nothing more offensive to a police officer than being accused of being on the take, and Pearce would calmly dissect their arguments until all the evidence and facts aligned and the officer was charged accordingly.

It drew the ire of his colleagues, many of whom saw him as an obstacle to true police work.

But what he had done was vital.

It had saved a lot of lives and eventually, it had brought him to the life he lived now.

But along the way, he had discovered that his gut was rarely wrong.

When everyone was looking to the streets for the person attacking criminals, he had looked inside. Whereas the rest of the police force had barely registered Sam's existence, he had pegged him as the man dishing out rough justice to those who had seemingly beaten the system.

It was that instinct that had led him to trust Amara Singh, even when she was bullishly stepping on everyone to get to Sam. Just as it had welcomed Sean into the youth centre when he had nowhere else to turn.

Pearce trusted what his gut told him, and the moment he answered the phone to Sean less than an hour before, his internal alarm bells were ringing.

He was certain the other voice had been Bowker.

The evening traffic had been particularly heavy, even for a Friday, and as he navigated the wet streets of London, he begged to be wrong. Although not a religious man, Pearce was willing to reaffirm his faith in a higher power if it meant his gut was wrong.

The blue lights told him otherwise.

He was two streets away from the estate. The large concrete building that Sean had grown up in rose from the bright lights and disappeared into the dark sky above. The police had cordoned off the road ahead and a few unlucky officers were stationed by the sign, their high-vis jackets soaked through. Pearce couldn't wait any longer and he rashly pulled his car to the side of the street, invading a bus stop and pushing the car up onto the kerb. As he stepped out into the rain, someone grumpily told him he couldn't park there, but Pearce didn't care.

He began to run.

Every slap of his shoe on the wet floor sent an echo of guilt through his body. He'd told Sean to be careful, to lay low until he and Sam could figure out what to do. When Sean called to say Lynsey had taken care of it, Pearce had just accepted it. He was too caught up with his own injuries, the unsettling pain in his stomach from Bowker's attack which was now hindering his every step.

But he pushed through.

As he approached the end of the street, he stopped to survey the situation before him.

The entrance to the estate had been blocked off by two police vans, where a number of officers were working to disperse the excitable crowd that had gathered. Beyond them, Pearce could see an empty ambulance, which told him the paramedics were bravely on the scene. A few more police cars were deeper into the estate, the officers working tirelessly to cordon off the area to give those who needed it the space to operate.

Beyond it all, Pearce could see the turning to an alleyway, his view blocked by a few officers who were standing guard, doing their best to block the view of whatever horror lay beyond it.

Pearce needed to get in there.

His gut told him he had to.

The crowd, made up mostly of eager teenagers from the neighbouring streets, were all trying their best to get a video of the scene, no doubt to upload to social media in a distasteful attempt to garner a semblance of relevancy. It angered Pearce, and as he barged his way through the crowd, he tightened his muscles, ensuring that whomever he collided with would know about it. A few phones slipped from hands, and he drew a few angry yells, but he ignored them, drilling further through the crowd until he reached the officer standing guard.

'Please get back, sir,' the young officer said, trying his hardest to exert authority.

'That's my boy,' Pearce snapped angrily, looking the officer dead in the eye. It was at that moment Pearce realised he was crying, the fear and guilt finally colliding and overthrowing his composure. 'I need to get to my boy.'

Pearce's raw emotion caught the young officer off guard, and he turned cautiously towards the crime scene, the rain dripping from the peak of his police helmet. After a few moments of consideration, he nodded and lifted the tape that had marked off the cordon.

'Go, quick,' the officer said, and Pearce patted him on the arm and slipped underneath. Years of experience began to flood back Pearce as he stepped onto the crime scene. Throughout his career, he had arrived at many, immediately taking control of the situation and demanding the officers on the scene to carry out their duty without question. With the downpour unrelenting, he had noticed that the SOCOs had already put a makeshift tent in the alleyway, doing their best to protect a scene that had long since been destroyed by the rain. As he approached, he noticed the paramedics carefully strapping a body to their stretcher, with a few officers helping to steady the device. Pearce approached, ignoring another officer who called out to him.

Pearce felt his heart beat faster as his legs picked up the pace.

It was Sean.

With his worst fears realised, Pearce rushed to the entrance of the alleyway, his eyes burning as the tears began to roll down his cheeks and camouflage with the rain. A few feet from the stretcher, an officer stepped in his way, throwing his arms around Pearce and stopping him from getting to Sean.

'Sean! Sean!' Pearce yelled, his words cracking with fear. Sean was a mess. A thick brace had been affixed around his neck, blocking most of Pearce's view, but he could still see the blood that was splattered across the young man's face. An oxygen mask had been placed over his mouth, with a paramedic holding it steady to keep him alive. His arm was also strapped heavily, locked in place with a splint, and Pearce kept yelling for him.

'You can't be here, sir,' the officer said, struggling with Pearce who, despite reaching his fifties, was still a physically strong man.

'Sean, I'm here,' Pearce yelled, ignoring the officer who roughly held him in place.

'Who are you?' A voice caused Pearce to turn. A bullish looking man, soaked to his skin, approached. He was in his mid- to late-thirties and wore the unfortunate expression of the man who was in charge of such a heinous crime scene.

'Is he okay?'

'Are you family?' the detective asked, looking back towards the paramedics as they carefully led Sean towards the back of the ambulance.

'No.' Pearce shook his head. 'But I'm the closest thing he has to any.'

The detective introduced himself, but Pearce didn't register anything he said. He watched in horror as his surrogate son was loaded into the back of the ambulance; the paramedics' haste told Pearce all he needed to know.

There wasn't much time.

Whatever Sean had been through, it had taken him close to the limit and they needed to act.

'What happened?' Pearce asked desperately, looking at the detective with dismay. The man sighed, and Pearce knew it wasn't his first rodeo. It came with the job, the horror and heartbreak, and the man reached out a wet hand and placed it on his shoulder.

'He should make it. But they need to get him to the hospital.'

'Which hospital?' Pearce demanded. The man sighed and put away the notepad he'd pulled from his pocket.

'Northwick Park...' Before the detective could finish, Pearce stepped away, rushing back towards the police tape. The detective waved to the officers to let him through, and Pearce barged his way through the crowd of people before racing as fast as he could to where he'd parked his car. As his feet slapped against the wet concrete, the haunting howl of the sirens echoed through the estate and the gathering crowd parted like the Red Sea, as the ambulance made its way carefully through. Once it was clear, it shot forward down the street, ready to run every single light in the hope of keeping Sean alive.

Pearce roared his engine to life, knowing he didn't need his thirty years of experience to tell him that Sean's life was in the balance.

His gut was telling him, and he gritted his teeth and wiped his eyes, hoping that for once, his gut was wrong.

When the call came through, Sam had an inkling it was going to be bad news. The entire situation had been escalating and there were always going to be repercussions to what he did.

Bowker was a dangerous man.

The fact that he marched into an unknown place and beat up a total stranger just to find Sean was evidence of that.

It was unlikely he was going to stop, especially since

Sam had got the drop on one of his men and pointed a gun in his face.

As Pearce's panicked voice explained to Sam that Sean had been brutally beaten and was on his way to hospital, Sam felt the guilt pulse through his body like a second heartbeat. Pearce was on his way to the hospital, but the place would be swarming with police officers, at least for the next few hours. They would be wanting to speak to anyone who knew Sean and the second the police began digging around into Sam's life, the gig would be up.

His second chance would have evaporated, and he would find himself locked in the deepest, darkest hole and the key incinerated.

It meant he wouldn't be able to do anything about it.

Sam scolded himself immediately for even letting his mind wander down that path and with the walls of his flat seemingly pulling towards him like a magnet, he picked up his raincoat and stormed out. As he marched down the stairs, he could hear the rain clattering down, along with the unmistakable smell of smoke, as he reached the bottom. As he opened the door from his stairwell, he was greeted by a smiling Jess who was standing in the front doorway, trying her best to blow the smoke out of their porch and into the rain.

'Sorry,' she said sheepishly. 'I know I'm not supposed to smoke inside but look at this weather.'

'Don't worry about it,' Sam said politely, locking his door.

'You're not going out in this are you?' She looked at Sam with concern and when he didn't respond, she took another puff. 'Are you okay?'

'I just need some fresh air,' Sam responded coldly. It annoyed him, as Jess was nothing but polite. With a sigh, he forced a smile. 'A bit of rain never hurt anyone.'

'Speaking of which, Lily told me what you did for her the other day. Thank you.'

'Don't mention it. She's a good kid.'

'Yup, but like her mother, she makes bad decisions.'

'We all do.' Sam stepped past Jess and into the rain, pulling his hood up for protection. Before Jess could continue the conversation, Sam strode out into the darkness of the estate, his mind battling his own internal conflict. For nearly two years, he had lived a quiet, peaceful life. One that he never thought would have been achievable once he had laid siege to the High Rise nearly three years ago.

Having gone from a life of such pain and devastation to one of purpose, he knew there was never going to be an easy way out. It was why he was happy to give up his freedom for Singh back when he had exposed Wallace and Blackridge for the horrific truth that they represented.

Good people had given him a second chance.

Etheridge.

Alex.

Joe Alan.

Pearce.

All of them had done whatever they could to offer Sam a pathway back to a world that didn't revolve around death and destruction. But as he marched through the rain-soaked streets of London, all he could hear through the downpour were the calls to return to it.

To step back into the life he'd left and put things right.

After walking for over two hours, a text came through from Pearce.

Sean is stable but critical. Severe skull fracture. Punctured lung. Other issues. Currently in a coma. Am here with his mother. Too many police for now.

Sam didn't respond. The message made his stomach turn inside out.

Sean was a good kid, but he wasn't a fighter. The fear he must have experienced when Bowker set upon him would have been palpable and having been in enough fights to last him a lifetime, Sam knew how much they hurt. His body was a walking exhibit of the damage caused by that side of the world. Whether it was fighting Oleg Kovalenko above the Port of Tillbury or squaring off with Ravi in the bowels of The Grid, his body bore the scars of success.

They were all reminders of the pain.

Sam was built to survive.

Now, he was hoping that somehow, Sean was too.

After another hour of walking, Sam approached a corner on the streets of Colindale in Brent, not too far from the Metropolitan Police training complex. His memory of the place was hazy. It had been a number of years since he had been a hopeful recruit, ready to make his now ex-wife proud when he put on the uniform. He recalled the large tower blocks where some of the recruits were housed. The driving track, where the expert drivers revelled in showing off their expert handling behind the wheel.

The faux streets set up to provide scenario-based training for all sorts of procedures.

Beyond that, that part of his life was distant memories, like fading fingerprints on an abandoned handrail.

Sam held his breath as he turned onto the next street.

It was empty.

The roads were clear, with most people safely tucked up in bed or sheltering from the rain. Metal shutters lined the streets, the shops behind them locked up for the morning's business.

To anyone else, it would have been any other street.

For Sam, it was where his life ended.

He stopped walking and stared at the kerb, remembering the broken body of his son after he had been mowed down by Miles Hillock, a man who had been drunk behind the wheel.

Lucy's sky piercing howls of anguish had never left Sam, penetrating his sleep on a regular basis.

Something about Sean's attack had drawn Sam to the place he had loathed to visit, to remind him of what real pain was. Throughout his war on crime, he had been shot, stabbed, beaten, and run off the road.

But he had survived it all.

But he had never fully come back from the pain of losing his son. There were some things you just couldn't come back from, and Sam gingerly lowered himself onto the nearby bench and stared out at the road. Although abandoned, Sam could remember the blue lights illuminating the horror for the world to see.

As he sat, Sam allowed all the pain to come rushing back towards him like an unstoppable tidal wave. He pulled back his hood and allowed the rain to infiltrate his long hair, saturating it like his beard.

He was a different man now.

He looked different.

Felt different.

Sitting in the exact spot where he had felt more pain than he will ever be able to handle, he continued to tell himself he was changed.

He couldn't return to that life.

There was no way back from it.

With the rain clattering the surrounding streets, Sam sat back, closed his eyes, and allowed his thoughts and the darkness of the night to engulf him.

CHAPTER FIFTEEN

Despite his best efforts, Adam Bridges was unable to force a smile. The charity event was in full swing and as one of Head Space's major weapons, he had been rolled out on the charm offensive. With the hatchet piece by Beckett fresh in everyone's mind, the company's reputation needed restoring and it had been made crystal clear to Bridges that he was on the front line.

But he couldn't keep his mind from Bowker.

The large room of the hotel was decorated in classy splendour and a variable list of London's richest people were in attendance, all of them dressed to the nines and eager to share their wealth in the hopes of publicity. Somewhere within the sea of the upper class, Nicola Weaver was working the room, using her magnetic charm to no doubt smooth the tension surrounding their reputation and to empty a few wallets.

Bridges sipped his glass of prosecco with disdain for the entire event and found himself staring at the promotional banner that emblazoned the wall.

Helping kids to a better, healthier future.

The hypocrisy made him feel sick to his stomach.

A waiter casually strolled past with a tray and Bridges took the opportunity to dump his empty glass and replenish himself with another, taking a few seconds to admire the handsome man serving drinks. The waiter smiled back, possibly offering Bridges an opening, but the situation caused Bridges to turn away.

He had been firm with Bowker, something that he was terrified would come back to haunt him. But Weaver had paid a considerable sum of money for a message to be sent and Bowker hadn't delivered.

Failure didn't seem like a result the man would tolerate, and Bridges necked his drink as he thought of the poor bastard caught up in a dispute he had nothing to do with.

Bridges' phone buzzed in his blazer, and he retrieved it with a shaking hand.

The message was from Bowker.

It's done.

Two words were enough, and Bridges scurried across the room and through the doors, rushing as quickly as he could to the gentlemen's toilets. He scurried to the nearest cubicle, dropped to his knees, and the vomit exploding into the toilet bowl.

Somewhere, some poor man was no doubt lying in a ditch, and he had given the go ahead for it to happen. As the contents of his stomach hit the water, Bridges felt his body contract, pushing all the anxiety up his throat and out in a burning stream of vomit. After a few moments, he heaved, gasping for air as the ordeal was over and he collapsed back on his bottom and tried to regain himself.

Guilt wasn't something he often paid much attention to. Sure, there were things Head Space and Weaver did that maybe he should speak out against, but the six-figure salary helped him to sleep soundly at night. His Egyptian cotton sheets ensured it.

But this was different.

This wasn't offering troubled kids a crutch or a potential problem.

This was sanctioning violence against a stranger and Bridges was certain that Bowker wasn't the type of man who gently wrapped people on the knuckles. Taking a few more deep breaths, Bridges hoisted himself to his feet, using the wall of the cubicle for support and he flushed the toilet, hoping the swirl of the bowl would wash away his shame along with the evidence of his guilt.

He opened the door and came face to face with Weaver. She was immaculately dressed, as always, in a resplendent red gown, a black shawl draped across her shoulders. Her jewellery shimmered under the bright lights of the bathroom and her make up accentuated her sharp, attractive features.

For an older woman, she was certainly eye catching, and having a husband fifteen years her junior was evidence of it.

'Jesus Christ, Adam. Get a hold of yourself, will you?'

'Sorry, ma'am.' Bridges offered meekly, feebly stepping past her to the sink where he began to splash water on his face.

'This is an important night for the organisation, and I need you front and centre.'

'It's just Bowker, he...'

'I'm assuming he did what we paid him to do. Now I need you to do what I pay you for. To get out there, wipe the mud off our name and get these fuckers to invest.' Weaver huffed in annoyance. 'I don't pay you to have a conscience, Adam. I pay you because you're an obedient little dog with a silver tongue. Now get out there and start licking.'

Bridges kept his head down, refusing to turn and face his monstrous boss. His hand gripped the shiny, gold-plated tap and he squeezed it in anger, his knuckles whitening.

Weaver turned and stormed out of the bathroom, her heels clicking across the tiles. As the door closed behind her, Bridges looked up into the mirror, staring a hole through the man looking back at him.

Usually, it was a picture of perfection. He knew he was attractive, but no matter how you sneak upon a mirror, the reflection never lied. What looked back at him was a picture of the truth. His skin was pale, the colour drained from the sudden bout of sickness, and his eyes wore bags from the sleepless nights. With a grunt of shame, he fixed his hair, took one of the complimentary mints and forced his million-dollar smile onto his face.

He still had a job to do.

But every step he took towards the door felt labored, as the guilt of his actions hung heavy from him, and he genuinely wondered how long he could carry it for.

Staring through a hospital window was always a morbid feeling. Pearce had done it plenty of times throughout his respected career for the Met Police, and it always filled him with discomfort. Casting an eye over someone at their most vulnerable, usually without their consent, always felt voyeuristic to him, but a necessary part of the job. Now, happily retired and staring at a young man he looked at as a son, he could feel the pieces of his heart detaching.

Sean was in a bad way.

As the evening played out in a blur, Pearce had followed the ambulance to Northwick Park Hospital, the large, grim building surrounded by rows of trees and neighboured a fancy looking golf complex. He was familiar with it, as many years ago, a rogue killer had murdered a criminal within the batting cage, leaving the man to his demise in front of an active machine. Pearce hadn't been involved in the case, but something always stuck in his mind about it.

Lucas Cole was a man who had been wronged and fought back. It reminded him of Sam, although unlike Lucas, Sam managed to find a way out.

But as Pearce stared at the body of Sean, lying motionless and surrounded by wires and machines, every fibre of his being wanted to urge Sam to return to what he did best.

By the time Pearce had arrived at the hospital, Sean was already in surgery. The paramedics had bravely kept him alive long enough for the seven-mile journey. As Pearce sat in the waiting area, the detective from the crime scene arrived to take his statement. Detective Mark Williams was an ordinary man, befitting his name, but he showed enough compassion that Pearce warmed to him. When he divulged that he used to be a detective himself, Williams became even more open with him, offering him a little insight into what they believed happened.

Gang related violence.

Pearce tried his best to turn them towards Bowker, citing his own injuries and the very real threat to Lynsey Beckett as evidence, but Williams was sceptical. Pearce hadn't reported an attack, and there was nothing to link Sean to Lynsey Beckett that they knew of. Unless she could corroborate it, Williams made it clear that Sean Wiseman was part of a notorious gang a few years ago and had returned to a patch where there was a new big dog roaming the yard. That dog set his own pack on Sean like a wounded animal and judging from the forensics, at least five people had been set on the poor boy.

Pearce felt sick, but he understood.

A young black man found beaten half to death in a known gang hotspot was never going to jump to the top of the list. That anger soon turned to anguish when Sheila

Wiseman was brought in, the old woman shaking with rage at the fate of her child. It was only then that Pearce realised that Sean had taken his mother's name. Having never known his father, it had made sense, and Pearce understood further the bond that had grown between him and Sean.

Sheila had demanded to see her son, but the police officers explained to her that he was fighting for his life on an operating table. Pearce stepped in, taking her to the waiting room and explaining who he was. The instant she heard his name, she calmed, recalling numerous times that Sean had spoken of Pearce with gushing pride.

Pearce held back his own sadness for her sake and got them both a coffee, battling with the run-down Costa Coffee machine that spat out something half resembling a latte. They sat for two hours, sharing stories of Sean, and Pearce smiled as she spoke about the troublesome scamp he was as a child, yet was too clever for his own good. How he had been taken advantage of by bigger, stronger kids who used his mind to get ahead.

Pearce countered by offering her stories of the work Sean had done with him, the children he had helped, and how Sean often spoke of his own poor choices to keep them on the straight and narrow.

Although the two of them had never met, Sheila and Pearce had never been closer, their love for Sean something they were thrilled to share. Pearce sat with her until the surgeon emerged through the doors, informing them of the very real situation before them. Sean had suffered severe trauma to his skull, which although surgically repaired, meant for now he was in an induced coma. As the surgeon spoke to Sheila about the possibility of him pulling through, Pearce could tell from the man's cadence the dire reality.

There was little chance of Sean waking up.

If, by some miracle, he did, he would most likely have severe brain damage. Despite the horrific situation, Sheila maintained her calm and thanked the doctor, who took them both through to see Sean. They weren't permitted into the room, but from the window, Pearce gritted his teeth at the state of his friend. There were so many tubes and wires connected to him he looked like a science fair project, and Pearce felt Sheila squeeze his hand. After a few moments of muttering, he realised she was saying a prayer, her other hand grasping the crucifix she wore round her neck. Pearce bowed his head, and for the first time in a long time, tried to get through to God.

Detective Williams offered to drive Sheila home and on Pearce's recommendation that she got some rest, she accepted.

Sean wouldn't recover.

Pearce knew that, and along with the broken bones and punctured lungs, he felt his eyes water as he imagined how scared he must have been.

He also shed a tear because it was unlikely anyone would pay for their violence.

After sending Sam a message to update him, Pearce's attention was pulled towards the door to the corridor, as a terrified woman barged in, her pretty face stained with tears. As she called out Sean's name, he immediately clocked the Northern Irish accent, and he approached Lynsey with an apologetic smile.

She either knew who he was from Sean's stories or frankly, didn't care, and she collapsed into his arms, and Pearce held her tightly as she allowed her devastation to take over. Pearce could feel her heartbreak through every shudder of her body, and he allowed it to reverberate off his own, and he cursed the world for the amount of pain that flowed through it.

The sun had been up for an hour, and Hicks readjusted himself in the front seat of his car. His back ached, an expected side effect of staking out the youth centre, but he didn't care. It would all be worth it.

Bowker had called him the night before to inform him that they had got to Sean Wiseman and the job was complete. They would be well paid, and their reputation enhanced, and the boys were going out later to celebrate. Hicks politely declined the offer on principal.

As much as he would have liked to have stoved Wiseman's skull in himself, he hadn't partaken in the event and therefore he didn't deserve the celebration.

He had other business to attend to.

Lifting the cup of coffee to his lips, Hicks was grateful to the early bird café that was one street away and he embraced the caffeine like a father welcoming home a lost child. Ever since the moment that janitor had humiliated him in front of Bowker, Hicks hadn't been able to sleep. His jaw still throbbed from the clubbing blow the man had delivered and the humiliation of having his gun confiscated had burned inside him like a furnace.

Hicks needed to put that right.

Scratching his beard, he stared towards the door of the youth centre, his eyes fixated on the entrance, willing the janitor to appear. His swollen lip ached as he sipped the coffee, but he used it as a reminder of why he was there.

He was going to kill the janitor and clear his mind.

Working for Bowker had given Hicks a purpose his violent urges required. The financial aspect of what they did mattered little to him. Like Bowker, he was drawn to a simplistic life, and his small apartment consisted of a bed and a chair.

What Hicks craved was violence.

Anarchy.

The feeling of another man's life drawing to a close by his hand.

Hicks had arrived the evening before, knowing that Bowker and his crew would have little problem eradicating Wiseman and collecting their bounty. For Hicks, this was so much more.

It was personal.

He wanted his gun back.

And he wanted to kill the man who had got the better of him.

Cars had begun to fill the streets as the Saturday morning rush began to flood the streets of London. A few dog walkers trotted by, all of them lost in their own lives, all of them oblivious to the cold-blooded murder he was there to commit.

Hicks was never scared of a fight. But there was something that Bowker had said that had burrowed through his bald head and nested in the back of his mind.

Bowker was sure he recognised the man.

It put Hicks on alert as the only people Bowker knew were as dangerous as he was and despite the inevitable death he was about to suffer, the janitor could clearly handle himself.

It meant Hicks would have to be at his terrifying best.

His most sadistic.

Just the way he liked it.

The creaking of the metal gate drew his attention back to the youth centre and Hicks's dark, beady eyes lit up. Closing the gate behind him was the teenage boy who'd stumbled onto them last time Hicks was there. Hicks racked his brain for the name, as usual, he just dismissed black people with the vitriol of a true racist.

Curtis.

That was it. And if memory served him correctly, it

was Hicks threatening Curtis that finally drew the janitor out. Not the beating Bowker was giving to that old bastard.

It was the threat to Curtis.

Realising the upper hand had just been served up on a silver platter, Hicks smirked as Curtis entered the youth centre, no doubt looking for one of the men who ran it. Knowing full well the centre was empty, Hicks did his best not to lick his lips as he stepped out of the car.

With a spring in his step, Hicks marched towards the gate, his hand gripping the handle of the serrated blade that rested inside his leather jacket.

Carefully, he slipped through the opening of the gate and made his way to the front door, with Curtis already inside.

CHAPTER SIXTEEN

The spring morning brought with it an icy chill, the remnants of the wet night still lingering in the air. Sam shivered beneath his raincoat, not realising he'd lost himself in his thoughts until the sun began to peek through the clouds to welcome another day.

All night spent on the bench, tossing the events of the last few days over in his mind and letting them wrestle with the archive of pain that the location held for him. As he walked back through the empty streets of London, he shook his head at the level of rubbish that littered the streets, the Friday night crowds showing defiance to the weather by indulging in another night of merriment.

It had been a long time since Sam had even tasted an alcoholic drink, knowing that his current mind state and new life was a fragile ecosystem, and a drunken evening could certainly unlock a door he had long since closed.

But as he ventured back through London, he knew that people were banging their hardest against it, pushing its hinges to breaking point.

Sean was in a coma.

Pearce had sent him updates throughout the night and

despite wanting to see his friend, Sam knew it would be too risky. The fact of the matter was his good friend had been beaten to near death by a group of paid mercenaries.

Which meant not only were they accountable, but that those who paid for it were as well.

Sam hoped beyond all hope that they would be brought to justice, that they wouldn't go unpunished for what they had done.

But it was unlikely.

It was why he had begun his assault on organised crime in the first place. Seeing powerful people get away with despicable things with no hope for those whose lives had been ravaged by their actions.

Someone had to fight back.

But Sam wasn't that someone anymore.

Despite every fibre of his being wanting to set the world right, he knew that he couldn't.

A few cars were on the road as he walked towards Bethnal Green, the early Saturday morning footfall of people on their way to work or heading out of the city for a weekend break. It had been nearly two years since Sam had returned to his new life and identity and sticking to his routine had embedded it into his muscle memory. With the youth centre empty, he would take the opportunity to get a few odd jobs done and then finish by late morning, before a stop at the local café and an afternoon at the gym, usually listening to the football scores on his phone.

It wasn't the most exciting life, but it was a peaceful one and as he trudged in wet shoes across a cold city, he didn't even realise that they were directing him to the youth centre. As he turned the corner onto the street where the centre was situated, a recollection hit him like a slap in the face.

Curtis was stopping by.

Sam had promised him that he could help with the

electrical work in the bathroom. Sam scolded himself, picking up the pace and completely ignoring the car that was parked out front. Usually, a suspect vehicle would raise an alarm, and he would take every step with caution. It was a nagging worry within the back of his mind that any day he could walk into the youth centre and be greeted by an armed response team and a smug detective who had rumbled his secret life.

Sam wouldn't put up a fight.

He knew there was a price to pay for the things he had done and if he couldn't try to lead a good life and help struggling kids to try to put things right, then he would accept a lifetime behind bars.

Throughout everything that had transpired over the past few days, he had completely forgotten about his promise to Curtis and as he pushed open the gate to the youth centre forecourt, he hoped he would have enough time to use the facilities and freshen up. If Curtis was already there, he would certainly have some questions as to why Sam had clearly not slept and was soaked through.

Sam checked the time on his watch.

It was ten past eight.

The cleaners would have already finished and as Sam tugged open the front door, he tutted to himself. They'd requested the cleaners lock up after they were done, but because they knew Sam was usually there, they never listened.

Sam stepped into the youth centre, his wet boots squelching against the wooden flooring and he slid his wet coat from his muscular frame.

'Hello?' he called out, hanging the coat on a nearby hook. 'Curtis?'

Sam's voice echoed through the empty building, and he marched onwards towards the main hall. The plan was to pop the kettle on and then head to his locker, where, as always, he had a change of clothes and back up toiletries. Pearce ribbed him constantly, calling him a boy scout, but today, Sam was happy his caution always won out.

As he stepped into the main hall, he looked across the room and stopped in his tracks.

The first thing he noticed was the glimmer of the serrated blade that was being held to Curtis's throat, the rising sunlight seeping through the cracks in the blinds and sparkling off the clean metal.

The next thing he registered was the sheer terror in Curtis's eyes, his body rigid with fear. By the stains on his cheeks, he had been crying.

Finally, Sam's eyes settled on the man who had one arm locked around Curtis's waist, pinning his arms in and the other hand clutching the blade dangerously close to the carotid artery in the young boy's neck. The man's eyes were filled with hatred, his bearded jaw distorted in an aggressive snarl. Sam recognised him from two nights before, when he disarmed the man and sent him spiralling to the ground with a well-placed blow.

Then, he was there for Sean.

Today, it was very clear, from the murderous look in his eyes, that he was there for Sam.

'Well, well, well...' The man chuckled, deliberately adjusting the blade in his hand. 'Look who decided to show up.'

Sam took a tentative step forward, his only focus on the terrified boy being held captive.

'Curtis. Are you okay?'

'Oh, he's fine. Aren't you, matey?' Hicks said with a chuckle. 'We've just been waiting for you to get here so we can get started.'

'Everything will be okay, Curtis.' Sam's focus shifted to the armed captor, his brow furrowing. 'Let him go.'

'See, I'm starting to get a little pissed off with you making demands.'

'This has nothing to do with him. He's just a kid.'

'That's right. He is. But he is also the reason you stepped out of your little hiding place to blindside me. Not when your friend was having his arse handed to him. No, you hid back there like a pussy. But this little guy…' Hicks pressed the blade closer to Curtis's throat. Another inch and he would draw blood. 'This right here is what we call live bait.'

Sam took a deep breath.

The entire night, he'd struggled with the decision he was going to have to make. Every fibre of his being was calling to the man he used to be, yearning for him to put right what these people had done to Sean. But now, as he processed the terror in Curtis's eyes, he felt his adrenaline decrease to a worrying calm.

The choice had been taken out of his hands.

'If you want me. Come and get me.' Sam held his hands out, goading Hicks from across the hall. 'Just you and me. Let the boy go and let's take our chances.'

'Chances?' Hicks chuckled out loud. 'You're just a janitor that got lucky. But this time, face to face, I'm going to take you apart.'

'Then prove it.' Sam's fists clenched. Hicks withdrew the knife from Curtis and pushed the boy aside. 'Curtis, go home. Right now, you hear me?'

'B-b-but…' Curtis stammered as he rushed across the room towards him. Sam rested his hand on his shoulder.

'Now. You run and don't look back.'

Curtis shot a scared look back towards Hicks, who was practically salivating at the fight to come. With his body shaking with terror, Curtis rushed to the door and pushed his way to freedom. Sam turned his attention back to Hicks, the width of the room the only thing between them.

The sun cut through several gaps in the blinds, lining the wooden floor in strips of bright light.

Sam took a deep breath, said a silent apology to his son for the promise he had to break once again and a regrettable goodbye to the life he had tried to lead.

'You ready?' Hicks cockily asked, tossing the blade between his gloved hands, the sunshine gleaming from his bald head.

Sam rolled his shoulders and cracked his neck in response and then offered one final warning.

'You're about to make a big mistake.'

His words seem to light a fire in Hicks who rushed forward, growling as he slashed towards Sam with his knife, the blade slicing through the air. Sam was quick on his feet, dodging the first few swipes, then managing to raise his right arm to block the next manic swipe. As he did, Hicks expertly pivoted on his feet and drove his knee into Sam's stomach. As Sam arched over to absorb the blow, Hicks swivelled from him and whipped his arm forward, the blade slashing Sam across his cheek.

A spray of blood hit the floor, and Hicks chuckled.

'This is going to be fun.'

Sam dabbed at his bloodied cheek with his fingers, pulling them away to reveal the blood trickling from the cut. Hicks was clearly dangerous, the way he moved was that of a man who had been trained to kill. Hicks sized Sam up, then lunged again, thrusting forward with the intent to kill. Sam stepped to the side and hooked his arm over Hicks's drawing him in and driving his head viciously into Hicks's nose. The bridge of it collapsed immediately, shooting blood and cartilage down Hicks's mouth and beard and knocking him off balance.

Sam wrenched the arm upwards, locking it in tight, and with his other arm, he drove a fist into Hicks's throat, crushing the man's larynx and driving the air from his body. Hicks stumbled back, gasping for breath as Sam stepped forward. Hicks sloppily lunged at him again, the knife swiping sloppily in every direction. Sam blocked the blow with his forearm and then returned with a devastating haymaker that sent Hicks spiralling to the floor.

Quickly, Hicks scrambled to his feet, trying his best to fill his lungs with air. As he did, he looked up at Sam with a look that was clearly alien to him.

Fear.

'Who the fuck are you?' Hicks spat. The blood gushing from his nose had stained his beard a dark red.

'The janitor,' Sam responded, drawing a furious roar from Hicks who swung his arm towards Sam, the blade aimed for his throat. Sam arched his head back, the blade missing his throat by a centimetre, before he reached out and grabbed Hicks by the wrist. Using the man's own momentum against him, Sam directed the arm back towards Hicks. The velocity of the swing, combined with Sam's strength, caught him off balance. Sam twisted Hicks's arm and then directed it to his own leg, plunging the knife into Hicks's thigh and extracting a roar of anguish from him. The burning sensation roared from the knife wound and travelled up Hicks's spine to his brain, causing him to buckle in agony as Sam released his grip. With his own knife embedded in his thigh, Hicks stumbled forward, and Sam helped him to his knees with a vicious kick to the back of the knee. As Hicks dropped onto the hardwood floor, he looked back up at Sam in wonderment. He opened his bloodied mouth to speak.

Sam gripped the man's head with both hands and twisted sharply, audibly snapping the man's neck and then allowed the limp body to crash to the ground.

Everything went silent.

Sam could hear the traffic from the streets outside, the

world continuing, completely oblivious to the life he'd just ended.

There was no feeling of regret or remorse.

The corpse at his feet belonged to a vile man who had threatened harm to people he cared about. And as Sam stared down at his handiwork, he knew within himself that there was no choice left to be made.

He had made it.

His train of thought was interrupted by the sound of the door slowly opening behind him, and he turned quickly. Curtis walked in slowly, his mouth agape as he stared at the dead man on the floor.

'Fucking hell, JC,' Curtis said, his eyes locked on Hicks's motionless body. 'That was insane.'

'I told you to go home.'

'Yo, you fucked this guy up. Where did you learn that shit? Can you teach me?'

Sam turned and grabbed Curtis by the shoulder, shocking the young man with his strength. With his eyes burning a hole in Curtis, he spoke, his voice aching.

'What I did wasn't okay. Do you understand that?' Curtis nodded. 'You need to go home, okay? You need to go home and wait for Adrian to contact you.'

Sam released his grip and Curtis looked at him with trepidation as he began to head back towards the door.

'What should I say? You know, if the police ask or summin'?'

Sam offered him a smile.

'You tell them the truth.' Sam nodded. 'It's the right thing to do.'

Curtis let that fester for a few seconds before he turned and stomped to the door. As he pushed it open, he turned back to Sam, almost embarrassed.

'Yo, JC. Thank you. You saved my life.'

Sam drew his mouth into a tight line and nodded once

more, accepting the appreciation but hated what it was for. The young man had looked up to him, had asked his advice and been pushed towards a career based on a multitude of tasks they had done together.

Now, all he would remember Sam for was when he brutally killed a man who had pulled a knife on them.

As the door to the youth centre slammed shut, Sam looked down at the man he had killed and pulled his phone from his back pocket. He raised it to his ear, begging Pearce to pick up.

After a few rings, he did.

'Sam?'

'We have a problem.'

CHAPTER SEVENTEEN

It had been a hell of a night.

Physically, mentally, and emotionally drained, Pearce stumbled through his door a little after five in the morning, trying his best to stretch out the dull ache at the base of his spine. The trauma of the evening had taken its toll on his body and Pearce walked gingerly to his kitchen and poured himself a glass of water. He popped two paracetamols into his mouth and knocked them back, before wiping his mouth with the back of his hand.

What a mess.

After Lynsey had calmed down upon seeing the broken body of her potential boyfriend, Pearce had sat with her. Similar to the time he had spent with Sean's mother, he shared stories about Sean with the young woman in a hopeful attempt at raising her spirits.

She appreciated it, and as they spoke, he understood why Sean had been so besotted with her from the moment he met her. Lynsey spoke eloquently, yet every word she spoke was laced with conviction. At around four o'clock, Pearce offered to drive her home, but he could see a determination in her eyes that she wasn't ready to leave.

Determination and fear. It was understandable, considering the circumstances and staying in the vicinity of police protection wasn't a bad idea. He offered her a warm smile and then told her to stop by the youth centre if she wanted to talk.

She handed him one of her business cards, offering the same thing if he was struggling.

Then he left.

As he weaved his way back home through the desolate city of London, Pearce tried to make sense of the last week. It had started with such hope and promise, with Sean's clear excitement at meeting a woman filling Pearce with joy. From there, it had spiralled.

All because Lynsey had done her job as a fearless reporter and rattled the wrong cage.

Someone didn't want her story to come out and they had gone to disgusting lengths to ensure it stayed hidden.

Pearce stumbled up the stairs of his home and collapsed on his bed before lazily trying to flick his shoes off. He was beyond tired, and despite the first inkling of sunshine daring to peek over the skyline, he could feel his eyelids dropping.

A few hours later, he was awoken by the buzz of his phone, accompanied by the bizarre jingle it had selected as his ringtone. Disorientated, he sat up, hoping that the previous night was just a bad dream, before he finally drew his weary eyes to the illuminated screen of his phone.

Sam.

Pearce slid the green button with his thumb and lifted it to his ear.

'Sam?'

'We have a problem.'

Pearce swung his legs over the side of the bed, pressing his feet to the floor.

'What's up?'

'I need you here, Adrian. I'm at the youth centre. Hurry.'

Sam hung up and just to add more terror into the current cocktail of events, Pearce was frightened. Sam sounded worried, an emotion that Pearce rarely associated with the man. He sprung from the bed, his concern for his other friend willing his body into action, and he rushed to the bathroom. He quickly brushed his teeth and splashed water on his face, hoping the brisk chill would wake him up further. Usually, he would have taken the time to shave, neatening up his white beard that framed his jaw. He checked his watch – it was a little before eight thirty and Pearce picked up his trainers as he dashed down the stairs, sliding his feet in as he got to the bottom.

Within minutes, he was racing through the streets of London once more, pleased that the weekend traffic hadn't hit its stride. Pearce kept his eyes peeled for an empty coffee shop, his body yearning for a caffeine boost to help pull it through its exhaustion. A few streets from the youth centre, he clocked an empty-looking Starbucks and whipped his car up onto the kerb, knowing his parking was a traffic warden's wet dream. Keeping an eye on the street once he had entered, Pearce ordered a double shot and waited impatiently until it was placed in his hand.

Pearce downed it before he left the premises, the heat causing a slight scalding to his throat, but he ignored it. Thankfully, the magnetic pull of a warden hadn't been strong enough, and he quickly hopped in the front seat of his car and navigated the final few streets to the centre. Pearce parked in one of the marked bays outside and then rushed through the gate and threw open the door.

'Sam?' His voice echoed through the empty building.

'In here.' The response emanated from the main hall and Pearce pushed open the door and stopped in his tracks.

Years of working for the Met informed the obvious

deduction that the man on the floor was dead, his limbs sprawled out, indicating he had been killed before he hit the ground. A knife was embedded in the side of his thigh, with a small puddle of blood forming. A clear attempt had been made at cleaning a larger pool. Pearce recognised the man from the other night, who had accompanied Bowker during their confrontation.

Standing against the wall, with his muscular arms crossed, was Sam. A painful looking cut sliced across his cheek, and he dabbed at it with a blood stained tissue.

'Jesus fucking Christ,' Pearce exclaimed. 'What the hell happened?'

'I had no choice.'

Pearce placed his hands on his head in dismay.

'Are you okay?' Pearce asked.

'I'm fine.' Sam was surprisingly calm, which clearly made Pearce uncomfortable. 'This wasn't planned, but like I said, I had no choice.'

'There is always a choice, Sam,' Pearce barked as he inspected the body. 'This isn't your fight, Sam. It's not who you are anymore.'

'He had Curtis,' Sam said sternly, drawing Pearce's attention.

'Is Curtis okay?'

'He's fine.' Sam assured him. 'A little shaken, but he's okay.'

'Did he see you do this?'

Sam nodded.

'I told him not to lie. If the police end up asking him any questions, I made it clear that he needs to tell the truth.'

'Sam… no.' Pearce took a step towards his friend. 'We can figure something out…'

'Adrian, it's over.' Sam looked at Pearce with a resigned smile. 'I did what I had to do.'

'So, what the hell happened?'

Sam took a deep breath and dabbed at the wound on his cheek.

'I went for a walk last night to clear my head, to convince myself that I wasn't going to get involved. Then I remembered Curtis was coming here this morning. I'd promised him he could help with the electrical repairs. I walked in and this guy had Curtis with a blade held to his throat.'

'Jesus.' Pearce blasphemed again, knowing his grandma would be turning over in her grave.

'Curtis was okay. Pretty brave, actually. But apparently, this guy held a grudge about what I did to him the other night and once I'd convinced him to let Curtis go, it was clear both of us weren't walking out of here alive. Me or him, Pearce. So, I killed him.'

'Look, Sam, we can fix this okay...'

Sam pushed himself away from the wall and approached his friend. Without saying a word, he wrapped his arms around him and held tightly, hugging his friend. Taken aback, Pearce quickly relented and reciprocated, embracing his friend with a tight grip.

It had been nearly two years since Sam had returned from America, supposedly a dead man and with a fresh start. In that time, the two of them had become the best of friends, with Pearce helping to guide Sam down a more content road. A calmer existence, one that wasn't dominated by grief or violence.

But as they patted each other's back and pulled away from their hug, they knew that road had come to an end.

'I can't ask you to cover this up, Adrian. You're a pillar in this community and you've got a thirty-year career that is held in high regard.' Sam looked down at the body. 'Besides, he was here for me. And I'm not ashamed of what I've done.'

'I'm sorry, Sam.'

'I know.' Sam turned back to Pearce. 'But I can't let this go, Adrian. After everything Sean has done to turn his life around, I can't just let them get away with what they've done.'

'Sam… don't go down this road. Leave it to the…'

'The police? Come on, we both know that a young black man beaten to near death in a crime-heavy estate isn't going to go any further. They'll chalk it up as another gang related incident and hope he makes any sort of recovery. Sean is better than that. He deserves better than that.'

'I know.' Pearce sighed. There was no argument to make.

'For a long time, Adrian, I've been content. Happy might be a stretch, but I was at least okay with who I was. Who I had become. But this needs to be put right… you understand that, right?'

Pearce could feel his eyes watering and he stepped away, his hands on his hips.

'You know if you do this, there's no way back?' Pearce said, looking out into the room.

'I know.' Sam shrugged. 'But someone has to fight back.'

Throughout the years since he had met Sam, Pearce had struggled to ever condone the things he had done. He had understood the necessity of them, and without Sam's approach, who knows what fate would have awaited the likes of Jasmine Hill. Or what atrocities General Wallace would have committed.

Sam was a necessary weapon that the authorities couldn't wield, and there were certainly some wrongs that would never be put right.

Unless Sam intervened.

After a few more moments of painful thinking, Pearce sighed with resignation.

'What do you need from me?'

'I need you to speak to Lynsey Beckett and tell her to meet me. Give her my address.'

'Sam, she's a reporter. The last thing you need is the world to know you're still alive.'

Sam held out his hand to Pearce who, with a tear in his eye, shook it for the final time.

'Believe me, when I'm finished with Bowker, the world will know anyway.'

With that, Sam stepped towards the motionless body of the man he had killed and removed the man's phone from his jacket pocket. He then marched through the corridor to Pearce's office, sliding open the drawer to his desk and retrieving the handgun they had confiscated from the recently deceased. With the gun tucked firmly in the back of his jeans, Sam returned to the main hall and strode towards the door, leaving a conflicted Pearce to his own thoughts. Just as he reached the door, Pearce turned on his heels and called after him.

'Take care of yourself, Sam. Please.'

Sam stopped and turned, offering the tearful Pearce a smile, struggling to hide the pain in his face.

'You too, Adrian. You saved my life.'

With that, Sam pushed through the doors and out into the rain, while Pearce made the first of a few phone calls, knowing in his gut that the situation was only going to get worse.

The rain greeted Sam with a wet embrace and with the clarity of his next steps rattling in his brain, he hailed a cab and directed it home. The driver tried to strike up a conversation as they navigated through the increasingly busy streets, but it fell on deaf ears. As Sam stared out of the window, his long, wet hair plastered to his face, the driver seemed to get the hint and left him alone with his thoughts.

They ranged from his son, Jamie, the innocent smile that always filled Sam with pride. Watching as his son connected pieces of Lego together with excitement as Sam held the instructions.

To Theo, and the time they spent overseas in the army, to sharing a beer at a pub.

To his funeral.

To Lucy, hoping she was happy in her new life, raising her new family in a stable marriage. To their good times, which were truly the happiest of Sam's life.

To Frank Jackson, Andrei Kovalenko, Ervin Wallace, and Harry Chapman. To every criminal that Sam had looked down the barrel of a gun at, knowing he was about to snatch them from this world.

To Amara Singh, and the life they could have shared.

To Paul Etheridge, who had uprooted his entire life because he believed in what Sam stood for.

To Alex Stone and her family, knowing that he had walked through hell drinking gasoline just to reunite them.

To Sean, who Sam had watched fight back against the world that moulded him to try to help others. A man who was now holding onto the fringes of his life by the loosest of threads, all for being the wrong guy in the wrong place at the wrong time.

And finally, to Bowker, and the murderous glint in the man's eye when Sam held him at gunpoint, knowing that he wouldn't pull the trigger.

But things had changed, and as Sam handed the driver his fare and a generous tip, he stepped out of the cab, knowing that when that moment came again, he wouldn't hesitate.

The estate was quiet as Sam walked through a few of the streets until he arrived at his house, and he slid in silently, not wanting to wake either Jess or Lily with an errant slam of the door.

Sam's flat was pristine. The military mindset of order was something that would never leave him. He placed the handgun and his phone on the small kitchen side unit and marched to his bathroom. It was a dingy room, with just enough room for him to stand, with the amenities crammed together as tightly as possible. He quickly brushed his teeth and then stared for a few moments into the mirror.

The man staring back wasn't the one he recognised.

It was Jonathan Cooper.

The long hair, though wet, hung down and tucked behind his ear. The strong jaw was hidden behind a thick, grey tinged beard.

Sam reached inside the mirror cabinet and removed the pair of clippers. He set the guard to a high level and without hesitation, he drove it smoothly across his scalp. As the machine buzzed, the hair fell in clumps, splattering the sink and murky, tiled floor. Sam moved in regimented strips, taking the grade down lower and lower until his hair was cropped close to his skull. He clicked off the guard, exposing the blades, and with the clipper set to its shortest setting, he guided it with precision across his jaw.

Minutes later, the thick beard that had hidden his face for nearly two years was no more. With nothing more than a light stubble gracing his face, Sam stepped into the shower and allowed the warm, mediocre burst of water to wash over him, clearing off the loose hairs and coaxing him from his drained state.

As he stepped out of the shower, he wrapped a towel around his waist and moved to his bedroom and stepped in front of the mirror.

It was Sam Pope looking back at him.

Apart from the additional muscle his gym routine had granted him, his chiselled body was still covered in the battle scars of his war.

He changed into a fresh set of clothes, and as he pulled the black T-shirt over his head, he heard the unmistakable chime of his doorbell. Pulling the T-shirt down to cover the war wounds, he marched through his flat, taking a deep breath.

He was about to give up his entire new life.

But for the right reason.

Sam bounded down the stairwell and into the shared reception area, reached for the front door, and pulled it open.

Huddled under an umbrella was Lynsey Beckett. Despite the wet hair and the clear exhaustion that hung from her eyes, Sam understood why Sean had been so smitten with her. Her face was sharp and striking and as she looked up at him, her eyes widened.

Not with fear.

With recognition.

'Holy fucking Christ,' she exclaimed. 'You're Sam Pope.'

CHAPTER EIGHTEEN

Lynsey had been asleep in the waiting area of the hospital for a few hours after Pearce had left. Despite the horrendous circumstances of their meeting, she was glad that they had. Sean had spoken highly of him a few times, and within moments of their first embrace, she understood why. The man offered a sense of calm, and Lynsey soon felt a semblance of hope when he spoke.

Sean was in a bad way.

A really bad way and despite all the evidence that he wouldn't make it through, Pearce told her that they needed to believe he would.

To will him back to life.

As they shared stories about Sean and Lynsey gushed about their blossoming romance, Pearce had watched on like a proud father and when it was time for him to go, he promised her he would be there whenever she needed. They exchanged numbers, hugged one last time, and Pearce set off to get some much-needed rest. Knowing what had happened to Sean was a direct result of her investigation into Head Space, Lynsey didn't feel safe venturing out into the night. Whatever message they had intended to be sent had been heard loud and clear, and looking at the police officer guarding Sean's door, she felt it was the safest place to be.

Besides, Pearce had got her to hope for Sean.

She wanted to be there if he woke up.

As the hours passed, she found herself uncomfortably slouched in one of the chairs of the waiting room, the emotion and exhaustion guiding her into a stop-start sleep. A rumbling noise soon woke her completely, her brow furrowed as she looked around the room for its source. It was her phone resting in her bag and she scooped it up and blinked to see the screen.

It was Pearce.

'Adrian, hi,' she stammered. Her throat was dry. 'Is everything okay?'

'Yeah, how's Sean?'

'About the same.' She sighed.

'And you?'

'About the same.' She half chuckled.

'Look, Lynsey. Something has come up and I think this situation is only going to get worse.'

Lynsey sat bolt upright and glanced nervously at the police officer by the door. She lowered her voice.

'What are you talking about?'

'It's best that you don't know, but I have a friend who can fix this for us. But he needs your help.'

'Adrian, you're not making any sense…'

'Trust me. Please. I need you to go to the following address…'

Pearce gave her the address and hung up, leaving Lynsey anxiously looking around the room. The man's unflappable calm had been replaced with an urgency that Lynsey knew was genuine, and with the severity of Sean's injuries, she was terrified at how the situation could get any worse.

She needed to trust someone, and Pearce was her best

option. She opened her Uber app, entered the address, and submitted. Her taxi was two minutes away, and she quickly scarpered back down through Northwick Park Hospital. By the time she emerged into the rain, her taxi had arrived, and she rushed into it. The man welcomed her but didn't press for her life story and Lynsey allowed herself the luxury of a small nap as the car navigated its way back into central London. By the time she arrived, the sky had opened, and she stepped out into the grim estate. The few converted houses were stuffed at the end of the road, hidden by the tall, unkempt pillars that comprised small flats at extortionate prices. It was an impoverished area of London and Lynsey knew it pretty well, having done a documentary highlighting the government's neglect of inner-city estates.

In one click, her umbrella burst above her head, shielding her from the downpour, and she marched up to the door Pearce had directed her to and pressed the doorbell.

Seconds later, her entire world was turned upside down.

Now, she was sitting in a pokey yet immaculately tidy flat, shivering slightly from the cold downpour and waiting patiently for her cup of tea.

A cup of tea being made by Sam Pope.

It was a surreal moment, and as the imposing vigilante stepped away from the small kitchen and back into the living room, Lynsey felt a tinge of apprehension. Her work had taken her to some of the most dangerous places in the UK, but she had never been in a room with someone of his ilk.

Sam Pope had killed a lot of people.

Despite the divisive reaction to him in the press, the man was still a dangerous criminal and as he rested on the edge of the chair opposite her and fixed her with a warm smile, Lynsey wondered just how her life had brought her to this moment.

'Are you okay?' Sam asked, surprising Lynsey with the softness of his voice. She grasped the tea from the coffee table and held it in her hands.

'I thought you were dead?' She finally stammered, drawing a wry smile from Sam.

'I was.' Sam chuckled. 'But for some reason, the quiet life just doesn't seem to be something I'm built for.'

Lynsey awkwardly smiled and took a sip of her tea. The warm beverage was welcome, and she looked around the flat. It was small, with minimal furnishings, nothing like her overly stylised apartment on the other side of the city. But from the things she had read, some of it expertly written by the late Helal Miah, soft furnishings were not exactly high on Sam's list of priorities.

After a few minutes, the silence between them became too obvious and Lynsey shrugged.

'So why am I here?'

'Because I need your help,' Sam replied instantly, setting his mug down on the table.

'You need my help?' Lynsey repeated in bewilderment. 'I'm not sure how I can possibly help you?'

'Sean is a friend of mine. He's a good kid who took the second chance I gave him and turned his life around. All he wants to do is the right thing by people who don't know what that's like.' Sam took a moment to compose himself, the weight of Sean's plight hitting him momentarily. 'Now I know who did this to him. They came to see Adrian the other night and left him with a split lip, and most likely worse had I not been there.'

'That's what happened to Adrian's face?' Lynsey looked distraught. 'He said he'd fallen over.'

'He would. But these guys, they're bad news. Have you ever heard the name Daniel Bowker?'

Lynsey sighed and nodded.

'Yes, I've met him. He threatened me outside a supermarket in town a few nights ago. Told me not to publish my article…'

Lynsey tailed off. Both of them knew that her publication of Head Space's nefarious business plans was the catalyst for Sean's horrendous beating. Sam could see her holding back the tears, the guilt bursting through like a broken dam.

'It's not your fault,' Sam said sternly.

'If I had backed down, then Sean would…'

'You are not responsible for the actions of bad people, Lynsey. They tried to set it up as a choice you had to make, but it was window dressing for them wielding their power. The things you have written, you can prove, right?' Lynsey nodded, dabbing at her eyes. 'Then I need you to use it to get me to Bowker.'

With a snap of her neck, Lynsey shot Sam a confused look.

'I can't do that.' Her words were laced with hesitation. 'I mean, I don't even know how to find the man.'

'I know this story will be a big deal to your career, Lynsey. But these people beat Sean in a dark alleyway and left him for dead. Even if he does pull through, the chances of him ever being the same are non-existent. If you need a better story, then you can have me.'

'What?' Lynsey sat up like she had just sat on a pin. Sam gritted his teeth and sighed.

'When I'm finished with Bowker and his crew, the police are going to be pretty sure that I'm back. So you can make it official. Take some pictures of me, lead them to this address. Whatever. But all I ask is that you get me to Bowker and give me a few days to put things right.'

Lynsey sat back in her chair, her mind racing. Two different sources of guilt were battling for supremacy, with her responsibility for Sean's attack being overwhelmed by her reluctance to throw her work away. But Sam was offering her the story of the year. It shouldn't have mattered to her, not in light of Sean's hospitalisation, and she hated the fact that it did. With a reluctant sigh, she turned to Sam.

'I don't know how to get to Bowker, but I'm pretty sure I know who does.'

'Who?' Sam stood, his muscular arms on his hips.

'Adam Bridges.' The name itself caused a bad taste in Lynsey's mouth. 'He's the face of Head Space. This all started when I confronted him.'

'Is he the head of the snake?'

'No, he's just a puppet for the CEO, Nicola Weaver. She's the one with the links to the drug companies. Bridges just takes whatever turds she feeds him and rolls them in glitter for the press.'

'And you can get me to him?'

'Probably. If he was the one who sent Bowker after me, then he'd probably agree to meet me if I told him I wanted to be paid off.' Lynsey shrugged. 'But there's little chance he will admit to anything.'

Sam's eyes narrowed.

'You leave that to me,' he said, stepping towards the small dining table and retrieving his jacket from the back of the chair. 'Can you schedule a meet this afternoon?'

'Today?' Lynsey raised her immaculate eyebrows. 'I can try.'

'Try.' Sam headed towards the door. 'Three o'clock. Somewhere discreet. Text Adrian the address.'

'Where are you going?'

'I have to go get something.' Sam offered her a smile. 'Look, this whole situation should never have happened.

You were just doing your job. But unfortunately, you rattled the wrong cage and now a good friend of mine is clinging to his life by a thread. It's not your fault, but you can help me put this right. So, make the call, send us the address, and I promise you, I will get you out of this situation by ending it.'

Lynsey bit her lip in confusion. Deep down, she knew she couldn't condone the actions that Sam was intending to carry out, but there was an imbalance of justice that was unfortunately swinging in Bowker, Bridges, and Weaver's favour. Someone had to tip the scales back so they rested evenly, and with the amount of money and power that Weaver possessed, Lynsey wasn't confident the authorities would do it.

Looking into Sam's eyes, she knew he could.

In the struggle of guilt erupting in her mind, a moment of clarity shone through.

If she wanted to bring them down, her way wasn't going to work.

Eventually, she nodded and pushed herself up from her chair, ready to follow Sam out of his apartment.

'Okay, I'll make the call.'

'Thank you.'

'But I don't want your story afterwards. I'm doing this for Sean and because people like Bowker and Weaver need to be stopped.'

Sam smiled, nodding his appreciation at Lynsey's breakthrough. As she stepped past him and headed to his stairwell, Sam checked the back of his jeans, feeling the cold metal of the handgun that was tucked tightly against his spine.

He had a few hours to make a quick collection, and then it was time to get to work.

Time to set things right.

It was a morning like any other and as Bowker stepped out of his shower and wrapped a towel around his portly stomach, he stared at himself in the mirror. The steam caused his reflection to blur, but he wondered how it was possible for him to care so little about what he had done.

They had beaten a young man close to death, all because he was a useful way to intimidate a young woman.

He shrugged.

It was just business.

The world needed people like him. Someone who was willing to do the dirty work to ensure the rich stayed rich. They were willing to pay obscene amounts of money and he was more than happy to cash the cheques to give himself and his crew a comfortable life.

As for the young man who he'd left to his crew, he just wasn't important in the grand scheme of things.

Expendable.

With such little regard for human life, Bowker had often wondered how his mental state would be classified. He was certain he was a sociopath, but his violent past and tendencies would probably give the top psychiatrists a hard day's work. As far as he was concerned, he was saner than most.

He didn't chase materialistic trophies to try to gain some sense of self appreciation.

Nor did he splatter himself across social media, pushing a fake life to the world in the quest for popularity.

Bowker saw the world for what it was, played the shit hand he was dealt, and used it to become a successful businessman. But unlike those who worked in boardrooms and dealt in money or paperwork, he dealt in blood.

Unfortunately, for people like Lynsey Beckett's

boyfriend, the world was a shit place, and men like Bowker had just cottoned on to that fact quicker than most.

Bowker moved to his bedroom and opened the wardrobe, his eyes gazing across the simple and fairly priced clothing that he had amassed over the years. Despite the small fortune he had made off the desperation of the rich and powerful, his simple approach to life meant his clothes reflected his mindset. He quickly changed into jeans and a dark T-shirt, before moving to his kitchen to make a coffee. As his Nespresso machine rumbled into action, Bowker checked his phone.

Still no word from Hicks.

Bowker wasn't concerned for his friend, but the lack of contact was odd. Hicks had taken the janitor's attack personally and although he had argued about returning to the youth centre on the pretence of retrieving his gun, Bowker knew it was a matter of pride.

Hicks had been bested.

And the man's ego couldn't take it.

As far as causing any further mess was concerned, Bowker saw the janitor as a loose end. The older man, who had taken his beating like a champ, would stay quiet, especially once Hicks had gutted his janitor.

But there was no word yet.

As the milk came to a frothy conclusion, Bowker lifted the mug and took a sip.

He wasn't concerned, but something didn't feel right.

There was something about the janitor that he couldn't quite place. The man was certainly familiar, and Bowker was certain he'd seen his face somewhere before. Maybe not with the beard and long hair, but those eyes were recognisable.

They were also focused, which meant Hicks's task may be a little trickier than they predicted, especially if Hicks lost his temper and gave up the element of surprise.

Taking another sip of coffee, Bowker decided to give Hicks until the afternoon to touch base, otherwise he would assume the worst and take the necessary steps.

Something told him he may just have to.

CHAPTER NINETEEN

Adam Bridges woke with a thumping headache.

Whether it was the excessive booze from the night before, or the sickening feeling of guilt that encased his brain, he stumbled from his bed to the medicine cabinet that was nailed to his bathroom wall. As he threw two tablets back and dipped his head to the tap, he hoped the gushing water would wash away the horrendous feeling in the pit of his stomach.

After receiving the confirmation from Bowker and subsequently emptying his guts, Bridges had drunk his way through the rest of the evening's festivities. While London's richest gushed at his spiel and fawned over the excellent work that Nicola Weaver and Head Space were doing, Bridges had to keep his mind right. With no information of how or what Bowker had done, Bridges tried to turn that into a positive. The less he knew, the less he had to feel guilty for.

But Bowker wasn't a tactful man, not in the same way Bridges was.

Bowker was a man of action and having failed to

intimidate Lynsey Beckett away from her story, it was only logical to assume the next step was physical.

But the lack of any Twitter news pertaining to her told Bridges that she was safe, which meant someone else had been brought into the situation.

Someone unconnected.

The thought made Bridges woozy, and he dipped down to the tap once more, lapping at the water like a thirsty hound. He scooped up some of the water with his hand and splashed it across his face before staring at himself in the mirror.

The reflection disgusted him.

The usual handsome, well-groomed face was replaced with bloodshot eyes, messy hair, and a five o'clock shadow that ruined his chiselled jaw. Despite his cracking mindset, Bridges had spent the evening doing his best to distract himself, knocking back the drinks in an effort to hide his disgust at what he and Weaver had put into action.

It hadn't worked.

As the night went on, he had seduced one of the young waiters into joining him in a storage room, trying to let his thoughts dissipate as the young man fellated him.

It didn't work and after an awkward exchange, Bridges left the young man to deal with his shame as he dealt with his own. Now, as he tried to ignite his usual morning routine, Bridges couldn't think of anything else.

He needed something to bring it all to an end.

It had gone too far now for him to just walk away. The things he knew and had initiated meant his hands were just as dirty as Weavers. For a time, the vast sums of money were enough to wipe them clean, but now all he could see when he looked at his pristine hands was the blood of so many people.

Young teenagers hooked on drugs.

Innocent people who had been set upon by Bowker and his dogs.

Somewhere within his bedroom, he heard the irritating chime of his work phone and, as he rummaged through his clothes, he managed to retrieve it from his blazer.

It was the office.

One thing about being the face of a company was that whenever you were needed, you had to be available.

With a sigh, he answered.

'What?'

'*Well, good morning to you, too,*' Janice barked. '*Too many drinks last night?*'

'Sorry, Janice.' Bridges turned on the charm as easy as the tap in his bathroom. 'Just a few too many.'

'*I heard it was a blast. The biggest fundraiser ever. Go you.*'

'Thanks.' Bridges shook his head in disgust. If only she knew. 'What can I do for you, Janice? It's a Saturday.'

'*I know, but as you always say, we are never off the clock. I have a call waiting for you. It's a journalist…*'

'Tell them to fuck off.' Bridges snapped.

'*Oh… I think you might want to take this call.*'

'Look, I'm hungover, and the last thing I want to do today is sing and dance for the press. Can't you schedule it for Monday?'

'*It's Lynsey Beckett.*'

Bridges stopped pacing his bedroom and stood upright. The mere mention of her name brought the guilt flooding back, but through the darkness of his self-loathing, it also offered a glimmer of light.

'Put her through.' Bridges needlessly ran a hand through his hair, as if readying himself for an interview. After a few moments, the call connected. The unmistakable Northern Irish accent crackled through his phone.

'*Hello?*'

'Miss Beckett,' Bridges said with his usual bravado. 'To what do I owe this displeasure?'

'We need to meet.' Her voice was stern, unmoving. Bridges felt slightly uneasy.

'I don't have anything to say to you or your company. Not after the smear campaign you ran…'

'It's about the assault of my boyfriend, Sean Wiseman. An assault you ordered through Daniel Bowker.' Silence, as Bridges stood, mouth agape. *'How am I doing here?'*

'How… what…' Bridges stammered.

'This has gone too far, and it needs to end.'

'I agree.' Bridges finally wrestled back some composure. 'I will need any and all evidence you think you have on us.'

'Deal.' There was a steely determination in Lynsey's voice that Bridges found discerning.

'When and where?'

Lynsey gave him the location and he let out a relieved sigh. It was secluded, away from the public eye. It meant not only would it escape the clutches of the press but also that she had relented. Despite the horrific nature of Bowker's actions, the message had finally got through.

'Meet me there at three.'

Before Bridges could respond, Lynsey killed the call. He cursed her under his breath and then looked up at the mirror before him. The same bedraggled man looked feebly back, but this time, there was a sense of relief in his eyes.

Soon, this would be over.

And once it was, Bridges would begin the tricky process of trying to sever all ties with the horrendous journey he'd ventured down.

Not having a car was never a problem for Sam, especially as he'd tried to keep his name off as many systems as possible. Plus, living in London gave him ample options for transportation, as well as saving on the eye watering costs of running one within the country's capital.

But with time very much of the essence, he found himself becoming frustrated as he hopped on the train at Neasden and rode the Jubilee Line towards North Greenwich Station. It was a long, dull journey, made all the more tedious by being almost exclusively within the confines of a tunnel, but Sam's patience was tested more by the task at hand.

Before he'd embarked on his final fight in America, he and Etheridge had collected the final remnants of Sam's arsenal, pulling together the remaining weapons that the Met hadn't seized from the stashes they didn't know about. Together, the two men had boxed them up and shipped them away, a gesture that Sam's fight was over and that he had put that part of his life behind him.

If he returned from America, it would be to a life of peace.

But there was a glint in Etheridge's eye that day, especially when Sam asked for confirmation that every weapon had been packed.

Now, as he exited the train and began his ascent through the glass structure of North Greenwich Station, he hoped that Etheridge's nonchalance equalled a genuine betrayal of Sam's wishes.

He was about to go to war with a group of violent mercenaries and all he had was the Glock 17 he'd taken from the recently deceased.

As Sam exited through the humongous opening to the station, he saw the O2 Arena in the distance, the sharp, yellow masts jutting into the sky like giant candles on a birthday cake. Tourists were flocking from the station behind him, and Sam made his way onto the main road, looking out to cable cars that offered transport across the Thames.

Having only lived in North Greenwich for a week while lying low with Etheridge, Sam wasn't familiar with the area, but by sticking to the main road he soon came across a small retail estate he recognised.

A large Odeon Cinema loomed over the restaurants and Sam followed the road to a metal flyover walkway that transported him across the large dual carriageway that sliced through the residential area.

Greenwich itself was a wealthy part of London, the small town offering a selection of quirky shops, a marketplace, and some popular drinking destinations surrounding the famous *Cutty Sark*. North Greenwich, however, was an overly crammed plethora of residential streets, with rows upon rows of thin, cramped houses available at eye-watering prices.

Etheridge had bought one during his excessive days, where money and property equalled fulfilment, but he had abandoned it once he had joined Sam's cause. The derelict flat was on the ground floor of an old house on Fingal Street, and as Sam approached the door, he looked around to ensure he wasn't being watched. Satisfied that the coast was clear, Sam drove his elbow into the small pane of glass above the door handle, reached in, and unlatched the door.

A year and a half's worth of stale air greeted Sam with a grim slap to the face, and he quickly lifted his T-shirt to cover his nose. The neglect had covered the entire flat in a thick layer of dust and the various piles of vermin droppings didn't help the aroma. As Sam ventured through the rooms, his hand instinctively reached to the base of his spine, his fingers clasping the handle of the gun.

Just in case.

As Sam cleared the flat in seconds, he slowly began checking the few storage cupboards, hoping Etheridge had lied to him.

Nothing.

Sam sighed.

Although he'd been committed to his new life, the current change in circumstances meant he needed to be right.

He needed a weapon and with Etheridge gone and the police swarming the second he rose from the dead; Sam was holding on to a hunch for dear life.

His phone buzzed in his pocket, and he lifted it.

Pearce.

'Hello.'

'Sam. Are you okay?'

'Just dandy,' Sam said dryly, carefully stepping over the rotten carcass of a long-deceased mouse.

'Lynsey called. The meet is set. Three at the Old Mill car park in Balham. Do you know where it is?'

'I'll find it,' Sam said, lodging the address in his mind. 'One last thing, you don't remember the name of the warehouse that Amara raided, do you? The one run by Harry Chapman.'

Pearce blew air out from his lips, challenging his brain to recall a memory.

'Wow. Not off the top of my head. Why?'

'Do you think you could find out?'

'I can look it up. Am pretty sure there will be enough about it online. Why?'

'I have a plan. But I'm going to need your help. This one final run and then it's over.'

Before Pearce could object, Sam explained the idea to him. Sam knew he was asking a lot. Despite being retired, Pearce had spent his entire adult life as a well-respected man of the law. By pushing him further across the line into pure criminality, Sam knew how conflicted Pearce was.

But this wasn't for Sam.

This was for Sean.

And despite every fibre of his being telling him to turn away, Pearce agreed and told Sam to call him when he was ready. As Sam hung up the phone, he turned to leave, stepping carefully over another pile of waste. As his foot hit the floor, he stopped and looked down.

He lifted his boot and stomped, confirming that the floor beneath the spoilt rug was hollow. Sam dropped to his knees, flipped the rug over, and, with the handle of the gun, bashed through the floorboards with haste. As the wood crumbled beneath his blows, he sat back on his haunches and shook his head.

'You bastard,' Sam uttered to himself, chuckling at Etheridge's insolence.

Although wrapped in several sheets to protect it, Sam immediately recognised the unmistakable shape of the assault rifle. He reached into the crawl space and lifted the weapon out, carefully unwrapping the covering to reveal a pristine SA80 Assault Rifle.

Sam held the weapon like a long-lost lover, cradling it in his hands with care and attention.

With his new life stripped away, Sam could feel the elite level marksman bubbling beneath him and, as he glided his hand up the body of the gun, he felt a new sense of clarity and purpose.

His plan was still a dangerous one, but thanks to Etheridge being a pain in the arse, he had a much better chance of seeing it through.

Sam ducked his head beneath the boards to scope the rest of the clearing and he noticed the wooden shoe box and removed it. He placed it on the floor and opened it, revealing several magazines of bullets, enough to arm Sam for a full-on assault.

Sam pocketed them and just as he was about to leave, he noticed the single sheet of paper, with Etheridge's handwriting scrawled across it. Before he left, Sam read the note and smiled, hating the fact that Etheridge was right.

Wherever the man was, Sam knew he owed him more than he could ever repay.

With the time ticking before someone noticed the shattered glass on the door, Sam dumped the assault rifle into a sports bag and headed for the exit, leaving the note on the ground to eventually perish in time.

The note read:

We are who we are, Sam. Keep fighting. PE.

Sam agreed with what was written on it and was ready to prove Etheridge right. Closing the door behind him and basking in the freshness of the brisk, wet Saturday afternoon, Sam headed to the nearest car rental outlet, ready to go to war.

CHAPTER TWENTY

The roof of the Old Mill parking garage offered a stunning view of Balham and further afield into the city of London. Usually a tremendous visual of large, shiny buildings and a cacophony of noise, the grim spring shower engulfed the city in a damp gloom.

As Lynsey stood, arms rested on the stone barrier of the parking lot, she felt the view was apt.

Somehow, just doing her job and beginning to fall for a young man had sent her life down a path she had never intended.

Most Saturdays were spent out with her friends, other thirty-year-old women who were too busy enjoying the freedom of London and decent salaries to want to be tied down to the responsibilities and repetition of relationships and parenthood. Afternoons usually consisted of trips to the Westfield Shopping Centre near her work, or bottomless brunches leading to a boozy afternoon that bled into a drunken evening out.

Random guys would come and go, and despite her semi-celebrity status as a TV reporter, Lynsey was never in any danger of her private life impacting her professional.

Until now.

Sean was a good guy; someone she had built an instant connection with and now he clung desperately to his life all because he had the unfortunate reality of being the closest person to her at that point in time.

Ever since she sniffed the corruption behind Head Space, it had become her life's work to expose them, knowing that pulling together a damning and comprehensive report would make her career. As she looked around the depressing, empty car park where she stood, she realised now how naïve she'd been.

The powerful don't stay powerful by playing nice.

That much had become obvious and with her regret sitting in her stomach like an undigested meal, she realised her life's work would be coming to an end.

Sam was right.

She had rattled the wrong cage and as the squeal of tyres echoed through the car park; she knew that there would always be another story to drag her to the top.

But only this one chance to set things right.

As she waited patiently for the car to make its way to the top of the structure, she wrapped her arms around her body, pulling her waterproof jacket tighter to her body. Her hair had been pasted to her head, darkened by the downpour, but she needed this to go down in private.

On a rainy afternoon in London, very few people would be looking to park in its downpour.

Eventually, the black Mercedes emerged from the concrete ramp, carefully navigating the tight turn and then rumbled casually towards her. As it pulled to a stop, Lynsey felt her body tense.

The driver's door opened, and a well-built, well-dressed man emerged, before he released an umbrella which exploded open like a firework. The back door flew open, and Adam Bridges stepped out, gratefully buttoning his blazer before taking the umbrella and striding towards Lynsey, a look of smug victory plastered across his handsome face.

'A little dramatic, don't you think?' Bridges said, sweeping his hand out in a grand gesture. 'We could have met in a Starbucks.'

'I don't want people to see us,' Lynsey responded.

'Well, I could have done with a coffee.' Bridges flashed his cheesy grin. 'First things first. Richard, search her.'

'What?' Lynsey protested as the broad man stepped towards her. Despite her attempts, he soon frisked her down and then stepped away, seemingly satisfied.

'I can't have you recording us now, can I?' Bridges stood confidently. 'So, to what do I owe this pleasure?'

'I need this to end,' Lynsey said defiantly.

'This?' Bridges shrugged. 'What do you mean?'

'You know what I mean, you smug prick. You're going to tell me that you didn't send Daniel Bowker to intimidate me because I found out the truth about your company? That you didn't send Bowker to nearly kill my boyfriend?'

Lynsey could feel her fist clenching in rage. She needed to keep her cool.

Stick to the plan.

But Bridges' smug, unwavering grin was severely testing her patience.

'Before I answer that, what's the trade-off here?'

'I have all my files on Head Space and the links to Lonoxidil distribution. Everything on you and Nicola Weaver. All in the back seat.' Lynsey motioned to her car. 'You can have them. I'll drop the story but you leave me and the people I care about alone and you give me Bowker so he can be arrested for what he did.'

Bridges turned to his muscle, Richard, and nodded towards the car. Like a good lap dog, Richard strode towards the vehicle, pushing past a defiant Lynsey who remonstrated violently.

'Actually, we will just take the files and leave you alone.' Bridges smirked. 'But as for Bowker, we kind of need to have him on our payroll to deal with problems from time to time.'

'Just tell me where he is, and I'll call the police.' Lynsey begged. 'Then you'll never hear from me again.'

'Listen, Lynsey. None of this is personal, it was all business. But there isn't a chance in hell I will tell you anything.'

As Bridges finished his arrogant retort, Richard reached for the door handle to the back of Lynsey's new model Clio. As his fingertips brushed the cold metal handle, the door shot open, the curved edge cracking him between the eyes and crushing his nose instantly. The sickening thud drew a panicked gasp from Bridges, and Richard stumbled back, falling on his backside and scrambling on the wet concrete to recollect himself.

Sam stepped out of the back seat, the rain clattering against his leather jacket, and he slammed the door shut behind him. The colour drained from Bridges's face, faster than the dissipation of his control of the situation. Whoever this man was, he looked menacing, and Bridges barked at Richard to do something.

Sam shook his head in disappointment as the man got to his feet and threw his fists up, goading Sam to engage. With a shrug, Sam stepped forward, ducking the first wild swing from the amateur before blocking the next with a firm forearm. As the impact shook the man's arm, Sam drove his other fist into the man's diaphragm, shaking the air from his lungs, before driving him headfirst into the side of Lynsey's car.

The man dropped to the floor, unconscious and Lynsey scowled at the fresh dent to her side panel. Sam turned his head and looked Bridges dead in the eyes and the man crumbled, holding up his hand in surrender as Sam marched towards him.

'Look, look...' Bridges stammered. 'We can work this out.'

Sam drove a thumping right hand into Bridge's stomach, sending the man hunching forward onto his knees and his umbrella scattering across the floor. Lynsey shrieked in horror, but Sam reached down and lifted the umbrella before gently handing it to her.

'Here you go.' He offered a smile.

'Jesus, Sam.'

Bridges drew in quick breaths, trying to replace the air that Sam had knocked clean from his body. He began to clamber to his feet, holding out both hands in protection as the rain engulfed him.

'Sam. Sam.' Bridges began, but Sam knocked his hands away and grabbed him by the scruff of his jacket.

'Maybe you'll talk to me, huh?' Sam said gruffly. 'My name is Sam Pope. Ring any bells?'

Bridges's eyes widened in shock. The man who'd terrorised the London underworld a few years ago had long since been declared dead. Now, risen from the ashes, Bridges looked into the eyes of a trained killer, and he felt his body weaken with fear.

'Look, we don't need to do this...'

'Unfortunately for you, we do.' Sam drove another hard punch into Bridges' kidneys, knocking the man unsteady. As Bridges wobbled, Sam tightened his grip. 'Sean Wiseman was brutally attacked last night by Daniel Bowker and his crew. Unfortunately for you, Sean Wiseman isn't just Lynsey's boyfriend, he happens to be a good friend of mine. Now, I'm going to give you one chance to answer the next question, or I am going to knock one of your lungs loose. Did you give Bowker the order to go after Sean?'

Bridges was crying, the realisation of his situation becoming too much for him to control.

'Not specifically.'

Sam drove his knee into Bridges' stomach and let him drop to the floor. Either through the blow itself or the sickening fear, Bridges vomited onto the concrete. Lynsey tried her hardest to find any sympathy for the man, but she failed. Sam squatted down next to Bridges, who was heaving.

'Tell me where I can find Bowker.'

Bridges didn't answer, and Sam slapped him on the back of the head.

'I don't know.'

Sam hauled Bridges up by the collar of his jacket and then roughly marched him towards the thick, concrete barrier that encircled the parking lot. Lynsey called out in protest and Bridges shrieked in terror as Sam hoisted him over the barrier, holding the lapels of the man's jacket.

Sam's grip was the only thing stopping gravity from hauling Bridges down the twenty-feet drop to his certain death. With his eyes wide in fear, Bridges looked at Sam for mercy.

'Where can I find Bowker?'

'I don't know. I swear.' Sam loosened his grip slightly, causing Bridges to jolt back. 'Fuck. All I know is he operates out of Mile End.'

'How do you reach him?'

'I have a number. I have a number,' Bridges wailed, looking back over his shoulder at the terrifying plummet beneath him. 'Just pull me back up, for the love of god.'

With an angry grunt, Sam hauled Bridges back over the barrier and tossed him recklessly onto the ground.

Bridges took a moment to appreciate his mortality and collect his thoughts as Sam paced, shaking his head.

'Subtle,' Lynsey said dryly. Sam shot her a look and shrugged, as Bridges pushed himself to his knees, reaching for the mobile phone in his pocket. With his hand shaking, Bridges thumbed through the contacts and then held the phone up to Sam. With the rain splattering the screen, Sam snatched it from the snivelling man, pressed the green button, and lifted the phone to his ear.

It rang three times before it was picked up.

'What the hell do you want?' Sam felt his jaw tighten with fury at the sound of Bowker's voice. *'Well?'*

Sam took a deep breath.

'Do you remember me?'

Sam waited for a few moments. He could practically hear the cogs turning in Bowker's brain.

'Well fuck me. The janitor.' Bowker chuckled. *'What the fuck are you doing on this poofter's phone?'*

'I wanted to speak to you.' Sam maintained his calm. 'I wanted to introduce myself to you. My name is Sam Pope.'

Sam heard Bowker slap his thigh, as if he'd just figured out a particularly hard clue on a crossword.

'I fuckin' knew I recognised you. Well, this is an honour. The big bad Sam Pope, back from the dead to speak to little old me. Tell me, has Benny been to see you yet?'

'Is he your friend? The one I disarmed when you decided to lay your hands on mine?'

'That would be the one. Ugly little fucker, but boy was he excited to see you again.'

'He's dead.' Sam's words were cold, sending a shiver down Lynsey's spine.

'Bollocks.'

'I killed him this morning. He thought it would be a good idea to hold a knife to a kid's throat to get to me. Turned out it was a bad idea for him as I broke his neck.'

Sam stared out over the city. 'Turns out it's bad for you as well.'

Sam could hear the shift in Bowker's tone. The anger at Sam's dispatching of his friend had certainly raised the stakes.

'Listen here you piece of shit. I do what I do because I'm the best at it. Usually, it's all business. But for killing my friend, you just made this personal.'

'You have no idea.' Sam felt his brow furrow. 'Years ago, I made a promise to my son that I would stop killing people. It turned out I had to break that promise to help others. To fight back against people like you. I was given the chance to walk away. To put that part of my life to rest. But the mistake you made, Bowker, was that you and your boys attacked a good friend of mine. I can't change that, but I can't let that go. You've brought the old me back from the dead, and I'm going to kill each and every one of you.'

Sam's threat hung in the air like a thunderous cloud, the rain clattering the car park and drenching Sam as he stood stoically. Bowker was processing the threat. Sam wagered the man was rarely threatened and coming from a man as dangerous as himself, it must have landed like a haymaker. Eventually, Bowker spoke.

'Time and place.'

Sam turned his wrist over, glancing at his watch. It was half three.

'Eight o'clock. The old JB Meat Co. factory in Aldershot. When you get there, call your friend's phone.'

'You have made a grave mistake, my friend.' Bowker spoke with murderous intent.

'I'll be seeing you.'

Sam hung up the phone and tossed it onto the ground next to Bridges, who was still on his knees. Sam leant down and hauled him up by the back of his collar.

'Please, I did what you wanted.'

'This isn't over for you.' Sam spat, a mere inch or so from the man's face. 'The people responsible for what happened to my friend are going to pay. Tonight. But his blood is on your hands also, so you have two choices. One, I take you with me and put a bullet through the back of your head. Or two, you hand over all the evidence, every little detail of what you, Bowker, and whoever else is involved in this, to Lynsey. Then you go to the police, and you confess to it all.'

'There has to be something else I can do,' Bridges begged, but Sam removed the gun from the back of his jeans, causing the man to squirm in fear.

'We're all accountable for the things we do.' Sam turned to leave and then looked back at him. 'Whether it was your decision or not, you made the call. So do the right thing. You have until tomorrow evening.'

With that, Sam marched past both Bridges and Lynsey, heading to her car. Lynsey looked at Bridges, his frail state almost drawing sympathy from her. But the implications of his actions had nearly cost Sean his life, and she shook her head in disapproval before chasing after Sam.

'What now?' she asked, a surge of adrenaline pulsing through her body.

'I need to borrow your car,' Sam said as he threw open the driver's door. 'And you need to go home.'

'Home?' Lynsey repeated in annoyance. 'You're kidding me?'

Sam shook his head and dropped into the driver's seat of the car and held his hand out for the key.

'Lynsey, you have everything you need. Go home, stay safe, and be ready for Sean when he pulls through.'

Sam beckoned for the keys again and Lynsey sighed before handing them over to him. Sam roared the engine to life, before tapping the postcode Pearce had sent him into the in-built satnav. Lynsey stood, arms wrapped around her drenched body.

'What are you going to do?' she asked, knowing that she already knew the answer. Sam looked up at her, his eyes full of purpose.

'I'm going to war.'

Sam pulled the door shut, flung the car into reverse, and headed towards the exit of the car park, the tyres ripping through the puddles as he headed to battle.

CHAPTER TWENTY-ONE

ONE YEAR AGO...

Despite the autumnal months, the weather had held out, with a cheeky burst of sunshine peeking through the cloudy sky and bathing the cemetery in a glorious shine. There was something always morbidly peaceful about a graveyard, the feeling of finality for all those who were resting among its ground offering a quiet solace that couldn't be matched elsewhere.

Taking great pride in the appearance of the surrounding area, the groundsmen were always out in force, ensuring those who had come to grieve could do so in a well-maintained and peaceful environment.

Sam often walked through the cemetery, hands tucked into his pockets, breathing in the air, and offering a sorrowful nod to anyone he passed.

It had been two years since Sam had begun his war on crime, and nearly a year had passed since he'd lived under an assumed identity, hiding in plain sight from a police force that thought him dead.

Death was a recurring theme in his life, from those he'd lost to those he had put in the ground himself.

It was also the catalyst for Sam's journey.

The death of his son, Jamie, was something that Sam had to live with. The guilt of not stopping the drunk driver who ultimately claimed his son's life was a responsibility Sam would carry until his final breath.

As Sam meandered down the gravelly path, he looked out at the gravestones, all of them different shapes and sizes and in varying states of decay. Some were clearly tended to regularly while others had been left to fade away, a poignant reminder that eventually, even the memories will eventually end.

Sam rounded a corner and saw Pearce, immaculately dressed as always, standing, arms folded, looking at one of the gravestones. Sam's hair hung down over his ears, his thick beard covering his jaw. His jacket and hoody were neat enough, but he knew he could never match Pearce for style. Dressed in a navy overcoat, grey jumper, and dark chinos, Pearce looked like something out of a catalogue. It baffled Sam how a man who looked as good as Pearce did at half a century still hadn't settled down. The echoes of the man's divorce had long since faded, but Pearce had dedicated his life to helping others.

Sam could appreciate that.

It was something they had in common.

And it was the reason they'd ventured to the cemetery, and as Sam approached his friend, he felt the sickening tightness in his gut.

Two years.

It had been two long years since Theo Jackson had been killed, sacrificing himself to save Amy Devereaux and her husband during Sam's escalating war with Frank Jackson. It was what eventually bound Pearce and Sam together, despite them being on opposite sides of the law and their commitment to honouring Theo's memory had solidified their friendship for life.

Sam took a deep breath and then looked at the grave where his best friend rested.

'How you holding up?' Pearce asked, turning to his friend.

'You know, I thought it would be easier now. Now that I'm at the youth centre, carrying on Theo's work with you. But it's not.'

'It never gets easier.' Pearce agreed. *'But the fact these wounds stay open for so long only shows how much people mean to us. I didn't even know Theo, not personally. But his spirit is alive in the kids who flock to that centre for a better path. And that's something special.'*

'It sure is,' Sam said, grateful for Pearce's kind words. *'The world was a better place with Theo in it.'*

'Which is why we remember him.' Pearce reached out and patted Sam on the back. *'Remember, he gave his life because he believed in what you were doing. In fighting back for those who couldn't.'*

Sam shook his head.

'You know, for the last few years, I always blamed myself for Theo's death. I took Amy and her husband to him because Theo was the only person I could trust. If I hadn't done that, then he wouldn't have been killed.'

'Sam, you can't carry that burden…'

'Oh, I don't anymore. Because I remember Theo as the proud medic he was when we served together. As the guy who would willingly run into a crossfire if there was a chance he could save one of his brothers. If I'd left Amy and her husband behind, Theo would never have forgiven me. So now, everyday I wake up, I try to make sure I do everything I can to make this world a better place, the way Theo would. By being there for people and living a good life.'

Pearce smiled to himself. Ever since Sam had returned from America with a new identity and without the shackles of his war on crime clinging to him, he'd been desperately seeking redemption for the things he had done. Pearce never condoned the act of killing, but he understood the necessary steps Sam had to take to get the job done. Without Sam, many innocent people would have had their lives destroyed.

Now, under his new, peaceful life, Pearce had noticed a sense of calm in Sam. It was as if he'd finally forgiven himself for the horrors that had led him to pick up the gun in the first place.

The two of them stood in silence for over fifteen minutes, allowing the surprisingly warm afternoon to envelop them as they collected their own thoughts. Honouring a fallen friend raised several questions about one's purpose and mortality, and both Sam and Pearce allowed themselves a quiet moment to reflect.

Sam eventually let out a sigh and Pearce patted him on the shoulder.

'Come on, Sam. Let's go grab a coffee.'

Sam smiled and nodded, and the two of them headed towards the exit, hands stuffed in their pockets, and ready to do whatever they could to help maintain Theo's legacy.

To do the right thing.

To help people.

It was as good a blueprint for life as either of them had ever known.

Pearce was thankful for the back gate of the youth centre and the heavy downpour. It had allowed him to bring his car as close to the backdoor as possible and ensured there was nobody on the opposite street when he dragged the lifeless body of Bowker's henchman to the boot of his car and dumped him inside.

Every part of him felt dirty, but he understood Sam's request. Sam was going to war with Bowker and his men and intended to kill them. The last thing he wanted was for the police to suspect Pearce had been harbouring Sam since his return, so bringing the dead body to the intended war zone meant it could be stacked up with the others.

It made Pearce's skin crawl and went against everything he had stood for while being a proud member of the Metropolitan Police. But Sam wasn't coming back, and he was adamant that Pearce continue the incredible work he was doing with the kids and that one of them needed to keep Theo's legacy alive.

Knowing that Sam Pope had killed a man in the youth

centre would see it most likely shut down, and Pearce would lose his freedom for the role he'd played.

As he drove to Aldershot, he ensured he stayed strictly to the speed limits, which wasn't a huge problem considering the Saturday afternoon traffic as he navigated his way through the city centre until he slipped through Richmond and Twickenham and made his way to the M3. It had taken over an hour and a half to get through the capital city, and Pearce was grateful for the empty motorway as he cruised uneventfully until he reached Junction 4 and turned off. He coasted through Farnborough and continued his descent into Hampshire before turning off and towards Aldershot.

Ever since it had been raided, the JB Meat Co. factory had been left desolate, with the surrounding industrial estate rotting in a hidden corner of the town. The notorious gangster, Harry Chapman, had used it as a front for his business and once exposed, it drove the value of the entire park into the mud. Chapman had owned some of the surrounding buildings to ensure privacy, but the entire estate had been neglected for almost two years.

Pearce brought his car to a stop outside of the factory's main shutter and exited the car. He scoped the surrounding area, ensuring that he was unseen, and then went to work on the nearby reception door with a crowbar. It didn't take him long due to his regular exercise routine and with the door pulled from its frame, Pearce let himself in.

The factory was a colossal space and since the raid, had been left harrowingly empty. Each footstep echoed off the thick corrugated metal walls and numerous pieces of machinery had been removed. The redundant machines that had been left behind had been covered in cloths and dust and the smell of old rust hung heavy in the air.

Pearce looked upwards, clocking the metal walkway that hung from the roof, suspended by metal beams that had seen better days. A rickety, metal staircase in the far corner led up to it, but Pearce didn't fancy climbing nearly twenty-five feet into the air, suspended by old metal.

But Sam would.

Pearce returned to his vehicle and hauled the dead body into the factory. It was a taxing endeavour, with the man's limp, lifeless body getting heavier and heavier the further Pearce dragged it. Taking it as far across from the door as possible, Pearce propped it up against an old machine and let the man's head slump forward.

He had no pity for the man, having witnessed him pull a gun on one of the kids that Pearce looked out for.

As Pearce stepped back, he breathed a sigh of relief. It was done. His final act to help Sam and now he could return to a life that had been irreparably fractured by Bowker.

Sean was on death's door.

Sam had stepped back into his old life.

As Pearce made his way to his car, he pulled out his phone and quickly clicked out a message.

All done. Body is as far in as possible. Good luck, Sam. I'm sorry it came to this.

Pearce clicked send and realised that a tear had formed in the corner of his eye. The emotional overload of the past twenty-four hours hit him like a sledgehammer to the gut, and he stumbled to the driver's door of his car and dropped in. Before he could pop the key in the ignition, Pearce angrily slammed his fist against the steering wheel, allowing the devastation of the last twenty-four hours to explode forward. As the tears rolled down his cheeks and his forearm throbbed from the assault of the steering wheel, he thought about the devastating effect that a single act of violence could have on so many people.

Needing something to snap him back to reality, his phone buzzed.

It was Sam.

Thank you, Adrian. For everything.

Pearce took a deep breath and collected himself. He brought the engine to life and pulled away from the factory, not wanting to be there when the blood began to flow.

―――

Sam felt guilty as he raced down the M3.

He had coaxed Pearce into breaking the law by moving a dead body and had asked his exhausted friend to drive the same route he was now just to give him a chance against whatever Bowker was bringing to his doorstep.

But it was necessary.

As he guided the car off the motorway and down through Farnborough, Sam focused his thoughts on the task at hand. Bowker was undoubtedly rounding up whatever crew and arsenal he had in a bid to exact vengeance for his fallen friend. They were coming for Sam and without being able to fully scope out the location or do any recon on Bowker's crew, Sam knew he was at a disadvantage.

He hadn't pulled a trigger in nearly two years and was heading into an unknown building, hoping that his element of surprise would be enough.

If it wasn't, it wouldn't just be Sam's life that would be over.

Bowker would want to tie up all loose ends.

Lynsey Beckett.

Pearce.

Both of them knew too much, and with Bridges most likely to follow Sam's instructions and go to the police, Sam knew that whoever was really pulling the strings would have Bowker silence him, too.

They would get away with it, and in the unlikely event that Sean pulled through, he would be left with nobody.

It had to end.

Sam needed to get it right.

As he pulled up outside of the factory, he checked the time. It was five forty-five.

Carefully, Sam exited the car, the Glock 17 locked between his deadly fingers. There was a chance that Bowker had got here first but, considering Pearce had messaged an hour ago, it seemed unlikely. Moving quickly, Sam pulled the SA80 from the back seat and jogged to the open door Pearce had broken through.

Sam scanned the factory. The lack of machinery was both a blessing and curse for what he had intended. It meant Bowker and his crew were afforded little in the way of cover, but it also meant should any of them manage to get to some, Sam would be a sitting duck.

As he approached Hicks's dead body, Sam pulled out the dead man's phone. There were over forty missed calls from Bowker himself, and Sam turned up the volume of the phone before placing it beside Hicks.

The trap was set.

Moving swiftly, Sam navigated the metal stairs that lead up to the overhead walkway, apprehensive at their solidity. The entire structure shook as he climbed, but he reached the top with little incident.

Sam walked across the narrow metal platform, knowing full well any misstep would see him hurtle to his immediate death. Once he was as far into the corner as possible and engulfed by the shadow of the ceiling, Sam dropped down to one knee. With expert precision, he pulled the SA80 into his shoulder, locking it in place, his eye drawn to the scope on top.

In his crosshair was Hicks's corpse.

It would be like shooting fish in a barrel.

The only question was, would he be able to shoot them all before they located him? If he didn't, then Sam wasn't sure if he was built to survive what would happen next.

CHAPTER TWENTY-TWO

'I'll be seeing you.'

As soon as Sam Pope had ended the call, Bowker hurled his phone as hard as he could against the wall of the Stonewall Security Ltd office. The expensive handset shattered into a multitude of shards littering the ground below. With an uncontrollable rage, Bowker let out a pained roar of pure anger, before reaching down to the edge of his desk and in a display of sickening strength, he flipped the entire thing over; the contents spiralling into oblivion.

Outside in the main gym area, the rest of his crew watched on, their eyes wide with confusion at the fury shown by their leader.

But Bowker didn't care.

He didn't see his outburst as a sign of weakness, more as a sign of his increasingly dangerous temperament. As he stood, seething with rage drawing in deep, calming breaths, Bowker began to acknowledge the gravity of the situation.

His confidant, Hicks, had been killed.

A man he'd known for many years. Someone he

trusted and had built a true bond with through their business together. The man may have been a vile racist and somewhat of a loose cannon, but Bowker had loved Benny Hicks like he was a brother. Pride goeth before the fall, and in the case of Hicks, his need to settle the score with the janitor had cost him his life.

Because he wasn't dealing with a janitor.

It was Sam Pope.

Despite playing it off nonchalantly on the phone, Bowker knew that the situation had changed drastically. He had known a few nights earlier, when Pope had pointed a gun at him, that the man was dangerous. The way he carried himself, the way he disarmed Hicks.

The way he held a gun.

All of it told Bowker that he was a threat, but not even he could have placed his finger on the man being Sam Pope. The man the press had both vilified and hero worshipped for his assault on organised crime.

But more importantly, a man that they had pronounced dead almost two years ago.

But here he was, hiding in a crummy youth centre and looking like a homeless man. But underneath the façade lived the brutal vigilante who had taken down some of the UK's most notorious criminals.

And by killing Hicks, had proven that he hadn't missed a step.

What should have been a simple intimidation job had turned into an assault. Bowker had been okay with that. It wasn't beyond the realms of his crew to deliver a physical message by maiming a loved one of the intended target. But now things had escalated.

There was no way back from this.

They would have to kill Sam Pope. Judging from the threats he'd just received and the cold, matter-of-fact tone in the man's voice, Sam Pope was back and Bowker and his crew had made the mistake of giving him a reason to rise from the dead.

There was only one way this could end, and Bowker took a deep breath, turned on his heels, and headed out of the office into the main opening of the headquarters. The Stokes brothers were sitting on the apron of the boxing ring, looking on with interest. Bezdek stood to attention, hands behind his broad back, ready for the update. Mickey Turner and Lemar were leaning against the ring posts, as Paul Creek, now assuming the role of Bowker's right hand, stepped forward.

'Everything okay, guv?' Creek asked, his eyebrows raised.

'Fan-fucking-tastic,' Bowker said as he approached them. 'Right, gather round. Benny won't be joining us today due to a sudden case of death. Now, before we all go getting emotional about it, we need to finish the job we were paid to do. Beckett's boyfriend, you boys done him over real good, but it turns out, that janitor who mugged off Benny the other night isn't just a janitor. It's Sam fucking Pope.'

The name caused a slight gasp to echo around the makeshift gym, like a spectre had just floated through the air. Bowker scanned his crew, looking for any flickers of fear before continuing.

'Now, obviously, this changes things in quite a big way. First, he killed a good friend of mine and as they say, an eye for an eye only makes the whole world blind. Well, I want to blind this fucker tonight. Second, he ain't gonna stop until we stop him. He's given me a time and address, so I say we go get him and make this cunt pay for what he's done to Benny.' Bowker clasped his meaty hands together. 'Oh, and Benny's cut of the money to whoever brings me Sam Pope alive.'

'Yes, guv.' A few of the guys piped up before they anxiously began to gather their things. Although they usually used their fists or knives, Bowker had given them all a Glock 17, similar to the gun Pope had taken from Hicks. It was from an illegal stash of unlicensed firearms Bowker had acquired from a bent copper years ago. What worried him wasn't them using the weapons, but who their target was.

Pope had fascinated Bowker during his crusade against the London underworld, with always a slight worry that perhaps he would knock on his door and shut them down permanently. But compared to the institutions that Pope burnt to the ground, Bowker and his business were small fry.

They didn't fit the brief.

But this wasn't about what Bowker and his crew did for a living. This about what they had done to Sam's friend.

It was personal for Sam, and Bowker was sure the man didn't let those things slide.

As his crew began to disperse to retrieve their firearms and get ready for the long drive to Aldershot, Bowker ran over their chances in his head. They had the numbers advantage, which meant Sam had little room for failure.

But Sam's reputation preceded him, and they were headed to a place that Sam had chosen.

Meaning he would be waiting.

As some of his crew filtered out of the building to retrieve their weapons or to partake in an anxious cigarette, Bowker clenched his fists in anger.

His friend was dead.

And he was certain he would lose at least one more in trying to even the odds. What Bowker needed was a safety net, something that could guarantee Sam's demise. Then, as if a lightbulb flickered in his skull, a grim smile spread across his face and he motioned for Creek to step into his office, to let him know why he wouldn't be joining Bowker and the rest of the crew on the trip to Aldershot.

The drive to Aldershot was full of tension.

Ever since Bowker had brought his crew of mercenaries together, they had existed as a tool for greedy corporations to manipulate their world. Not one member of Bowker's crew had ever been challenged, as their targets were usually innocent people who were just unfortunately in the wrong place at the wrong time.

It had given each member a sense of invincibility. On the rare occasion that one of their targets had the stones to fight back, it wouldn't take much for them to dish out a sadistic beating. Each one of them had ventured down a dark path to end up in Bowker's employ, all of them having survived violence, whether it was sought out or not. They were some of the most dangerous men who walked the streets of London, and their seeming dismissal of the health and wellbeing of others kept their egos strong and their bank accounts full.

Usually, a constant stream of banter would be thrown back and forth between them, especially when they were all heading to a job together.

Individually, they were dangerous.

Together, they were unstoppable.

But this was different.

Split out across two cars, each travelled in near silence as they weaved their way through London towards the motorway towards Hampshire.

This wasn't a normal job.

It certainly wasn't a normal target.

Sam Pope was a legend. A spectre that had hung over their way of life until the confirmation of his death. While some of them were sceptical that the man who had killed Hicks was who he claimed to be, Bowker's insistence had made them uneasy.

He had looked the man in the eyes.

Bowker had known there was more to him than just a lucky shot.

Bowker rode in the passenger seat as Turner took the wheel, with the stoic Bezdek sat in the back. In the other black Range Rover that followed, Lemar was behind the wheel, accompanied by the sneering Scouse overload that was the Stokes brothers. As they were the most sceptical, Bowker demanded they travel in the other vehicle, his temper not willing to accommodate their disbelief or their accents. He could only imagine the frustration bubbling in Lemar as the two brothers continued to bicker.

'You think it's really him, guv?' Turner asked, navigating the exit from the motorway and following the signs towards Aldershot.

'I do,' Bowker said coldly. 'I looked him in the eyes, and I saw a man who had been to war.'

'Well, he's gonna go to another,' Turner said with a sneer. 'No one takes a shot at one of us and lives.'

Bowker appreciated the loyalty and then shot a glance at Bezdek in the rear-view mirror. The man was emotionless, staring out of the window and no doubt reliving the horrors of his own country before he came to the UK. Bezdek was a cold, calculating soldier and Bowker felt better for having him along for the ride.

One on one, Sam Pope would likely dismantle his entire crew.

But as a unit, the man's chances of survival were minimal.

As the sun set on a cloudy, wet afternoon, the headlights of the car illuminated the factory as they turned onto the abandoned industrial estate. Turner headed towards the giant structure, slowing the car to a stop some thirty yards from the front of the building. Behind them, Lemar did the same. Bowker glanced in the side mirror, watching as an agitated Lemar stepped from the driver's door, his hand clutching his pistol. He was soon followed by the Stokes brothers, the two of them holding their guns to attention and scoping out the area.

Bowker flung open his door and joined them, his dark eyes scanning the building. As the crew gathered around, Bowker retrieved his phone from his pocket and dialled Hicks's number.

The faint chime of a ringtone echoed from the factory, the noise travelling from somewhere within and out through the office door which flapped in the wind.

Sam was beckoning them into the factory.

'Right, boys. In you go,' Bowker commanded, his arms crossed over his broad chest. 'Try not to kill him just yet.'

'What if he doesn't give us a choice?' Lemar questioned, readjusting his grip on his weapon.

'Like I said. Try. But either way, that piece of shit is going to die tonight. Mickey, you cover the door. The rest of you, use your fucking heads. He isn't going to make this easy.'

A palpable apprehension was shared among the group, except Bezdek who turned on his heel and marched towards the door, his weapon still strapped to his hip. Following his lead, Jimmy and Connor Stokes scuttled after him, followed by Lemar, who was cautiously looking around the estate, both hands clasping his gun and ready to open fire.

'You not coming, boss?' Turner asked.

'I'll be in shortly.' Bowker grinned. 'I'm just waiting on a call.'

Turner shrugged and then fell in line, bringing up the rear as Bezdek was the first man to enter the building. As they all disappeared into the darkness, Turner hung back by the doorway, gun in hand and obliging the direct order.

Bowker took a deep breath.

Sam Pope deserved to die for what he had done to Hicks.

But he couldn't help feeling concerned that his men were walking to their death.

CHAPTER TWENTY-THREE

The sound of car doors echoing in the distance snapped Sam into focus. With one knee planted on the ground and his other raised closed to his chest, he locked himself into position, his solid frame unmovable. The assault rifle had fit snugly into the arch of his shoulder, and he drew the weapon up once more with expert technique.

The safety lights that clung to the metal walls and hung from the iron ceiling bathed the factory in a dull, orange-tinged glow, illuminating most of the factory floor but casting multiple pockets of shadow throughout. It was the only light the factory afforded, with the main electrical supply being cut off once Chapman's empire came crumbling down. Once the backup generators finally ran out of gas, the place would be plunged into permanent darkness.

It was rather fitting.

From up in his vantage point, he was afforded a clear view of the floor below, all the while being bathed in the dark corner.

Sam was certain Bowker would send the entire crew.

A man as calculating and as successful as him wouldn't leave things to chance and the very clear, unspoken agreement between the two of them was that only one of them would be walking away from this encounter.

Sam had been in his position for a little over two hours, allowing himself to bleed into the shadow and to become fully acquainted with the location. Not knowing how many men were on their way to kill him, he wanted to become familiar with the arena of death that he'd chosen.

Throughout his illustrious career as a deadly sniper, Sam had been in many stand-offs requiring him to stay prone for days on end in the hope of an opening. Sam had the ability to commit details to memory instantly. His experience also allowed him to logically and accurately estimate the distance between his gun and his target, as well as the time taken for a bullet to travel or a getaway to be made.

It's what had made him such an elite soldier and what made him a proficient killer.

Hicks's motionless body was still slumped against a covered machine on the far side of the factory, meaning he had at least two clear shots before anyone ducked for cover. To the left of the body, it would take roughly eight paces for someone to make it behind the next abandoned machine, meaning Sam would most likely have one attempt to cut them off at the pass before they were beyond his reach. To the right of Hicks, it was ten paces to an old forklift truck, which would provide enough cover but little room to manoeuvre.

Sam would need to be quick.

He would need to be clinical.

In the few minutes after the final car door had slammed shut, Sam had deduced that two cars had been taken, meaning that there were at least six people encroaching on his position. Right now, they would be discussing their plan as Sam had only left one way into the factory and they would no doubt be cautious about walking in blindly.

Just then, the jingle of Hicks's ringtone echoed through the factory.

Bowker was here, and now they would follow the phone's metallic chimes and walk straight into his crosshairs.

Sam pulled the rifle in tight, his hand locked on the grip and his finger delicately placed on the trigger. The magazine jutted out behind it, with thirty bullets ready to be sent hurtling towards his enemies.

His other hand steadied the gun, grasping underneath the body of the weapon that fed into the barrel.

A slight concern spread through Sam's brain like a forest fire. His SA80 rifle had been neglected beneath Etheridge's floorboards for two years. Without the time to properly check and tend to the gun, Sam was hoping it would still operate to a high level. Etheridge had been careful to wrap it up, but the cold could have reduced its efficiency, and Sam hoped that the weapon hadn't become too dry. Without oiling the breech extension or the chamber, there was a chance the gun could misfire, meaning his position would be given away and all he would have was the Glock 17 beside his standing foot.

There was a lot that could go wrong, and Sam knew that getting out of the factory alive was a long shot.

But there were things worth fighting for and things worth dying for.

And having lost so many people along the way, he was willing to fight until his last breath to make sure the people who had nearly killed his friend were made to pay.

Footsteps echoed through the factory, and Sam gripped his rifle tightly. Slow and calculated, Sam could envisage the men traipsing through the office and down the corridor to the main factory. Judging from the disorganised pattern, he predicted at least four men were entering the factory, meaning his chances of a quick and clean execution were unlikely.

Sure enough, emerging from beneath the walkway he was perched on, he made out the first figure as he stepped carefully into shot. The man was tall, with a strict buzz cut, and judging by the way he held his gun and moved with tactical efficiency, Sam could tell he was well trained. Two more figures emerged, their movements sloppy, and one of them broke the silence with an angry yell.

'Hicks. Jesus fucking Christ.'

The man's voice was laced with a Scouse accent, and without any regard for Sam's position, the man pelted across the factory to the motionless corpse.

Sam had the man's skull in the centre of his scope.

The concerned member of the group was quickly joined by another, similar looking man, who Sam assumed was related to him. The low lighting made it difficult to get a clear identification, especially as they were facing away. A fourth man, with darker skin, came into view, straying further afield than the other two and checking behind the forklift truck, his gun drawn.

Sam took a breath.

His body went completely still as he effectively merged with the rifle.

He pulled the trigger.

The bullet was already halfway on its trajectory before the clap of the rifle exploded in the factory. The sound caused three of the men to turn in surprise.

The fourth dropped to the floor dead, the bullet burrowing through the back of his skull and exploding through the forehead in a devastating explosion of bone and brain. With his blood splattering Hicks's corpse, Jimmy Stokes collapsed to the ground, his eyes still wide open.

Watching his brother die was not something Connor

had ever imagined happening, and the effect of it was terrifying. Every sane part of his brain told him to run.

To get to cover.

But he was seeing a mist redder than the one that had been blown from his brother's skull, Connor Stokes turned towards the metal balcony that ran the length of the far wall, and while screaming profanities at the top of his lungs, wildly unloaded his pistol towards the corner.

Sam realigned the rifle with his eyeline, the kickback causing a slight re-emergence of his previous shoulder injury, and he pulled the furious man into his scope. The man was shooting blind, engulfed by rage, but one of his errant bullets clattered the metal a few feet to Sam's left.

Sam tightened his grip and fired, gritting his teeth as his shoulder absorbed another stern impact. The shot was pinpoint, ripping through Connor Stokes's chest and sending him spiralling to the floor. Landing face down on the concrete, Connor gasped for air, the bullet having torn through his lung, and he could feel it filling with blood. As the pain stifled his movement, he looked to his already deceased brother and tried to reach out for him as he clung to his final breaths.

Sam scanned the factory. The erratic onslaught from the man he'd just killed had taken his full attention, and now the other two men were nowhere to be found. Carefully, he rose to his feet, shimmying carefully to the edge of the walkway before looking over the lone, metal railing that ran the length of it. Besides the two bodies that were now surrounded by pools of their respective blood, there was silence.

Nothing but the smell of burning from the gunpowder and Sam kept the rifle up.

Out of the corner of his eye, he saw the movement, but before he could react, he saw the flash of the gun barrel. The bullet whizzed past the rifle and grazed the top of his bicep, shaving off a few layers of skin and sending Sam spinning to a seated position.

Lemar ducked back down behind the forklift truck, hoping that the shot had been fatal.

Sam quickly flattened himself to the walkway, doing his best to remove any part of him from the shooter's eyeline. His arm was burning, but luckily for him, the bullet had grazed him rather than penetrated, and despite the searing pain, he would be fine. He tried to extend his arm to retrieve his rifle, but it failed, the wound doing sufficient damage to render it semi-useless.

'Fuck,' Sam uttered. The rifle was too big to wield in one hand. He glanced back to his original spot a few metres away, his eyes locking on the Glock 17. As he pushed himself and darted for the gun, Lemar took aim, unloading a few more bullets that ricocheted off the metal railing, missing Sam by a matter of inches. Sam picked up the handgun and breathed a small sigh of relief that the wound was on his left arm.

Without the scope, it would be harder, but Sam had the higher ground and as he peeked his head over the railing, he saw another flash of the handgun explode from the forklift truck, and Sam hit the deck as the bullet slammed into the iron wall behind him. Sam popped up, his arm extended, and he blasted two bullets that hit the truck, causing Lemar to duck for cover. The two men were in a stand-off, and Sam knew it was a bad idea to keep wasting bullets, especially with his rifle out of use.

After Lemar had blasted another two bullets in Sam's general direction, Sam popped his head up, his eyes scanning the forklift truck for anything. Just as Lemar was swinging his arm around to fire another couple of shots, Sam saw what he needed and ducked down.

Seconds later, as Lemar dropped down, Sam sprung to his feet, brought the handgun into his line of sight, and sent a pinpoint bullet at the rickety pillar that the back half of its tyre was rested on.

The bullet obliterated the pillar upon impact, and the sudden loss of support caused the back end of the forklift to dip by a few inches.

Enough to expose the top of Lemar's skull.

Enough for Sam to hit.

The timing between the two shots was a matter of seconds, and as an astonished Lemar realised what Sam had done, the bullet clapped him directly between the eyes, hollowing out the back of his skull and pushing his existence clean out of his body.

Sam spun back to a seated position and discharged the clip.

Empty.

He was a sitting duck and he needed to get moving, but just as he pushed himself to his feet, a footstep shook the entire walkway.

Bezdek may have been the first one into the room, but he made sure he was the one who hung further back. There was something about the whole situation that didn't sit comfortably with him.

They were walking into a gunfight with an apparently deadly man, but they were feeding off raw emotion and not sensible thought. Bezdek had long since removed nigh on all emotion from his life, existing to live a better life than the one he was afforded in Czechia, and he knew that a trap had been set. Unfortunately, the only way for him to succeed in bringing down Sam Pope was for him to know the location.

That meant he watched on as Jimmy and Connor

approached the body of Hicks, knowing that they were going to die.

Sure enough, two bullets were sent their way and both of them hit the ground.

Sam was on the above balcony and behind Bezdek, in the far corner, was a metal staircase that led up to him. All he needed to do now was move as silently as he could, allowing the darkness of the corner to envelop him as he made his slow ascent up the stairs.

Luckily, Lemar had managed to pin Sam Pope down and had him locked in a gunfight, meaning the distraction and the noise would mask his footsteps.

As the two men traded bullets back and forth, Bezdek made his way to the top of the stairwell, peering out from the shadow as Sam sent one bullet to the base of the fork-lift, followed by another that eliminated Lemar permanently. It was a shame.

Bezdek liked Lemar. He was one of the more palatable of the crew.

But Bezdek had no time for grief, and he watched with the vicious snarl of a pitfall, as Sam Pope checked his weapon.

He was out.

Deflated, Sam tossed the gun onto the metal and had clearly decided to make a break for it. But as he scarpered to his feet, Bezdek stepped out onto the walkway, his eyes locked on Sam who was twenty feet away.

Sam held his hands up, showing he was unarmed.

Bezdek took another step closer, admiring the fighter before him. Having made his way into Bowker's world through his proficiency and lethality on the underground boxing scene, it had been a long time since Bezdek had felt any semblance of competition.

Until now.

CHAPTER TWENTY-FOUR

Pearce had returned from Aldershot with his entire body begging him for sleep. He stopped at the café down the road from the youth centre upon his return, buying two double-shot espressos in a lame attempt to keep his body moving.

There were still things to take care of.

He needed to keep his mind occupied, to ensure he didn't think about the warzone Sam was creating.

How did it get to this?

It saddened him that he'd lost both Sean and Sam to the same despicable group and, although he tried his best to settle upon peace, there were some people who deserved more than the law could throw at them.

Pearce unlocked the youth centre and entered, making his way to the cleaner's cupboard and pulling out the strongest disinfectant he could find and a scouring pad. He'd already spent the majority of the afternoon mopping up the blood that had flowed from Hicks's knife wound in his leg, and luckily, Sam never removed the blade, meaning it wasn't too big a puddle.

But Pearce knew a crime scene like the back of his

hand, and he rolled up his sleeves as he lowered himself to his knees and began to ferociously scrub the floor clean, hoping to burn away any remaining evidence.

As he scrubbed, he felt the soreness in his body courtesy of the clubbing blows from Bowker, but he soldiered on through the pain. Eventually, his attention was drawn by the opening of the door. Quickly, he scrambled to his feet, tossing the pad and disinfectant into the corner before turning to the corridor where the footsteps were approaching.

Lynsey stepped in, offering a sheepish grin. Courtesy of the rain outside, her hair was stuck to her forehead, and she was shivering slightly.

'Lynsey. This is a nice surprise.'

'I hope you don't mind…' Her words trailed off.

'Not at all. Come in… over here.' Pearce rushed towards the stack of chairs in the corner and pulled a seat from the top of the pile. 'Tea?'

Lynsey smiled and nodded, taking her seat as Pearce scarpered to the kitchen. After a few moments of rattling around, the kettle was switched on and he got two mugs ready.

'Do you take sugar?'

'Just milk, thanks,' she responded, looking round at the hall. It wasn't anything special, but it was as neat as a pin, and the walls were covered in wonderful posters and inspirational quotations. It warmed her heart to see the place Sean had spoken so frequently about and as Pearce stepped back into view with a cup of tea in each hand, she shook her head.

'You didn't tell me Bowker did that to your face.'

Pearce shrugged.

'Must have slipped my mind.'

'I'm a big girl, Adrian. I know what's going on.' She

took a sip of her tea, welcoming the warmth that ran through her. 'So... Sam Pope is your friend?'

'Ah,' Pearce responded sheepishly, taking his own seat. 'I thought this might come up.'

Lynsey leant forward in excitement.

'What the fuck? The police confirmed his death a few years ago. Has he been here the whole time?' Pearce nodded. 'Did Sean know?'

'Yup. Sam's the reason Sean is here in the first place. I don't know how much Sean told you, but he used to run with a very bad crowd. Bad enough to end up garnering Sam's attention. But I guess Sam saw the good in him and he sent him to me.'

'As if this situation couldn't get any crazier.'

'I take it you helped him?'

'I introduced him to the guy who set Bowker after me. Sam can be... persuasive,' Lynsey said cautiously, drawing a chuckle from Pearce. 'Will he really do what I think he will?'

Pearce set his mug down on the floor and gingerly sat back up, grimacing at the aches his body groaned with.

'Sam is a man of principle and conviction. In his mind, the law let him down when his son died and the more he tried to put his faith in it, the further it dissolved. Eventually, he decided to fight back and, well, you know the rest.'

'He's going to kill Bowker?'

'He'll try,' Pearce said confidently. 'I spent a long time in the Met, and despite their best efforts, they are fighting a losing battle. Budget cuts, paperwork. There are only so many crimes they can focus on. Unfortunately, Sean's will most likely fall down the ladder if he survives. Besides, Bowker made a big mistake.'

'What was that?'

'He hurt someone Sam cared about. If there was

anything that was going to get Sam to step out of the shadows, it would be personal.'

Lynsey blew through her lips, exasperated.

'It's going to make one hell of a story.'

Before Pearce could respond, the door to the youth centre flew open once more, and as Pearce rose from his chair in annoyance, a man decked out in a black bomber jacket marched in. Instantly, Pearce knew it was one of Bowker's men, and the gun in his hand told Pearce this wasn't a social visit. The man pointed it at Pearce, who held his hands up in surrender.

'He's not here,' Pearce said firmly.

'I know.' Creek snapped. 'I'm here for you and… well… who do we have here?'

Lynsey sat, frozen in fear.

'You're here for me. Let her go and we can handle this between us.'

'Bollocks to that, mate.' Creek chuckled. 'Two for the price of one. Now both of you, car's out front. Let's fucking move.'

Pearce turned to Lynsey and nodded to her assuredly. There was no point trying anything stupid. The man was armed and judging from Pearce's first-hand experience with Bowker's crew, they weren't mucking around. Lynsey eventually rose from her seat and Pearce waited for her, the two of them walking side by side, their arms raised. Creek stepped to the side to let them past, then fell in line behind, prodding them both in the back with his gun. The rain clattered all three of them as Creek ushered them through the gate to the black BMW that he'd parked up onto the kerb.

'Grandad. You drive.' Creek pulled Lynsey towards him, locking his arm around her neck and pressing the gun to her temple. 'Nothing stupid, yeah?'

Lynsey shrieked in fear.

'Everything's going to be okay, Lynsey,' Pearce said, as he slid into the driver's seat. His mind raced, wondering if there was anything he could do to fight back. Improvise.

But the man dropped into the backseat with Lynsey, the gun still pressed roughly against her temple and as they squeaked against the now wet leather, Pearce knew any stupid move would result in her death.

The man had come for him.

Meaning she was expendable.

'Drive,' the man commanded. 'I'll direct you. And don't fuck about. I just had this car cleaned.'

Pearce shot a glance in the rear-view mirror, sickened by the smirk on the man's face. He looked to Lynsey, who tried her hardest to hold back the tears.

With no other option, Pearce turned the key in the ignition and pulled the car out into the road and drove into the downpour.

―――

Bowker sat in the comfort of the leather passenger seat of the Range Rover, the door open as he held the cigarette between his fingers. It wasn't often he smoked, but knowing that he had essentially sent his men into a metal prison with Sam Pope had been too much of a lure to the nicotine.

With each puff, he felt a sense of calm rush through his body. Allowing the smoke to simply drift from the side of his mouth, Bowker just wanted the day to be over.

He hadn't had time to grieve for Hicks.

There was too much at stake, but the death of his friend had caused him to react instead of plot. He didn't feel one step ahead and as soon as the first gunshot echoed through the abandoned factory, he began to regret his decision.

This wasn't the way to get to Pope.

The man was too dangerous.

Too well drilled.

But before he had departed, he'd sent Creek on an errand that could potentially turn the tide in his favour. If the only thing that could lure Sam Pope out of his hiding place was the assault of a close friend, then doing it again could lure Pope into Bowker's domain.

It would put Bowker in the only place he felt comfortable. In full control.

As he flicked the end of his cigarette into the ether, his phone buzzed. He looked down at the screen and he felt a twinge of excitement.

It was Creek.

Bowker raised the phone to his ear.

'What's the update?' Bowker snapped impatiently. Through the phone, he could hear the whirring of a car engine moving at speed.

'*Heading back to base now,*' Creek said confidently. '*Our boy is driving the car and guess who else I picked up? I think he said her name was Lynsey?*'

'Lynsey Beckett?' Bowker sat up, a smile creeping across his face.

'*Yes, sir. I'll get them nice and comfortable.*'

'I'm on my way. If the boys can't handle Pope now, I'll have Mickey tell him what we have.' Bowker hung up the phone and tossed it into the side compartment of the door. He stepped out of the car, lit another victorious cigarette and ignored the repetitive gun fire echoing within the factory. 'Oi, Mickey.'

Turner was standing at the door, and he looked back. Bowker summoned him over. The diminutive man shuffled over nervously.

'Don't sound good in there, guv.'

'I'm heading back,' Bowker stated, drawing a confused

look. 'Stay out here. If Pope comes out alive, tell him we have Lynsey and his friend. I'll have Creek send you a picture to prove it.'

'You're leaving?' Turner remonstrated.

'You're damn fucking right I am.' Bowker stepped forward, looming over his employee. 'I want him brought back to me. I want to face him on *my* turf, and I want him to feel every remnant of his life seep from his body. Is that clear?'

'Yes, guv.' Turner nodded.

The gunfire stopped.

Both men looked towards the building and Bowker slapped Turner on the back, pushing him a few steps forward.

'Go and get him and bring him back to base.' Bowker dipped into the driver's seat of the Range Rover. 'I need to go and greet our guests.'

Slamming the door shut, Bowker spun the car round in reverse and then shot towards the exit of the industrial estate. As the lights of the car disappeared around the corner, Turner shook his head and spat on the floor.

He had never witnessed cowardice in Bowker before, and although there seemed to be a plan in motion, Turner wasn't thrilled to see his boss leave before the job was done.

But the plan had changed.

Pope was needed alive.

Quickly, Turner scurried back towards the broken door to the factory.

There had been no further gunshots, yet he walked carefully, his hands clasped around his gun, and he rounded every corner like a trained soldier. As he cleared every possible hiding space, he ventured further into the factory, taking measured steps as he approached the door to the main factory.

Already, he could see the motionless bodies of the

Stokes brothers. He felt his knuckles tighten around the gun and gritted his teeth at the deaths of his poker buddies. Whatever they had walked into, they had been eliminated in cold blood.

Turner stopped in his tracks, trying his best to listen out for something.

Anything.

A large clang of metal rang out through the factory, its sound elevated from the echo between the metal panels that comprised its walls.

He heard footsteps up high, and then nothing.

Turner edged forward, his gun held up, ready to aim and if necessary, shoot.

Then, a mere few feet from the door, he heard the sickening splat of a body hitting the concrete and he stepped into the factory to bring Sam out alive.

CHAPTER TWENTY-FIVE

With no bullets in his gun, Sam looked up at the daunting prospect before him. Bezdek stood over six feet tall and was a solid wall of lean muscle. His buzz cut was neat and tidy, and he held his gun with the precision of a man who had no hesitation in using it.

Sam pushed himself to his feet, blood dripping from his right arm, and he gingerly held his hands up in surrender.

This was it.

To Sam's surprise, Bezdek tossed the gun over the side of the railing, allowing it to clatter loudly on the concrete a few seconds later. Sam raised his eyebrows in confusion, before he realised what awaited him. Bezdek slowly unzipped his black bomber jacket and wriggled his muscular arms free. Wearing short sleeves, the rest of his arms were covered in tattoos. As Bezdek hung his jacket over the railing, he began to roll his shoulders, limbering up.

'This job, it can get tiring.' Bezdek spoke in slow, partially broken English, his thick Eastern European accent clinging to each word. 'All we do is hurt people who cannot fight back. It has been long time since I have been in actual fight.'

Bezdek stomped towards Sam and threw a rocket of a right hand, which Sam managed to duck, the man's fist grazing the short hair on his head. Before Sam could move, the left hand shot upwards into his ribcage and Sam felt his organs rattle on impact. As Sam stumbled back in pain, Bezdek threw two more clubbing blows down, both of which Sam absorbed in his upper arm that he had raised above his head. The man was relentless, and Bezdek drove two hard knees into Sam's stomach and then once again, went for a thunderous right hook.

Sam managed to duck and slip around the side of his attacker, his foot coming dangerously close to edge of the walkway which was rocking from the heavy movement.

'Fight me,' Bezdek demanded as he turned around. 'You have no choice.'

Sam sighed.

The man was right.

They were suspended over twenty feet in the air with no weapons to use. At the far end of the balcony was the SA80, but Sam knew without the support of his left arm, it wouldn't be half as effective.

It was just the two of them, suspended at a fatally high height, and Bezdek had made it perfectly clear that there was no alternative.

Sam's plan had been as successful as he could have hoped, and the three dead bodies that littered the factory were testimony to that.

But he was out of options.

He had to fight.

As Bezdek stood, fists clenched and looking every bit the prized, underground boxer he had been, Sam took a second to remind himself that this man had been there when Sean was attacked. That a man who could hit this ferociously and accurately had decided to unload on his friend.

An act that the man said was 'tiring'.

As if nearly killing his friend was tantamount to boredom.

Sam nodded to himself more than Bezdek and cracked his neck.

'Let's do this,' Sam said and raised his fists, ignoring the burning pain in his left bicep. Bezdek grinned and then launched forward, aiming a teep kick straight into the centre of Sam's chest. Sam swivelled to the side, his back touching the railing, and he lashed out with a quick strike, his fist cracking Bezdek clean in the jaw. The man absorbed the blow as if he had received a peck on the cheek and he drilled Sam in the side of the face with a clinical elbow strike, the sharp bone crunching into Sam's cheek and reopening the cut that ran across it. Immediately, Sam felt the man lock his taut arm around his neck, and Sam struggled for balance, before drilling his own elbow into the man's midsection.

It was like colliding with a brick wall.

Regardless, as the man tried to shut off Sam's air supply, Sam repeated the swing, he eventually loosened his grip and Sam broke free and swung a hard right.

Blocked.

The man drove his head forward, his skull catching Sam flush in the face and sending him spiralling to the hard metal beneath them.

'This is good.' The man chuckled.

Sam couldn't agree, and he clawed away from the man to try to get to his feet, aware that the width of the metal balcony was dangerously small. As Sam got to his feet, the man drove another knee into the side of his ribs, before hauling him up straight and rocking Sam with a hard right.

Sam refused to fall and as the man followed up with a

left hook, Sam drove his elbow into the centre of the man's forearm, disabling it momentarily. As the man tried to shake off the impact, Sam rocked him with a couple of jabs and then a hammer of a right hook, sending the man collapsing against the railing. Sam took a step back, planting his feet firmly in place and raised his fists. Bezdek raised a hand to his mouth and then looked at the blood that had stained his fingers.

To Sam's horror, the man smiled, as if pleased Sam had drawn blood. The smile soon dissolved into a scowl and the man threw an overhead right hook, drilling down towards Sam's skull. Sam raised his wounded left arm and absorbed the entire blow in the centre of the bicep.

The pain was disabling, and Sam momentarily dropped his guard, meaning the next relentless fist drilled down into the side of his head, knocking him dizzy, and he stumbled back. Bezdek leapt forward, and using one leg for momentum, drove the other foot into Sam's chest, taking him off his feet.

Sam landed back first on the metal and gasped for breath. The man loomed over him, refusing to give Sam a moment's recovery, and he rained down on Sam with a few savage punches, drilling Sam in the face a few times before Sam managed to latch onto the man's arm, locking it in place. As the man struggled, Sam drove a boot into his stomach and then leant back with all his strength, taking the man off his feet and flipping him over onto the hard, unforgiving metal behind him.

As Bezdek hit the walkway, the entire structure shook and Sam wondered how much more punishment he, and the walkway, could take. Like a machine, Bezdek sat back up, taking deep breaths to replenish his lungs, and he gave Sam no respite as they both clambered to their feet at the same time.

He threw a left jab that Sam blocked, but instantly

caught Sam with the follow up right. Then another. And then a solid punch to Sam's gut, followed by a stiff knee to the head.

Sam collapsed onto the metal, his brain spinning, and he realised that stepping back into this world wasn't like riding a bike.

There were people who spent every day of their lives being as dangerous as humanly possible. His two years of solitude and peace had hindered him, and as Bezdek hauled him to his feet, Sam tried desperately to find any last remnants of the fight within him.

But he was overpowered, and Bezdek, with blood dripping from his lip, nodded at Sam respectfully.

'Thank you,' he said, and then he placed his elbow against Sam's throat and Sam gasped for air. Bezdek shuffled Sam backwards, so the base of his spine was pressed against the railing and then pushed further.

Sam could feel his feet beginning to lift from the safety of the metal and his back began to arch, sending him closer and closer to his death. A few more inches, and gravity would do its job and lure Sam to a high-speed collision with the concrete below.

Sam threw a few limp punches, but with his air supply being dropped, they barely registered.

Bezdek's eyes were alive with excitement. The cruel, deliberate push towards Sam's death was his way of asserting his dominance.

With seconds left before it was over, Sam searched desperately within himself, looking for the last scrap or morsel of fight left in him.

He thought of Sean, and how these men attacked him in the dark, wet alley the night before.

It wasn't enough.

Then, with the final push beginning, Sam thought of Jamie.

His son.

His reason for living and his reason for fighting back.

'I love you, Daddy.'

His son's voice echoed in his head, a distant sound from memory that Sam clung to.

It was enough.

In one final swing of his arm, Sam drove his thumb as hard as he could into Bezdek's eye, pushing the eyeball backward and he then twisted his thumb in place, hooking it in behind the socket. Bezdek roared in agony, relinquished his grip, and fell back. But he didn't pull Sam with him, and despite his best efforts, Sam felt himself flip backwards over the balcony, and gravity reached up to claim him.

Sam's hands slammed against the edge of the walkway, and he clung on for dear life, his shoulder popping slightly out of its socket, but he gritted his teeth as he held on. With his feet swinging beneath him, Sam grunted as he pulled himself upward.

His shoulder threatened to separate entirely, and the blood pumping from his bicep was burning in tremendous pain.

Sam was built to survive.

Bezdek was on his knees, his hand clasped to his eye that was oozing blood, and Sam managed to haul himself back onto the platform, letting out a sigh of relief as he did. Blood trickled from a gash across his eyebrow, and he spat a mouthful of blood through the grated metal below him. He pushed himself up, doing his best to steady himself, and then through gritted teeth, he jolted his shoulder back into the socket. Sam grunted with pain and then turned to his opponent, who was dealing with the loss of his sight in one eye. As Sam hauled him to his feet, Bezdek flailed his arm, but Sam hooked it behind the man's back and with his other, drove him face first into the metal railing with all his might. The collision caused the man's nose to explode, and Sam spun him round to face him. Despite Bezdek's physical advantage, he stood limply, his face a bloodied and broken mess and with all the anger and emotion of what this man had done to Sean, Sam dipped down and then swung all of his body weight upwards, channelling his entire momentum into a sickening uppercut.

It connected flush on Bezdek's jaw, lifting him off the metal walkway and over the side of the railing.

Sam didn't watch the man hurtle to the ground, but he heard the sickening, wet thud as he hit the concrete twenty feet below. Sam dropped to his knees, his body screaming for a rest and his mind racing.

He had killed five people in one day.

But none of them was Bowker.

What concerned him was he had no idea how many more men were in Bowker's employ, and even more pressing, how many more awaited him. The sound of footsteps clattering up the stairs told him at least one more and Sam rocked back on his knees and looked to the stairwell, where a smaller, gruff looking man emerged, his gun trained straight on Sam.

'Fucking hell, you're a pain in the arse,' the man spat. He then motioned with his gun. 'Come on, on your feet.'

Sam sighed.

'Do I have to?' Sam shook his head. He was physically drained. 'Can't one of you just shoot me instead of pointing one of those at me?'

'Oh, I'd love to, mate. But Bowker wants you face to face.'

'Is he outside?'

'He's on his way back to our office.' Turner smirked. 'He has some business to attend to.'

The man took a step towards Sam and held up the

screen of his smartphone. It was a picture sent by Creek, showing Pearce and Lynsey tied to two chairs, with a boxing ring just off to the side. Pearce had a savage cut across his head, with blood trickling down his cheek and staining his neat, white beard red.

Sam lunged forward with anger, but the man stepped back, smart enough to keep enough distance between them.

'Uh-uh. Don't be a prick, mate. Now slowly, you're gonna follow me down these stairs and you are going to drive us back so you can join them.' The man backed down the walkway to the stairwell. 'If we aren't back there within the next couple of hours, then your friends are going to be killed. And trust me, the boss ain't going to do it quickly.'

Sam felt his jaw clench with anger. Every fibre of his being wanted to disarm the man and shut his lights off, but he knew he didn't have a choice. Nor did he have the energy. The brawl with Bezdek had sapped the life out of him and he ached all over.

This was his fight.

Lynsey and Pearce were innocent, and after what had happened to Sean, there was no way Sam could lose anyone else.

With a resounding acceptance, Sam struggled to his feet and followed the ratty man down the stairs, the gun trained on Sam every step. They reached the bottom, and Sam glanced at the sticky pile of blood and bone that had previously been Bezdek. Then he followed him out into the rain, towards the black Range Rover and the man demanded Sam get behind the wheel as he slipped into the back, the gun locked on Sam's skull for every second.

Sam started the engine, knowing that at the end of his journey, there was nothing but death waiting for him.

But he didn't have a choice.

Pearce and Lynsey's lives hung in the balance.

And it was the only way that Sam could get face to face with Bowker.

The car exited the industrial estate and cut through the rainy villages, heading towards the M3 and back towards London, where all of this would come to an end.

CHAPTER TWENTY-SIX

Bridges reached for the bottle of wine that sat on his marble topped kitchen counter with a shaking hand. His body was still aching from his introduction to Sam Pope, with one of the pinpoint kidney punches causing him to piss blood. The entire afternoon had been the most terrifying ordeal of his life.

Not because he'd taken a small beating. Nor because he had been threatened with a three-storey fall to his death.

But because he had finally been made accountable for his actions. To admit to himself the part he had played in numerous violent crimes, despite always placating his doubts with the fact he never got his hands dirty himself.

The fact his actions had drawn Sam Pope, one of the most notorious vigilantes in history, out of his supposed death, told him all he needed to know.

That underneath the expensive clothes, the flashy apartment and the million-dollar smile, he was a criminal.

Adam Bridges had been responsible for the deaths of a few people, along with the ripples of pain that those deaths had caused. It didn't matter that he never signed off on the payments, nor that he himself had never held a gun in his life.

Those long felt doubts about how responsible he was had now overflowed and he didn't even use a wine glass as he brought the expensive bottle of red to his lips. As he gulped back the sour wine, he prayed that he could drink away all of it.

The pain that was bouncing around his body like a pinball.

The inevitable prison sentence he would face.

The agony and devastation he had orchestrated for so many by letting Bowker off his leash.

Bridges woozily placed the bottle back on the counter and blew out his tear-stained cheeks. Everything about his home now sickened him, from the expensive art that hung on the walls to the handmade furniture purchased from exclusive boutiques. All of it was a reminder of what he'd done to amass his small fortune, and all the lies he had spewed to people who were truly looking for help.

It wasn't guilt that was holding him back from pressing the send button on his laptop, but fear.

One thing Sam Pope's assault had done was wake him up to true nature of evil that existed within Nicola Weaver. By blinding Bridges with an extortionate salary, he had looked the other way at what she was truly doing. Through meticulous planning, she had developed an almost bullet-proof public reputation as one of the country's biggest philanthropists, and her role in building Head Space had garnered her rave reviews from the press. A media darling, she had amassed a vast fortune but had used Bridges to shield the world from what she really was.

A drug dealer, feeding off the innocence and desperation of young adults who were trying their best to cope with mental health issues. While the world was more accepting and understanding of it nowadays, the majority of these kids were still being guided by a generation who thought that *'they just needed to cheer up a bit'*.

'Keep quiet and deal with it.'

They were hungry for something more and while Head Space offered numerous solutions and support, most of it was just a funnel to the eventual subscription and inevitable addiction to Lonoxidil.

Weaver was creating the problem to sell them the drugs that would solve it.

In a way, it was genius.

But in every way, it was pure evil.

With his hands shaking, Bridges lifted his phone, found Weaver's number, and dialled it.

It answered after one call.

'What?' Weaver snapped, angered by the intrusion to her Saturday evening.

'It's over,' Bridges said morbidly.

'I know. You told me last night. Like I said, Bowker is the best…'

'No, I mean this. Everything. It's over.'

'What the hell are you talking about?'

'We went too far, Nicola.' Bridges heard her tut at the use of her name. 'Bowker went too far.'

'You're drunk and quite frankly, Adam, becoming a bit of a liability.'

'Do you know who I met today? Sam Pope.'

'Who?' Weaver chuckled before a realisation kicked in and her tone changed. *Don't be ridiculous. Sam Pope is dead.'*

'He's very much alive. And the guy Bowker put in the hospital. The one who might never wake up… he was Pope's friend.'

'This is ridiculous. You need to put the bottle down…'

'I'm calling you to let you know that Sam Pope has gone after Bowker. Which means Bowker is likely going to be dead by dawn.' Bridges took a deep breath. 'As part of the deal so Pope didn't kill me, I am giving everything to the press. Every message. Every phone call. Every person we sent Bowker after.'

'Listen here you little shit...' The venom that rang through her every word sent a shiver down Bridges' spine.

'All the evidence of the truth behind Head Space and Lonoxidil. The truth needs to come out, Nicola. I'm sorry. I'm willing to pay the price for the things we've done, but I wanted to let you know so you can decide what you do next.'

Silence.

Bridges waited patiently for a few moments, and then the call disconnected. He held the phone to his ear for a few more minutes before it dropped into his lap. He wiped away a few tears from his eyes, reached forward and tapped the *Enter* key on his laptop.

The email sent.

Lynsey Beckett would receive every shred of evidence she needed to bring the entire thing crashing down. Most likely, within the next few days, Bridges would be arrested and while there was the window of opportunity to run, to disappear, he didn't want to.

There was a price to pay for things he had done, and he was tired of refusing to foot the bill.

A sudden wave of calm washed over him, as if a weight had been lifted from his shoulders. As he reached out for another swig of the expensive wine, he found his hand wasn't shaking anymore.

It was over.

Sam kept one eye on the road and one on the rear-view

mirror. Blood was still trickling from his eyebrow, joining the stream from the slash that ran across his cheekbone.

The M3 was relatively clear, and judging from the signs he was passing, it wasn't long until they'd be entering the capital and the phenomenal skyline of London was etched on the horizon. Through the rain-soaked windscreen, Sam passed the penultimate junction.

'Off at the next one.'

Turner prodded Sam in the back of the head with the pistol, a timely reminder of who was in charge of the situation.

It had been a hell of a day.

From spending the night dealing with the pain of Sean's assault to dealing with his own guilt when it came to the death of his son, Sam had been awake for nearly forty hours, and it was nothing but adrenaline that was keeping him going.

The morning had started with a confrontation with Hicks, the man using one of the local teenagers as a hostage to try to get one up on Sam. He had failed, and it had cost him his life. Now, Sam had eradicated four of Bowker's crew, but it didn't matter.

They had Lynsey and Pearce, and right now, he was out of options.

If he drove back to wherever they were based at gun point, he would be marched inside and executed. His friends would be nothing more than loose ends and would likely face the same fate.

Sam couldn't let that happen.

Under the pretence of keeping his eyes on the road, Sam watched as Turner looked down at his phone, no doubt trading messages with Bowker regarding their ETA. What Sam confirmed was that Turner wasn't wearing his seat belt.

They were two miles from the turning.

The stretch of motorway was clear, with no lights ahead or behind them.

Sam had one chance.

He took it.

Driving at a swift eighty miles an hour, Sam slammed his foot on the brakes, momentarily pulling the car to an almost juddering stop. Turner was thrown forward between the two seats, colliding face first with the touch screen display built into the dashboard. Sam swiftly threw the car back into second, his foot maxing out the acceleration pedal and he shifted up through the gears as quickly as he could to keep going. Woozily, Turner clambered onto the passenger seat and tried to take control of the situation.

'You're a fucking dead man,' Turner shouted, but before he could raise the gun, Sam drove his elbow down hard into the man's jaw.

He swung it again and again.

Turner raised the gun and pulled the trigger.

The bullet blasted out the driver's window, the deafening sound rocking both men as it obliterated the glass which danced across the motorway. Sam tried to keep the car steady, giving Turner enough time to readjust, and he shoved the gun in Sam's face.

He pulled the trigger.

As he did, Sam reached out and grabbed the man's wrist, directing the gun upwards and the bullet ripped through the roof of the car. As they struggled, Sam did his best to keep the car in the lane, thankful for the solitude of the motorway. Sam gritted his teeth, ignoring the pain in his bicep and the hard knees that Turner was driving into his ribs. Sam managed to slide his finger over Turner's, and he applied pressure to the trigger, emptying the magazine through the roof of the car and into the night sky.

Turner finally wrestled control of the gun, but Sam drove his elbow into the man's throat, before slamming his head against the dashboard as hard as he could. Woozily, Turner slumped back into the passenger's seat, trying his best to realign his thought process. His gun clattered to the floor, lost in the darkness underneath the seat.

Now or never.

Sam drove another vicious elbow into the man's temple, scrambling his brain and sending him further into a dazed slump. With his head resting against the window, Turner slurred a grotesque threat in Sam's direction, but Sam, holding wheel steady, delivered another devastating blow. Sam pulled the car onto the hard shoulder, bringing it to a shrieking stop before unbuckling his belt and stepping out.

The wind whipped against him, and in the distance, he could make out the fast approaching headlights of another vehicle.

He had to be quick.

Sam wrenched open the passenger door and Turner flopped towards him, the side of his skull swollen from the brutal assault Sam had administered. With all his upper body strength, Sam caught the man before he slumped to the hard tarmac below and in one heave, he hurled Turner towards the metal barrier that separated the motorway from the woodland.

With his consciousness fading, Turner's shins collided with the barrier and he toppled over, lost to the darkness. With the severity of his head wounds, he needed medical attention and as Sam hopped back into the drivers seat and brought the engine to life, he knew Turner didn't have a chance.

He'd be dead by morning.

Carefully, Sam picked up speed on the hard shoulder and then re-joined the motorway. He drove for the next eight hundred yards and only as he turned off of the motorway did he try to slow his heart rate. The speed limits of the local streets required him to reduce his speed and, as he stopped at a red light, he took a deep breath.

He had bought himself half a chance of survival.

It's what he did.

As he turned onto a residential street, Sam pulled the car to a stop by the kerb and raised the handbrake.

After a few moments of quiet retrospection, he was able to calm his breathing, amazed that he'd been able to remove his captor from the car in time. He leant across the passenger seat and pressed his hand to the floor, feeling around until his fingers touched the cold, unforgiving steel of the gun. He drew it up, discharged the magazine, and checked the ammo.

One bullet.

Sam was heading to Bowker with one bullet remaining.

It didn't sit well with him. He had no idea where he was headed, no clue how to get in and couldn't even hazard a guess at how many men Bowker still had, locked and loaded and out for his blood.

But Pearce and Lynsey's lives were at stake.

They were live bait, and if Sam didn't show up to take it, then they would become surplus to Bowker's requirements.

There was no way out of it.

No way back.

Sam had to fight for them, otherwise he would lose them.

He turned his attention to the screen on the dashboard and brought up the inbuilt satnav, working through its clunky interface to bring up the list of frequent journeys. He scrolled through until he found what he was looking for.

Work.

Sam tapped it, waited for it to load; the address given was a building in Mile End.

Stonewall Security Ltd.

He was just outside of Twickenham, which meant he was still an hour away. Bowker would be expecting a knock on his door by then and Sam slammed the magazine back into the gun, fired up the engine, and pulled back out into the rain, eager not to disappoint him.

CHAPTER TWENTY-SEVEN

The moment Bowker unlocked the door to the Stonewall Security Ltd office and was greeted by Sam Pope's restrained friends, he smiled. On a day that had proven too costly for it to be worth anything, and a situation that had spiralled wildly out of control, it was the first time in hours that he felt his grip tighten on the reins.

Never had he been challenged in such a way.

Throughout his years as a boxer, Bowker had been a devastating force, fully earning his moniker of 'The Reaper' and certainly never once felt like he was threatened. When that career ended and he took up his vocation as a hired gun, usually, a stern warning was enough for the desired result. If the pressure needed to be raised, then a serious beating would do the trick.

It should have done here.

As he locked eyes with Lynsey, who looked terrified in her restraints, part of him wished that she had just crumbled under his first warning. Going one step further and putting her partner on life support should have drawn a line under everything.

It hadn't, and for all of the collateral damage and bloodshed, a new opportunity had arisen.

Bowker would be the one to actually kill Sam Pope.

On the drive back, Bowker ran the scenario through his head. For years, he had been happy to collect his payment from the rich and pathetic and do their bidding. But how much power could he garner if the underworld knew that Sam Pope, a man who had them all quaking in their boots, had been killed by his hands?

It was a juicy prospect, and one that aided the smile that Bowker greeted both of them with.

'Well, it's nice to see you both again,' Bowker said dryly, removing his damp coat and tossing it onto the sofa in the recreational corner. He looked at Pearce. 'How's the eye?'

Pearce grinned.

'A little sore. How's the ego?'

Bowker chuckled. For a man who was in a very dangerous place, Pearce certainly had a sense of humour.

'Oh, it's been better.' Bowker approached Pearce and leant down to his level. 'Nothing I can't fix though.'

Mockingly, he ruffled Pearce's grey, cropped hair and then stood, turning to his henchman.

'Any word from Turner?' Creek asked, seemingly taking his role as the new right hand seriously.

'He's sent me a few messages. He has Sam and they're on their way here.'

'Here?' Pearce interrupted; his bruised eyebrow raised. Bowker turned impatiently.

'What are you, an echo? Yes, he's coming here and I'm going to take great pleasure in killing him in front of you both.' To everyone's, including Lynsey's, surprise, Pearce began to chuckle. Infuriated, Bowker lifted a bottle of water and took an angry swig. 'Did I say something funny, mate?'

'Let me get this straight. You put one of Sam's friends in the hospital, kidnapped us both, and have already sent God knows how many men after him and he's still standing. And your great plan is to invite him into your home?' Pearce shook his head in disbelief. 'You're a dead man.'

Bowker's face flushed with rage, and he stomped towards Pearce. Lynsey squealed in terror, and Pearce braced himself. With the back of his hand, Bowker struck Pearce venomously across the face, rocking him on his chair and sending a trail of saliva from his mouth. Bowker flashed Lynsey a threatening glare and let Pearce slump forward in his seat. As he collected himself, Pearce heard Lynsey's terrified voice register as a whisper.

'Adrian. What are you doing?'

Pearce shook the cobwebs.

'Buying us some time.'

Lynsey shook her head. It was an honourable thing for him to do, to direct all of Bowker's rage in his direction, but Pearce was on a fool's errand. Strapped to a chair, and already hurt, the man stood no chance against Bowker. Least of all with his lapdog stood watching, his handgun resting in his lap as he sat on the edge of the boxing ring.

Bowker took another sip of water and stretched his shoulders behind his back. Despite the additional weight, he was still an imposing figure and his back rippled against his T-shirt. After a few more minutes, Pearce eventually lifted his head and looked Bowker in the eyes.

'So, what's your plan?' Pearce interrogated. 'Bring Sam in here and put a bullet in his head?'

'Hey, buddy. Less of the questions.' Creek piped in, gesturing with his gun regarding the possible consequences. Bowker held up his hand.

'It's fine, Paul.' Bowker folded his arms and regarded Pearce with interest. 'That's pretty accurate, Sherlock. I can tell you were a detective.'

'One of the best.' Pearce grinned, causing another grimace from Bowker. Agitated, Bowker turned to Lynsey.

'You know all this is your fault, right?' Lynsey's eyes widened in surprise. 'If you'd just deleted that fucking article, then none of this would have happened.'

'I was just doing my job.' Lynsey snapped back. Bowker launched forward and got right in her face, causing her to recoil in fear.

'So. Was. I.'

'Hey, Bowker.' Pearce desperately clamoured for his attention. 'Leave her alone.'

Bowker ignored him. He reached out and stroked the side of Lynsey's face, causing her skin to crawl.

'Come to think of it, all of this blood that's been shed, it's on your hands. You prodded the wrong person and now, your little boyfriend is in hospital and a lot of my guys are in the ground.' Bowker snatched up a handful of her hair and yanked her face a mere millimetre from his. 'For that, I should just fucking kill you right now.'

Pearce took a breath, knowing full well that his next move may very well be his last.

'Hey, dipshit,' Pearce yelled. 'How's about we get in the ring?'

Bowker, still clutching Lynsey's hair, arched his neck to look at Pearce, his eyes wide with intrigue.

'You what?'

'You always said you wanted to get in the ring with a pig, right? Well, I was a detective for thirty years. Take your shot.'

Lynsey looked on, mortified by the challenge, and Bowker slowly relinquished his grip. With a smile on his face, he turned to Creek and shrugged.

'I think I hit him too hard.' Bowker chuckled.

'If I recall, last time, I put you on the floor, didn't I?'

Pearce goaded. Bowker's nostrils flared. It was working. 'Or do you only get your reputation by scaring women?'

That was the trigger.

The tried and tested dent of the male pride.

Angrily, Bowker stomped towards the ring, pointing at his sidekick.

'Cut him loose and keep the gun on him.' Bowker reached up and hauled himself onto the ring apron before looking back at Pearce. 'This is going to hurt, son.'

Pearce knew he wasn't lying.

As Bowker stepped through the ropes and then bounced against them, limbering up, Creek stepped behind Pearce's chair and cut through the bindings that had locked him in place. Pearce turned to Lynsey, whose eyes were watering at what was to come. He offered her a warm smile, but gingerly got to his feet.

There was little to no chance he was going to step back out of that ring once he entered. Bowker had already proven to him that he was a devastating fighter, and with the likelihood that he and Lynsey were to be killed once Bowker had executed Sam, it meant Bowker was unlikely to go easy on him.

But Pearce had done what he needed to do.

Kept Bowker away from Lynsey.

If Sam was on his way, Pearce could only hope that he wasn't too far.

In his prime, Pearce was quite the boxer, winning a number of competitions within the Met's boxing league.

But that was a long time ago, and as Creek shoved him forward towards the ring, he felt like a man being made to walk the green mile. Pearce reached up and grabbed the ropes, hauling himself up onto the apron as Bowker patiently stalked him from the other side of the ring.

'Go easy on me,' Pearce said with a wry smile that tried to mask his fear. 'It's been a while.'

Bowker ignored him, waiting patiently against the corner pad as Pearce stepped in the ring. As he did, he took a deep breath and then lifted his fists.

Bowker grinned.

Then launched across the ring.

A thunderous right hook was sent Pearce's way, but to the surprise of Bowker and the two spectators, Pearce weaved underneath it, slipping out from the corner and stepping away into the middle of the ring.

Bowker had a four-inch height and a minimum three stone weight advantage over Pearce. As he shuffled away from the behemoth, Pearce knew his best chance was to keep moving.

With an impressed smirk, Bowker faced Pearce and then stomped towards him, not even throwing a guard up. Pearce tried to weave a little more, but Bowker reached out, hauling him in with a firm grip and he thrust his head full force into Pearce's face.

Lynsey gasped in horror.

Pearce stumbled backwards, colliding with the ropes, and before he could gather his thoughts, Bowker unloaded with a series of precise shots, the first cracking Pearce in the jaw. Gritting his teeth, Pearce got his arms up to block the next one, but it was swiftly followed by one to his solid mid-section.

Then another.

And another.

As he buckled under the onslaught, Bowker threw the rule book out the window, grabbed a hold of Pearce's collar and his belt and hurled him dangerously into the centre of the ring. Pearce clattered against the canvas, the impact causing a sharp pain in his wrist. Bowker, not even breaking a sweat, shook his hand out mockingly.

'Isn't it nice when something is just as satisfying as you always thought it would be?'

As Pearce pushed himself onto all fours, Bowker drove a ferocious shin into his ribs, taking him clean off the mat and flipping him over onto his back. Pearce groaned in agony, and then, as he hauled himself up via the ropes, he spat a mouthful of blood onto the floor.

'Jesus Christ. You're killing him!' Lynsey screamed.

'That's the point,' Bowker replied, cockily lining up his next punch as Pearce leant on the ropes, as if he was reaching the finish line.

He turned.

Bowker swung.

Pearce ducked underneath. Caught by surprise, Bowker turned, and Pearce rocked him with a right hook, splitting the man's lip open and rocking him back on his heels. Bowker shook it off, dabbing at the blood with the back of his hand, and to Pearce's surprise, he looked impressed.

'Nice shot.' Bowker spat onto the mat.

'Let's go, big guy,' Pearce said, knowing that kicking a hornet's nest was never a wise move. As Bowker clenched his fists, Pearce sent a silent prayer that Sam was nearby.

There were only so many chances he was going to get.

Angered by Pearce's apparent skill, Bowker charged forward, looking to catch his opponent with a haymaker. But Pearce defied his age, shifting to the side, shuffled his feet and caught Bowker with a vicious uppercut to his portly body.

It was like hitting a punching bag and had minimal effect.

Bowker swung his arm out, catching Pearce on the jaw with his elbow, before rocking Pearce with a nasty left hand that knocked him to his knees. As soon as the fist collided with his nose, Pearce knew it had been broken, and blood poured down his lips. Trying to get to his feet, Pearce saw

Bowker drive his knee forward and he tried to absorb most of the blow in his arm.

The knee drove into the joint of his wrist, cracking the bone, and Pearce grunted in pain.

He hit the mat, knowing that there was little chance of fighting back.

His ribs were cracked, the pain rendering him almost immobile. His eye was swelling, the throbbing ache joining that of his broken nose, and he looked up at Bowker in defeat.

As the burly man approached, he offered Pearce a look of respect. It was rare that a man was foolish enough to step into the ring with him, but the ex-copper had shown the type of fortitude that Bowker could appreciate.

However, there was no room for sentiment.

Not tonight.

'It's been a pleasure watching you die, mate.' Bowker smiled evilly, and then placed his boot on Pearce's throat. Desperately, Pearce tried to lodge his working hand underneath it, knowing that if he failed, the man would literally squeeze the life from his body. Fighting with all his might, Pearce managed to get a little purchase underneath, but Bowker, using the ropes for support, lifted himself up and applied his entire weight.

'Stop it. Please.' Lynsey begged.

Creek watched on, a little disturbed by the violence but understanding of the reason why.

Pearce fought and fought, but as he looked up at Bowker, with his vision fading, he didn't see a man staring back at him with sickening pleasure.

He saw the devil.

As everything started to go black, Pearce heard the thunderous pounding of metal, and then nothing.

CHAPTER TWENTY-EIGHT

The satnav beeped and welcomed Sam to his destination as he pulled the hijacked car to a stop. The Stonewall Security Ltd sign hung above the door to the nondescript building, which was unremarkable in its simplicity. As the engine purred to a stop, Sam removed the key and slid it into his pocket.

If he wasn't too late, there was a chance that both Pearce and Lynsey would be able to get away.

Every part of his body ached, and Sam remembered why he had stepped away from this life in the first place. Every blow that he absorbed was beginning to take more and more of a toll on his body and he felt like he was running out of room for new scars.

He had been through hell, most of the time willingly, and now he had one more demon to put down.

As he stared at the metal door to the building, Sam lifted the Glock 17 from the passenger seat and once again slid the magazine smoothly from the weapon.

One bullet.

It wasn't a lot, but it was something.

Sam slammed the magazine back into the gun and threw the door open, the rain greeting him with a surprisingly cooling soak. The briskness of the weather seemed to ease the pain that was thrashing through his body and, holding the gun down by his side, he strode across the vacant road and to the door.

There was no way of knowing what was awaiting him on the other side of the door. For all he knew, there could be six men, armed with assault rifles, ready to blow him to kingdom come.

Pearce and Lynsey could already be dead.

But there was no retreat in Sam. No walking away. As he slammed his fist against the solid metal door, he heard it echo through the room beyond.

Sam shot glances in both directions, glad that the weather had removed any witnesses from the street. The last thing he needed was the police showing up, as despite the heinous crimes that befell Bowker, Sam knew that their attention would immediately turn to him.

One of the bolts on the door jolted loudly.

Sam drew his other hand to the gun, locking it securely between both palms, his deadly finger gently resting on the trigger.

Another bolt slid open, and with a little resistance, the door was pulled open.

'It's about fucking time. You're missing the fun.'

Creek stood on the other side of the door, his hand still fastened to the handle and by the look of shock on his face, he was expecting Turner to be waiting, holding Sam at gunpoint.

Sam was happy to disappoint him.

'Oh fuck,' Creek stammered, and in his haste, he fumbled with his own handgun as he tried to raise it at Sam.

Some things never left you, and Sam's instincts and muscle memory combined in deadly unison as he swiftly drew the gun up, pulled it in line with Creek's forehead, and squeezed.

The man's head snapped back, blood splattering into the room and he collapsed to the floor with the bullet hole still smoking in the centre of his forehead.

There was no smart way to play it, and Sam jumped forward over the body, turning in the air and allowing himself to land on his shoulder. If there was a barrage of bullets headed his way, he hoped he could miss them, but as he rolled into the room, there was nothing. Before he rose to his feet, he whipped up the fallen man's seemingly loaded handgun, rolled through onto his knee, and lifted it to face the room.

All he got was a round of applause.

Bowker stood in the ring, slapping his meaty and swollen hands together. Beneath his foot, he saw the motionless body of Pearce. Sam aimed the gun squarely at Bowker.

'Get off him.'

Bowker held his hands up, pushed out his lip in a mock apology and stepped back. Pearce stirred slightly, his face a bloodied mess and his left hand hanging sickeningly off kilter. Sam felt his heart drop at the sight of his friend, but as he stepped further into the room, Pearce began to regain his breath and he opened his one good eye and looked at Sam.

His face was a picture of relief.

'Adrian. You okay?' Sam called out, stepping carefully towards Lynsey, his gun still trained on Bowker who stood arrogantly in the corner of the ring, his arms resting on the ropes.

'Quite the entrance,' Bowker called out.

'I'll live,' Pearce chimed in, shuffling under the bottom rope.

'Thank God you're here,' Lynsey blurted, her eyes red with crying. Sam pulled the car key from his pocket and with considerable force, tore it through the tape that had pinned her to the chair.

'There's a car parked on the opposite side of the road.' Sam explained. 'Get him to the nearest hospital.'

Lynsey stood, turning to Sam in shock. The man was certainly in worse shape than when she'd last seen him, with half of his face bruised and splattered with blood. She reached out and touched his arm.

'Come with us.'

'I can't,' Sam said sternly, his eyes and gun still trained on an eager-looking Bowker. 'I have to finish this.'

Lynsey went to remonstrate but realised it was useless. Sam's focus was squarely on Bowker and with a heavy heart, she walked away from him held her hand out to Pearce, helping him slowly from the ring apron. He thanked her with a grimacing smile and then limped slowly beside her, leaning on her for support. As they approached Sam, he stood to the side, the gun trained on Bowker as he leaned in.

'I'm sorry, Adrian.'

'Just do me a favour,' Pearce replied, straining through the agony to shoot one final look at the man who had assaulted him. 'Make it hurt.'

It was the first time Pearce had ever vocally condoned Sam's actions, and Sam was putting it down to the trauma he'd been through. It was pretty clear to see what Pearce had done. He had drawn Bowker's focus entirely to himself, keeping Lynsey safe and buying Sam time. It had worked, but it had come at a heavy price, and Sam responded with a firm nod. With his good hand, Pearce reached out and gently rested it on Sam's shoulder. A silent goodbye.

Sam swallowed the heartache.

The tension in the room was thick as Sam and Bowker patiently waited for the two hostages to make their escape, and as soon as the door slammed shut, Bowker spoke.

'So, the great Sam Pope. What an honour.'

'Honour is a concept that you don't understand.'

'Oh, spare me the sanctimonious bullshit, will you, mate? It's just the two of us so you can drop the fucking act.'

Bowker pushed himself out of the corner and Sam emphasised the readjustment of his grip.

'You hurt and kill people for money,' Sam said sternly. 'You put my friend in hospital because someone sent you their name and a cheque.'

'Actually, they sent me her name. Would you rather I kick seven shades out of a woman?'

'You're a monster.'

'And what the fuck does that make you?' Bowker's voice boomed loudly, reverberating off the walls. 'I know about you. When you were putting fuckers in the ground left, right, and centre, I wondered what kind of sick bastard does that. Now the press, they were keen to paint you as some kind of hero, but don't get it wrong, mate, you've buried more people than I have.'

'I didn't have a choice.'

Bowker burst out laughing.

'Give me a break. You did have a choice, and you chose what you knew best. You were trained to kill, just like I trained to step in this ring and beat the shit out of people. When we both stepped away, we both couldn't give it up. The only difference between us is I was smart enough to get paid.'

Bowker took another step into the centre of the ring, his arms outstretched as he continued.

'But you, you actively went looking for blood. You gunned down criminal after criminal in cold blood and you justified it with some holier than thou bullshit to keep your conscience clear. So, who is the real criminal here? Because as far as I can see, I haven't actually killed anyone this week. Your friend, he's alive. He might be a fucking vegetable when he wakes up, but he's alive. But you, Sam. You've killed my crew. My friends. You killed Benny, Jimmy, Connor, Bezdek, Lemar, Mickey, and that poor fucker on the floor over there is Paul. All of them people. All of them someone's son. And you of all people, you should know what losing a son feels like.'

Sam felt his finger flicker on the trigger. He knew Bowker was actively goading him. The twisted smile on the man's face told Sam the truth.

Bowker was out of ideas.

Out of back up.

His only play now was to get under Sam's skin. Make him lose his composure. Refusing to play along, Sam lowered his weapon.

'We are all accountable for our actions.' Sam spoke calmly, much to Bowker's agitation. 'I've made my peace with the path I took, and I tried to put things right. But all you've shown me, Bowker, is that sometimes someone has to fight back. Sometimes, men like you and all your crew, need to be stopped. You have friends in high places, people who put a lot of stock and value in what you offer. Which means when the police come knocking on your door, you don't have to answer it. So if you don't answer to the law, then you can answer to me. The world thought me dead, and I was more than happy to play along. But I didn't come back because I wanted to or because I enjoy it. I came back because I needed to. For people like you.'

Bowker blew out his lips in exasperation and shook his head. He stepped back towards the corner.

'You tell yourself what you need to, mate. You're a killer. A cold-bloodied killer who enjoys the power it brings. With that said...' Bowker slowly turned his back on Sam, stretching his arms out as if accepting the Lord himself. 'Shall we stop pussyfooting around and get this over with?'

Sam lifted the weapon, his eyes trained on the back of Bowker's skull. It would have been one simple squeeze of the trigger and the man would be put down for good.

Another criminal organisation broken.

But this wasn't about resetting the balance that the scales of justice was incapable of.

This was personal.

Sam slipped the magazine out of the handgun and spilled the bullets onto the concrete floor, the metal clattering like a tambourine. With the gun empty, he tossed the now redundant weapon into the shadows. Bowker turned around; his eyebrows raised at the display.

Sam cracked his neck, doing his best to ignore the impact of the war he'd been in. Whatever pain was hiding in his body, he ignored it. With careful steps, Sam made his way towards the ring, his eyes locked on Bowker.

'You were wrong when you said I enjoyed what I do,' Sam said coldly. 'But for you, Bowker, I'm willing to make an exception.'

Sam's words were met with an eager grin by Bowker, who seemed to relish the challenge.

'Attaboy,' Bowker said with a strange sense of pride, waiting patiently as Sam stepped up onto the ring apron before stepping between the top and middle rope. All that separated them was the space of the ring.

No guns.

No crew.

Just the two of them. Without any further words, the

two men sized each other up, knowing that what was to come was the final destination of the collision course that fate had sent them on.

And as the two men slowly circled the ring, weighing up their first move, they both knew that there was only one way the night would end.

Only one of them would be walking away.

CHAPTER TWENTY-NINE

As they had made their way outside, Lynsey clicked the unlock function on the keys, following the sound and flashing lights to the Range Rover that Sam had promised was waiting. She had Pearce's arm draped over her shoulder, his other hung limp and useless by his side. Despite his best efforts, he couldn't keep himself up and Lynsey strained under the additional weight. Both of them ignored the rain that pounded them as they shuffled uncomfortably across the road. Pearce lost his footing and fell to his knee.

Instinctively, he threw out his shattered wrist and roared in agony on impact.

'Come on, Adrian.' Lynsey begged, squatting down and doing her utmost to hook his arm again. After a few moments, Pearce managed to get to one knee, and with all her might, Lynsey pulled him back to his feet. They eventually made it to the car, and Lynsey leant Pearce against it as she opened the back door.

'Thank you,' Pearce said. His words were soft and painful. Lynsey turned to him and felt a sea of guilt flood through her. Not just for him.

But for everyone.

Sean was lying in a hospital bed, his mother not knowing whether she will ever speak to him again. Sam Pope, a known criminal, but one who had fought through hell to bring down the people responsible.

And Pearce, who, despite trying his best to hide it, was in pure agony. His face was swollen and bloody, and his nose was a crushed mess. His broken wrist hung limply, resting in his other hand, and she could only imagine the state of his body after the blows he had absorbed.

All of it for her.

It was her questions and her article that had lit the fuse that caused the explosion of violence, and as she helped Pearce to lie on the backseat, she could feel the tears flooding down her immaculate cheekbones.

'Thank you, my dear.' Pearce sighed as he collapsed on the back seat, his body relaxing as he melted into the leather. Lynsey wiped her eyes with her already soaked sleeve.

'I'm sorry.'

Pearce either didn't hear her, or chose not to respond, but Lynsey ensured his feet were in before closing the door and jumping into the driver's seat. She fired up the car and then tapped the nearest hospital into the satnav. As the screen turned into a map, she indicated and pulled away, knowing full well she was leaving a murder scene. Nausea sat in the pit of her stomach as she contemplated the possibility that Sam wouldn't make it out alive.

What would Bowker do then?

A rush of panic surged through her, and she pulled out her phone, keeping one eye on the road as she thumbed in her passcode and then opened her keypad.

'What are you doing?' Pearce murmured, his voice strained.

'I'm calling the police,' Lynsey responded, her voice shaking as she cried.

'You can't...' Pearce began, before groaning in pain.

'We can't just leave them.' She remonstrated. 'What if Bowker kills Sam? Then what?'

'You can't send the police. If they find out Sam's alive, they'll lock him away for good.'

'Then what the hell am I supposed to do?' Lynsey yelled, reaching the end of her tether and realising that underneath the hard-nosed facade she'd put on, she was terrified. Pearce collapsed back onto the leather seat and took a deep breath.

'Have faith.'

Lynsey wiped her eyes and then threw her phone onto the passenger seat. Pearce was right.

Sam had gone to war with Bowker and his crew to avenge Sean and to keep her safe. Calling in the police would most likely render both Bowker and Sam in cuffs, with both of them locked away in the deepest, darkest hole. She would be safe, but with her cup already overflowing with guilt, stripping Sam of the chance to keep his freedom wasn't something she could carry.

Not after everything he'd done.

'How about a little music?' Pearce suggested. Lynsey smiled inwardly. Despite the anguish he'd been put through, she knew he was still trying to keep her calm. She nodded, wiped her tears once more and clicked on the radio. A nondescript pop song that was no doubt dominating the charts began to play and, as she stopped at a red light, she turned to look at Pearce.

His eyes were closed, but he was breathing.

He looked content, and it was in that moment that she realised why the world needed people like Pearce.

And like Sam.

People who, despite the worst of the world arriving on

their doorstep, still put others first. Pearce had kept her safe and was subjected to the brutality of a violent criminal in doing so.

Sam had been fighting back.

For Sean.

For her.

As quick as a flash of lightning, her mindset changed, and she realised it wasn't about the story or about exposing a criminal enterprise to climb the corporate ladder.

It was about doing the right thing.

She turned onto the next street, knowing there was no way back from the clarity she had just realised. If being in the presence of Pearce and Sam Pope didn't hammer the message home, then nothing would.

———

It was Bowker who nailed the first blow.

After circling the ring a few times, both he and Sam realised that there wasn't a strategy. It was whoever could hit the hardest. Bowker, having spent the majority of his youth within the squared circle, rose to the occasion, stepping to Sam, bobbing one way before drilling him with a hard uppercut to the ribs. Sam absorbed the blow like a brick wall, grateful for the hours he had spent in the gym.

This was Bowker's habitat.

Sam was trained.

Deadly.

Put a gun in his hand and his eye to the scope and there was nobody more dangerous on the planet.

But this wasn't his world.

Shaken by the blow, Sam stumbled back, keeping his guard up and he ran through the times he had engaged people like Bowker in hand-to-hand combat. Despite his impressive physique, Sam still gave a few inches and a few stones in weight, which combined with Bowker's prowess, put him in a very precarious spot.

Three years ago, when he had fought Mark Connor on the top floor of the High Rise, he had used the environment to his advantage, jamming a knife into the man's eye and drilling his head into the wall. When faced with the relentless Oleg Kovalenko at the Port of Tillbury, Sam had been subjected to a brutal beating, only to once again use his surroundings to impale and hang the man from a suspension hook.

With the body of his dead mentor, Sgt Carl Marsden, still warm, he had taken on the mercenary, Buck, the jewel in Blackridge's crown and only survived by putting a bullet between the man's eyes. Farukh, the Hangman of Baghdad, was also beaten when Sam slit his throat. He also needed a weapon to defeat Ravi inside 'The Grid', as well as a gun to blast the monstrous Edinson to hell in a bar in South Carolina.

Sam was good with his hands, but as Bowker rattled his ribs with another blow, followed by a swift knee, he realised that Bowker was better.

Judging from the smirk on the man's face, he knew it too.

'Come on, Sam. Hit me.'

Sam obliged, snapping out a sharp right like a coiled snake and rocking the big man's jaw. It seemed to only excite him, and Bowker responded with one of his own, drilling Sam in the face and sending him back into the corner pad. With a roar of anger, Bowker dived forward, his colossal shoulder crashing into Sam's stomach. The air exploded from Sam's lungs, and as he attempted a weak knee strike, Bowker held the rope, leant back, and drilled his shoulder into Sam again.

Sam gasped for air, and Bowker wrapped his thick arms around Sam's thighs and then hoisted him into the air, turned and drove Sam down onto the mat. Sam's back and head clattered on the canvas, rattling his brain and blurring his vision.

He was getting beaten to death.

'This is disappointing.' Bowker spoke cheerfully. 'You know you hear such stories about people. Things you couldn't possibly believe. But then when it comes to the truth… well, it's nothing but a fucking let down.'

Bowker's voice growled the last two words with hatred, and he threw a vicious boot into Sam's ribs, knocking him back to the mat and he immediately mounted, raining down on Sam with clubbing blows. Battling the dizziness, Sam tried to fend them off, but Bowker caught him with three ferocious punches to the face, each one drawing more blood and each one drawing the fight nearer to a close. As if offended by how easily he was winning, Bowker hauled Sam up by his neck and then carelessly hurled him across the ring.

Sam hit the mat hard.

Trying his best to unscramble his brain, every part of him was telling him to get up.

But his body wouldn't let him. Irritated, Bowker spat onto the canvas and shook his head.

'The big bad Sam Pope.' His voice was laced with disgust. 'You know, I'm ashamed this is so easy. But I guess I can reunite you with your son, huh? Give you chance to explain to him that the reason you couldn't protect him was because you just didn't have what it takes to fight back.'

Sam's eyes shot open. He knew Bowker was antagonising him, wanting Sam to mount one last empty attack before he dismantled him for good.

But Sam couldn't stop himself. By mentioning the death of his son, Sam's self-hatred and guilt took over, driving his fists into the mat and pushing him up to his knees. Bowker watched on in excitement as Sam got to his feet, his war-torn body aching but now running on adrenaline. His entire body was covered in scars, all of them a permanent reminder of the battles he had fought and the journey he'd taken.

But there was one scar that had never healed.

Never closed.

Jamie.

Sam turned to face Bowker, whose eyes sparkled like a shark that had just inhaled a pint of blood.

'Let's go.'

Bowker grinned as he spoke and he lunged forward, his right fist hurtling through the air. Sam ducked it and swung his left hand upwards, his knuckles cracking as they clattered into Bowker's jaw. Biting his own tongue, Bowker grunted in pain and threw another desperate punch. Sam blocked it with his elbow, caught Bowker with another solid left, and followed it immediately with a right hook that sent the large man to his knee.

The blow split Bowker's eyebrow and blood splattered the canvas.

For the first time in his life, Bowker looked across the ring with concern. Trying to mask it, he got back up and stretched his shoulders. Sam didn't relent, ducking under the next punch attempt before leaping off the mat and swinging a thunderous haymaker that sent Bowker sprawling, his nose obliterated from the impact. With blood gushing down his face, Bowker scrambled to the ropes and hauled himself to his feet.

Sam stared at the man, wondering how terrified Sean was when he was in the same position. About how many people had been beaten down by this man, and how he had done it without remorse.

Bowker could sense Sam's hatred and with gritted teeth, he reached into his pocket and pulled out a pen knife, which he flicked open, the halogen lights shimmering off the metal blade.

'This ends now,' Bowker growled and then shot forward, slashing wildly at Sam who dodged a few swipes before one caught him across his shoulder. He buckled slightly, gritted his teeth, and ignored the crazed smile on Bowker's face.

The man was desperate.

And desperate men make mistakes.

Bowker feigned one way but then slashed the other, but Sam ducked, grabbed the arm and with all his might, snapped it against his own shoulder. The crunch of the bone echoed loudly off the walls, and Sam shut down Bowker's squeal of anguish with a brutal forearm to the throat. Bowker dropped the knife and then to his knees, courtesy of a vicious kick to the back of his legs. With his options limited, Bowker refused to give up and he collected the blade with his functioning hand and in his final act of defiance, he swung upwards at Sam.

But Sam caught the arm with both hands, staring down at the big man who had been reduced to his knees, staring up at Sam for mercy. Bowker's eyes widened in realisation.

There was no mercy.

Not for him.

Using all his power, Sam locked his grip around Bowker's knife-wielding hand and then began to twist it back towards him. With his other hand defunct and his body gasping for air through a crushed windpipe, Bowker tried to fight for his life, but had none left.

Sam had beaten the fight out of him.

Slowly and deliberately, Sam directed the blade towards Bowker's throat, and at the last second, directed it upwards. The blade pierced the skin beneath Bowker's chin and his eyes widened as his slow death began.

Holding the man's head in place and slowly driving the knife upwards, Sam made it his mission to stare into the man's eyes as the knife continued its slow, painful trajectory upwards.

As the blood began to fill Bowker's mouth and his eyes began to flicker, Sam gritted his teeth and spoke.

'This is for Sean.'

Sam pushed the blade in at full force, slicing through Bowker's tongue and piercing the top of his mouth. He relinquished his grip and Bowker hit the canvas, his eyes wide, his body twitching.

Within twenty seconds, he was dead.

With his face bloodied, his knuckles broken, and his body battered, Sam took a deep breath and then rolled under the rope, taking a few seconds to sit on the apron and collect his thoughts.

Everything had changed.

His new life was over and as soon as the police discovered the bodies and connected the dots, they would soon come looking for him. Especially if Lynsey released the article and the proof of his re-emergence.

The only silver lining from all the devastation and pain of the last week was that he realised, once and for all, there were people out there who needed him to fight back.

That needed someone to set the wrong things right.

There was no way back now. Etheridge couldn't have put it any better.

'We are who we are.'

With that thought playing in his mind, Sam made his way to the door, knowing that nothing but a cold, wet night awaited him and his next step unknown.

The only thing that was certain was the moment he stepped outside he would need to disappear.

The fight had begun.

Again.

CHAPTER THIRTY

As Sheila Wiseman sat at Sean's bedside, she clasped her hand around the small, beaten *Bible* that she had owned for over four decades. By reading it out loud and praying with her son, she hoped that divine intervention would help him pull through.

Sean needed something.

It had been two days and still no movement.

The last thing she wanted to do was lose faith, but as every minute passed, and every machine that was plugged into her son beeped, Sheila found her grip on her religion slipping. Sporadically, she would get an urge to touch him, and as one of them took control of her body, she lifted herself gingerly from her chair and gently stroked the side of Sean's mutilated face with the back of her hand.

'How's he doing?'

Pearce's voice startled Sheila.

His appearance nearly floored her.

'Adrian. My goodness.' Sheila rushed to him as quickly as she could. 'Who did this to you?'

'Take a guess.'

Sheila guided him to a chair, and he painfully

lowered himself into it. Lynsey had taken him to the local hospital as fast as she could, and fortunately for Pearce, all the damage was superficial. His nose was broken, the swelling around his eyes and the thick, white plaster that was keeping it in place gave that away. His wrist was in a sling, the fracture likely to take up to a month to heal.

As for his broken ribs, the only advice he'd been given was to take it easy. He also had some internal bruising in his midsection and was under the advice that if the blood didn't clear from his urine within the next few days, he needed to come back pronto.

Besides all that, he was fine and as he explained his injuries to Sheila, she shook her head and gestured with the *Bible*.

'If you go looking for trouble, you will always find it.'

'Amen.' Pearce sighed. He nodded to Sean. 'Any update.'

'He's just resting.'

Pearce clocked the tear forming in Sheila's eyes as she stared at her son with pride. With his functional hand, Pearce reached over, ignored the pain in his chest and the doctor's advice, and clasped her hand.

'We'll get through this.'

'It just makes me sad to know that good people like you, like my boy, they go through life trying to do the right things, yet they still get caught up in this horrible violence.' She dabbed at her eyes. 'These people, these nasty, violent people, they need to be stopped.'

Pearce gritted his teeth and drew his lips into a thin line. Every part of him wanted to tell her that the people who were responsible had paid the biggest price for their misdeeds. That their crimes hadn't gone unpunished, and that Sam had sought and delivered justice to them all. It pained Pearce to think it, but for the first time since they had met, he was glad Sam saw the world in black and white and was willing to paint it red with blood.

What Bowker and his crew had done to Sean was despicable and now, as Sean clung dearly to life, the people responsible would never see another day.

'They will,' Pearce finally said, patting Sheila's hand and trying to stifle a yawn. 'I'll make sure of it.'

Sheila smiled at the joke and then turned her attention back to Sean. Pearce stretched out his legs, sinking further into the chair and abandoning the fight against his exhaustion. As soon as Lynsey had taken him into A&E, his bloodied face and clear anguish had seen him jump the queue. After being checked and treated, Pearce was told he needed to be observed for eight hours to ensure there was no further head trauma.

Lynsey checked her phone and clearly had received a message that put her on edge. As soon as Pearce gave her the okay, she kissed him on the cheek, told him she would see him soon and then darted out. After a few hours of rest, Pearce checked himself out and got a cab to Northwick Park, trading one hospital for another and now, sitting in the room with Sean and hoping above anything that his surrogate son would open his eyes, Pearce felt his close.

It had been a hell of a week.

He was asleep within seconds.

———

'Let me get this straight. You're not going to run this?'

Lynsey's editor sat at his desk, his arms out in confusion and his portly stomach pressed against the wooden edge. His laptop was open, the email that Lynsey had forwarded was open on the screen and his brow furrowed.

With her arms crossed, Lynsey nodded. A few hours of unbroken sleep had done her the world of good, coupled with a long, hot shower. For the first time in her career, she had arrived at the BBC offices in White City without bothering with her make-up, catching the security guards by surprise. Her editor, Tom Alderson, didn't appreciate the early call, but he had agreed to meet her.

Lynsey was already waiting for him in his office when he arrived. Although the coffee she had bought for him certainly improved his mood, nothing could prepare him for the story she relayed in excruciating detail. When Lynsey had first raised the question of her safety with him, he followed the usual protocol of arranging protection and a safe place for her.

Investigative journalists were subjected to threats all the time and as the media outlet was paid for by the British public, they were worth protecting.

But Lynsey told him everything.

About the sickening attack on her new boyfriend just to get to her.

The vile men who had carried out the attack and later kidnapped her and her friend.

The evidence, which was now splayed across his screen, of Nicola Weaver and Head Space's involvement in the attack.

And, most sensational of all, the re-emergence of Sam Pope.

It sounded too far-fetched to be true, but as Lynsey pointed out the details, he checked them on his phone. It had only been a day, but two bodies had been discovered within a private office in Mile End.

Just as she had said.

Soon enough, the rest of the bodies would be found wherever Sam had pitched his battle against Bowker's crew. It was the type of story that would propel Lynsey to the top of the organisation, making her the most in-demand reporter the BBC had on the books. As her chief editor, he would most likely ride her coattails, hoovering up the compliments and the pats on the back that would come his way.

The only thing more unbelievable than the story itself was the fact that Lynsey wasn't going to run it.

'I think I just need some time off, you know?' Lynsey responded with a meek shrug. 'Get my head straight.'

'Of course, of course.' Alderson said enthusiastically. 'But Lyns, come on…we have the chance to get ahead of this before any other outlet.'

But Lynsey wouldn't budge. She had already handed the evidence that Bridges had provided her over to the police and as far as she knew from her source within the Met, Bridges had already been arrested. He had been more than cooperative and knew that assisting them would likely reduce his sentence, maybe even suspend it.

Weaver had gone dark.

Not at her home or office and uncontactable, apparently Bridges was directing them to possible places the CEO of Head Space may be.

They would catch her, and her life and reputation would be shredded to a million pieces by a betrayed public.

'It's not about the story,' Lynsey said as she headed to the door. 'What happened is much, much more than a story, Tom.'

Lynsey pulled his door open and went to leave. He scrambled from his chair, desperate to keep the story alive.

'But what about Sam Pope? I mean, that's big news and the public has a right to know that a man that dangerous is alive and roaming the streets again.'

Lynsey shot him a scowl. She was aware of how the BBC represented Sam to the public during his initial war on crime. While respected journalists such as the late Helal Miah offered a balanced take on the man's actions, the BBC had a strict view that the man was a dangerous criminal. While not strictly false, Lynsey was aware of political pressure from Westminster to ensure that Sam Pope was not praised in any way.

Alderson was just doing his job and toeing the company line, but he didn't have a clue.

Lynsey had watched Sam go above the law with her own eyes, but for the right reason. He didn't do it for his own satisfaction.

He did it to right a very traumatic wrong.

He had also saved her life. The least she could was give him a few days head start before the police cottoned on. Eventually, she answered.

'Do you have any proof that Sam was involved?'

'Well, no… but you said…' Lynsey cut him off with a raised eyebrow and he got the message. The air had been let out of his balloon and he shook his head. 'I don't know why you're throwing away this opportunity, Lynsey. Why would you try to protect Sam Pope of all people?'

Lynsey chuckled to herself and shook her head.

'Because it's the right thing to do.'

Sam had used the cover of darkness and the inclement weather to make his way back to Hackney undetected. Whenever car lights illuminated one of the streets he used to weave his way through the city, Sam would duck his head, shielding the driver from a view of his battle scars.

The rain had helped, cleansing his face of the dried blood and also washing some of Bowker's from his hands.

The walk was brisk and wet, but offered Sam a chance to reflect.

Life had reverted back to what it had been, only this time there was no one on the inside of the Met Police looking out for him.

Pearce was retired.

Singh had been recruited and was out of his life.

All that awaited him from the boys in blue was a set of handcuffs and a cell as heavily guarded as the Crown jewels.

There was Etheridge.

After breaking Sam out of prison nearly two years ago, Etheridge had dropped fully off the grid, with no contact whatsoever and no numbers to be reached on.

Sam was alone.

Etheridge had left him an eye watering fortune to continue his fight, which had remained untouched since Sam had returned from America. It would help, but Sam knew that this new fight wouldn't be like the others.

He was older.

Wiser, maybe, but certainly older. The gym had kept him in phenomenal shape, but he felt every bone in his body ache for rest as he turned onto the Blackstone Estate, the looming towers jutting into the night sky like intruding concrete weeds.

Sam certainly wouldn't miss the area, and as he rounded the corner, he noticed that the front door to his building was open. The light in the shared hallway was on and as Sam marched towards it, he could see Jamal and his entourage crammed into the space, gesticulating wildly. Raised voices could be heard, and he quickened his pace as Jess's voice roared angrily from behind them.

'Get the fuck out!' Jess screamed, lodging herself in her doorway.

'What's the matter, Lily?' Jamal called out, ignoring Jess completely. 'You not gonna tell your mum that you're a skank whore who loves sucking dick?'

'I'm warning you...' Jess said with a seething rage. Jamal turned to her, pulling a knife from his pocket to make a statement.

'You what?' He snapped, his friends all cheering him on.

Jess's eyes widened with fear, as Lily gasped from behind her.

Then a voice startled everyone.

'Get out.'

All heads spun and all eyes locked on the haunting image of Sam, standing in the doorway, soaked by the thrashing downpour. It took Jess a few seconds to realise who it was since he discarded the long hair and beard.

But her relief was obvious.

Jamal, however, looked like he'd seen a ghost. Gone was the helpful stranger who had embarrassed him when retrieving Lily's bag. With his T-shirt stuck to his muscular frame, Sam looked twice the size of all of them.

His knuckles were split, clearly from fighting, and his forearms were stained with blood. His face, a mishmash of bruises, swelling and dried blood, was emotion free, but his eyes told Jamal and his crew what they needed to know.

They needed to listen.

Jamal held his hands up as if in surrender, and then lunged at Sam. Reading the situation, Sam thrust a powerful right hand forward, cracking the young man square in the jaw before he had even known what happened. Jamal lost consciousness immediately, and his friends caught him as he slumped to the floor. Sam looked at them all, their eyes wide with fear.

'If you come anywhere near this family again, I will personally kill each and every one of you. Is that understood?'

A few of them nodded instantly, and then, with the struggles of moving an unconscious body, they shuffled out of the house. Sam waited until they'd rounded the corner and disappeared from sight before he slammed the door.

As he marched towards his stairwell, Jess leant against her door frame, arms folded and a confused look on her face.

'Do I want to know?' she asked playfully, pointing at Sam's battered face.

'Nope.' Sam smiled back.

'I take it you have to leave now.' Jess was a smart woman. She had always suspected there was more to Jonathan than he let on. Sam raised an eyebrow. 'Oh, come on. I had my suspicions when you had the hair and the beard, but now I can see you clear as day, Sam.'

'Don't tell anyone.' He joked.

'Thank you, Sam.' Jess stepped forward and rose on her tiptoes. Tenderly, she planted a kiss on his cheek. 'For everything.'

'And you.' Sam reached for her hand and squeezed it. 'You look after yourself, and Lily. She's a bright girl.'

'Oh, I know.'

Sam looked up the stairs to his front door before reaching into his back pocket. He pulled his keys from his pocket, taking one of the two front door keys off the chain.

'Take this. Rent out the space upstairs for as long as you want. It's not great, but you'll get a good price for it. At least until my lease is up.'

Jess looked at Sam, her mouth open in shock at the gesture.

'Oh, I couldn't…'

'Please.' Sam pressed the key into her hand. 'It will help keep my leaving under the radar.'

Jess knew that wasn't true. Sam was doing what he could to help her out and despite his offers of money over their time as neighbours, Jess was a proud woman who didn't want charity.

She would rather work her fingers to the bone and know she earnt it than be handed life on a platter. Eventually, she pulled her hand away, her fingers wrapped around the key.

'Thank you, Sam.'

'I'll post the other key through your letter box on my way out.'

Sam began to ascend the staircase, and Jess called after him.

'You're a good man, Sam. This world needs people like you. People willing to do the right thing.'

Sam appreciated the words and headed up to this flat. It would only take him thirty minutes to shower and collect his things. Then, he had one stop to make and after that, he didn't know.

All he did know was that the fight was out there, waiting.

But it didn't have to wait much longer.

EPILOGUE

It had been a weird twenty-four hours for Curtis.

He woke on Sunday morning in his bed earlier than usual and he used those few hours to replay the events of the day before through his head. Ever since the movie night, where that horrifying man pointed a gun at him, his world had been turned upside down.

Not only did it make him question his own mortality for the first time in his life, but he had seen a side to Jonathan Cooper that he had never seen before.

A side he saw in full force the day before, when he watched JC kill the same man.

Curtis had been excited for his session working with JC, especially as the man was so open and honest when it came to talking about the world. Despite his long hair and scraggy beard, Curtis was amazed at the shape JC was in, asking him for tips on how to build muscle onto his scrawny, teenage frame.

The advice was clear. Just wait until you're a bit older and pay attention to what you eat.

JC was cool and whenever Curtis shadowed him around the youth centre, he was always amazed at the skills the man had. Whether it was putting up a shelf or fixing a sink, the man knew his stuff, and when Curtis showed his interest in an electrician apprenticeship, JC had been very supportive.

Behind it all, Curtis sensed the man was a little lonely, but by choice. He spoke about exercise and reading books, but never had he mentioned anything to do with his family.

In fact, he had never mentioned his past once and Curtis had always questioned why.

Until yesterday morning.

When the bald man had held that knife against his throat, Curtis was sure he was going to die. The man was unhinged and told Curtis that once he'd murdered JC in cold blood, he couldn't leave any witnesses.

That was it. Everything over.

No more girlfriend. No more future.

But JC was a different man when confronted by danger and despite telling Curtis to leave to bravely face the man alone, Curtis couldn't bring himself to. A morbid curiosity had caused him to peer through the crack in the door, where he witnessed JC systematically take the man apart before snapping his neck as easily as halving a chocolate bar.

It was something that Curtis couldn't stop thinking about and with his parents beyond useless in the advice stakes, as soon as his alarm went off at eight, Curtis was already dressed and heading out the door.

The weather was still a little on the blusterous side, so he took shelter at the bus stop and waited patiently for the morning ride to come. It was a twenty-minute walk to the centre but in this weather, it would feel like hours.

He needed to talk to Pearce.

The man was a fount of knowledge and seemed to be pretty tight with JC.

Pearce would know what to do. He always did.

The bus journey was pretty quiet, and he arrived outside the front gate in no time. It was open as usual, and Curtis knew Pearce usually came in early on a Sunday to get the following week in check. The door was open, and Curtis strolled in.

He called out to Pearce, his voice echoing through the empty building. A little flashback of being snatched by the man the day before flickered in his mind like a showreel, but Curtis overcame it.

That man was dead.

He saw it with his own eyes.

He ventured further into the building, deducing that it was empty. With a shrug, he walked towards the storage room, where JC sometimes sat and read.

Maybe he was lying low?

It was a long shot, but after knocking a few times and getting nothing, Curtis opened the door. Apart from the usual apparatus and junk, the room was empty.

Except for JC's pristine toolbox, something that he took great pride in and explained to Curtis the importance of preparation. Within its contents were top of the range tools, worth well over a thousand pounds and Curtis had made bold claims about having his own one day.

A note was taped to the top of it and Curtis snatched it off the box and began to read:

To Curtis,

With all my heart I am sorry about what you witnessed yesterday. It was never my intention to bring that side of my life into yours and I hope you can get past it. If you need to reach out to someone, speak to Adrian.

. . .

Keep walking your path. You have no idea what you are capable of, but I do, and I want you to have these tools to find out.

Be better than me.

JC

Curtis wiped his eyes. With absent parents, belief wasn't something he had felt through his life. But he clutched the letter tightly, knowing that despite whatever he was going through after killing a man, JC had kept him in mind.

After a few moments and a couple more reads of the letter, Curtis opened the toolbox to learn each and every tool within it, determined to prove JC right.

Determined to not be better than him, but to be like him.

A good man.

GET EXCLUSIVE ROBERT ENRIGHT MATERIAL

Hey there,

I really hope you enjoyed the book and hopefully, you will want to continue following Sam Pope's war on crime. If so, then why not sign up to my reader group? I send out regular updates, polls and special offers as well as some cool free stuff. Sound good?

Well, if you do sign up to the reader group I'll send you FREE copies of THE RIGHT REASON and RAINFALL, two thrilling Sam Pope prequel novellas. (RRP: 1.99)

You can get your FREE books by signing up at www.robertenright.co.uk

SAM POPE NOVELS

For more information about the Sam Pope series and other books by Robert Enright, please visit:

www.robertenright.co.uk

ABOUT THE AUTHOR

Robert lives in Buckinghamshire with his family, writing books and dreaming of getting a dog.

For more information:
www.robertenright.co.uk
robert@robertenright.co.uk

You can also connect with Robert on Social Media:

- facebook.com/robenrightauthor
- x.com/REnright_Author
- instagram.com/robenrightauthor

COPYRIGHT © ROBERT ENRIGHT, 2021

All rights reserved. No part of this publication may be reproduced, stored in a retrieval system, or transmitted in any form or by any means, electronic, photocopying, mechanical, recording, or otherwise, without the prior permission of the copyright owner.

All characters in this book are fictitious and any resemblance to actual persons living or dead is purely coincidental.

Cover by The Cover Collection

Edited by Emma Mitchell

Proof Read by Lou Dixon